E H

o 7 7 2 i 7 8 c

THE ROAD TO EDEN

IS OVERGROWN

Dan Wheatcroft

ISBN: 9781521942239
Acknowledgements:
Fabiana: contributions, perseverance and her love.
Dexter Petley: advice and encouragement.
Firearms advisor: Mike Olley
Cover: Phil Harris

NOTES

AWOL: Absent WithOut Leave

CCTV: Closed Circuit Television

COMMS: Communications

CROPS: Covert Rural Observation Posts

HUMINT: Human Intelligence

IPA: International Police Association

MIT: Major Investigation Team

OPPO: Colleague or friend

OSD: Operational Support Division

PNC: Police National Computer

PPU: Public Protection Unit

SFO: Specialist Firearms Officer

SK: Station Keeper

Holy Corner: junction in Liverpool's pedestrianised centre where Lord Street, Church Street, Paradise Street and Whitechapel all meet.

Matrix: Police unit specialising in overt/covert disruption of organised crime

Signalling stick: Wooden 'stick' approx 3ft (90cm) with flat metal tip. Traditionally used in many City Forces, pre-use of radios, to tap on pavement signalling to the 'Beat Officers' that their Supervisor required to meet them at the source of the tapping.

The Met: Metropolitan Police

West Mids: West Midlands Police

Knowledge is sorrow, they who know the most

must mourn the deepest over the fatal truth

Acknowledgement: Lord Byron

CHAPTER 1

Nicks took several mouthfuls of his Dreher beer, sat back and surveyed the bar. He liked this place, always had. A hint of 'student' reminded him of Keith's, on Lark Lane in his hometown of Liverpool.

Tonight it was not as vibrant as usual. A young couple sat at a small table on the far side, an old guy sat watching the TV and a group of four played pool in the back room.

The large, shaven headed, middle aged man had been looking at him intently. Foreign Legion, Nicks speculated. Never one to back out of a 'situation', he engaged him with eye contact and nodded. The barman nodded back and raised an empty glass. Nicks nodded again and downed his remaining beer.

He lit a cigarette and promised himself he would give up smoking soon then put the earphones to his iPod back in his ears. There was no music, just a vestige of the isolation he needed.

Placing a Dreher on the table, the 'Legionnaire' accepted payment with a hint of a smile. Nicks gulped the beer down, sucked heavily on the cigarette, rested his head wearily against the wall and closed his eyes.

He was remembering the letter she'd written, hidden amongst her things for him to find; when the time was right. Imprinted in his memory, each word bore the soft inflections of her voice, each sentence softly crushing his heart. The tears, almost imperceptibly, filtered through his eyelashes, gathering together as if unsure where to go next.

He sat up with a start to the pain of the burning cigarette and self consciously eyed the room for any reaction. There was none. He was invisible to all but the Barman who stood before him; another beer on the table. Nicks removed an earpiece and stared up at him. "You look as if you could do with this," the Legionnaire said in Hungarian "It's on me."

The following day he left the hotel, walking along Eötvös Utca to the Oktogon. The sun was shining and, with undertones of Paris, Budapest felt welcoming.

Usually, he'd spend time in Berlin, harvesting cash from the ATMs, but this time he *needed* to get home. He couldn't linger in admiration; one more call to make and a train to catch.

He took the Metro to Batthyany tér station and walked across to the nearby man in the wall. It should be enough; anyone tracking the use of his bank cards would think he lived in the Buda part of the city or was on his way to Déli pályaudvar, the Budapest railway terminal serving the west of the country. Job done, he re-crossed the river.

As he entered Keleti station through the grand portico, he checked the departures board then bought a kávé from a small shop close to the entrance; walking with it to the side exit. He liked this coffee. It was strong, that's why you didn't get much of it. With two sugars it tasted near perfect. At the benches he dropped the rucksack whilst he had a smoke and finished his drink.

He clicked a playlist and sat down to watch Budapest life trundle by. Ingrid Michaelson sang 'Soldier'. It was the song he'd played the very first time he'd made this trip. He smiled.

She was waiting for him as he stepped down onto the platform. With barely time to drop his rucksack, she flung herself upon him, showering him with kisses.

"Thank you for coming back to me."

Every time, she thanked him, as if his returning home was a gift she never took for granted. Her eyes filled with tears which trickled down her cheeks as he hugged her as hard as he dared.

Anca was 36 years old, fluent in six languages and a sought after literary translator, so why she had chosen him, a man 20 years her senior, was beyond Nicks. Perhaps she'd chosen him because they were both broken, sharing a common bond of sadness; the feeling of needing to be saved from themselves.

They walked to the station's small café where she bought them coffee. It was a little ritual of theirs. She always said it was like meeting each other for the first time over and over again. On the bench outside Anca told him everything that had happened whilst he'd been away: the new neighbours, her progress translating yet another novel and the flowers she was planning to plant in the window boxes of the tiny flat they called home. And it *was* home. Anca and this quirky Romanian town. His refuge.

He of course told her the same story every time; visits to his parents, places he'd seen. She would listen attentively, nodding and smiling every now and then. She neither wanted nor needed him to tell her

3

more. She'd never asked him what he did when he went away. It wasn't because she was foolish, or stupid, far from it, but simply because she loved him. He was her love, her best friend, her peace of mind. The rest was of no consequence.

CHAPTER 2
3rd February 2014

Derek Drayton returned to the MIT office in Police Headquarters with a cheese roll from the canteen.

"He's here, in his office," one of the staff said.

Derek nodded and went to his desk, placed the cheese roll in his top drawer and removed two sheets of A4 from the top of his in-tray.

The door was open, but he knocked anyway. "Good morning, Sir, Derek Drayton, Detective Sergeant. You probably don't remember me."

Thurstan Baddeley, his new DCI, looked up from the paperwork on his desk and smiled. "Derek. I remember you. Admiral Street, wasn't it? I know I was a DS. Always thought you were a very promising trainee detective and I see I wasn't wrong." He got up and shook Derek's hand.

"That's right, Sir. Admiral Street. Happy days," Derek replied. "Do you prefer we call you Sir or Boss?"

"I prefer Boss, Derek, but when the Chief and his mates are around it'll need to be Sir," Thurstan replied. "You know what they're like," he added.

"No problem, Boss," Derek said, "I've got you a list of the personnel on the team. This one's the team we actually have now, and this one's a list of those who would normally be here if they hadn't been drafted to the other syndicate working on the serial killings out in

5

St.Helens." He handed his Detective Chief Inspector the two sheets of A4.

Thurstan perused them as Derek continued: "I've included their nicknames, Boss, because you're going to hear them used around the office and I thought it would save any confusion."

"Very sensible," Thurstan murmured still reading the lists.

"It may help if I point them out to you. The only one not here at the moment is Chalkie White, he's your DI. He'll be in at twelve, had some family stuff to sort out."

He walked across to a large window that looked out onto the main office. Thurstan followed him.

"Right. It'll be easier if I do it in the same order as on the list if possible."

Thurstan handed him the sheet of A4.

Derek looked at it briefly, then pointed to an individual sat at the desk nearest the DCI's office, his sleeves rolled up exposing two hairy forearms. "This chap we call Chewbacca, or just Chewy. As in the wookie from Star Wars. The very thin guy over there at the back is the Strolling Bone, but we only call him that when he's out of earshot. Otherwise it's just Bob.

"The one eating the sandwich is Gandalph a.k.a The Wizard. He's very good at finding evidence and intel the rest of us can't seem to find, hence the name and the girls in the far office are Lizzie and Spud. Lizzie's the black girl and she's your other DS. She's also called Lizzie the Bizzie, a nickname she picked up from the 'bucks' at Admiral Street."

Bucks was a local name for people who provided the Police with most of their work. They in turn referred to the Police as 'The Bizzies'.

"Her real name's Elizabeth, but she doesn't like it and Betty's not a name she responds well to either. We only use them when we want to 'wind' her up and then only from a safe distance."

"The other girl's DC Murphy I take it?" Thurstan offered.

"That's right and the guy sat on the desk is Mark Sandon, a.k.a. Sando, or as we're currently calling him, Glando the Strolling Erection. Let's just say he's *very* fond of the ladies."

"I see. Why not have done with it and just call him Shagger?" ventured Thurstan.

"Already taken by someone on the other team, Boss" Derek replied matter of factly.

"Morning, Sir, *and* you, Sarge!" chirped a happy looking chap as he passed by carrying a pile of papers.

"That's Soapy," Derek said, then added, "Don't ask, Boss."

Thurstan frowned in thought then chuckled. "I suspect I know where you're going with that one. Are the girls aware?"

"Possibly not, but it's not something I feel the need to clarify, Boss," he grinned back before pointing once more. "That guy, on the far desk to the right, is Sparky, used to be an electrician. If you ever need something doing, he does a great job at *very* decent rates. On his left is Polo, after the 'mint with a hole'. Give it a couple of days and you'll get that one." Thurstan nodded.

"Then there's the group over by the water cooler. Left to right: Fast Eddie, very meticulous but if you're in a rush give it to someone else. Fred, the bald guy, weightlifter, looks like the singer from the group Right Said Fred. The chap next to him we just call Arthur."

"Why Arthur?" Thurstan asked.

"It's his name, Boss," smiled Derek.

Thurstan raised his eyebrows in a gesture of surrender. "Ah, well, fair enough. How old is he? He looks about seventy five?"

"I know," Derek laughed, "but he's a good ten years younger. Ex DS, retired now and the Office Manager. I'd suggest, if we get a job whilst the other enquiry is still at full speed, we use him as the House to House enquiries co-ordinator, running the control, especially if the local uniformed sergeants haven't done it before. We won't be able to use Matrix Disruption because they're tasked to the other enquiry. Anyway, Arthur's very good and a stickler for detail. Next to him is Taff, Welshman, unpronounceable first name. There's some dispute as to whether even he's pronouncing it properly."

He pointed to the two officers who had just walked out. "The black lad is Devon – as you might have noticed, another weightlifter. He and Fred like to take the same lunch breaks so they can train together. The other guy is Ikky. Iqbal Hameed." He looked around the main office and then said, "Ahh! And over there – the Indian lad is Sandy. Short for Sandeep. The other one is the newest and youngest on the team, the Foetus." He didn't add anything further, preferring to wait for the response.

8

"Good grief!" Thurstan exclaimed. "How long have we been employing twelve year olds?"

"I know," he laughed again. "No point sending him up to the bar to get a round in if we go for drinks, he keeps getting refused. Well, that's it, Boss. They're a good bunch. All very keen, and they know their stuff."

"Well, thank you for that invaluable information," Thurstan replied with a smile, then added in a more businesslike tone of voice: "Right, Derek. Can you get the team together, including those that've just left the office?"

"Yes, Boss. Not a problem. They'll only have gone to the canteen for an iced bun or a sandwich. No one's due out anywhere today. We're putting the finishing touches this week to the last job. I'll ring the canteen." He looked at his watch. "Shall we say... 15 minutes?"

"Fine," Thurstan replied as he returned to his desk. He hadn't needed to ask his DS what his nickname was. Coming from Liverpool, he already knew Derek would be called 'Degsy'.

CHAPTER 3
3rd March 2014

He was sitting outside Costa's at the corner of Old Hall Street and Tithebarn. Chewing the last of his almond slice, he sipped the remains of his caramel Latte and tapped his foot in rhythm to the music in his earphones.

The surveillance team interrupted: "Subject approaching Fazakerley Street. Fifty metres."

He stood up; with the strap over his left shoulder the messenger bag lay on his right hip. Across the pavement into Old Hall, he walked casually away from the city then stopped outside a sandwich bar, took out his spare phone and pretended to make a call as he took in the surroundings.

Within seconds he'd identified his target: White male, 40s, muscular build, shaven head, casual sports jacket, merino jumper, jeans and shades. He named him 'Sunglasses'.

"Subject crossing Old Hall ...entering Fazakerley Street ... now."

A voice: "Yes, yes."

It was narrow, one car's width, a thin footpath on either side. A hundred metres long, it connected Rumford Place to Old Hall carrying one way traffic towards the latter. Stepping into it he said quietly: "Elvis has entered the building," and activated the CCTV disruption device he carried in his pocket. Sunglasses was ahead of him. Nobody else was in sight. It was all down to him now. The voice: "Yes, yes."

He took out the smartphone, clicked music, playlist, then 'Fly With Vampires' *play all* and put it back in his pocket. Immediately the opening chords of 'Puppet Master' resounded through his head.

With twenty metres between them, he knew Sunglasses was heading for his car in the little side street at the far end, to his right. He knew exactly how it was parked. He'd seen it earlier. The cul-de-sac had once been bounded on three sides by buildings, but the left and far end boundaries had long been demolished. The BMW sat about fifty feet from the junction.

Sunglasses was in a happy place. His recent meeting had gone well. The problem of his ex-mistress would soon be resolved, permanently, leaving him to concentrate fully on his current business interests and plans for an early retirement. He looked back and saw only a businessman talking on his phone. That reminded him, he needed to speak to Tommy, his main enforcer and close friend. They needed to sort out that weasel Kehoe before he caused them any further problems. Then *he* needed to sort out Tommy. He was getting too cocky, assuming too many things. Sunglasses felt uneasy. He felt possible change in the air. He took out his mobile and turned the corner.

Quickening his pace as Sunglasses disappeared; he narrowed the gap between them back to fifteen metres. It gave him accuracy yet distanced him from the result and provided an adequate space between him and the target in which to react. He crossed over to the left hand pavement opening up his view. Sunglasses was walking towards the driver's side of the car, keys in his right hand, phone to his left ear. The vehicle's indicators flashed.

He registered both the scene *and* his peripheral vision: no immediate threats. Three workmen off to his left across the wasteland and adjoining road. One stood in a hole; the other two standing idly by. A white van drew up alongside them, obscuring him from view.

Briskly now, he crossed back over the narrow roadway, stuffed the phone into his trouser pocket and took the suppressed Sig 226 from the messenger bag. Taking two paces from the junction into the cul-de-sac, hidden from anyone looking up the 'alley' from Old Hall Street, he brought the weapon up in a weaver stance, paused momentarily then gently squeezed the trigger.

Tommy wasn't picking up. Sunglasses placed his hand on the car door handle glancing back along the street at the businessman who was pointing at him. No. He *wasn't* pointing. It was the last thought he had. His phone bounced off the cobblestoned roadway and into the gutter.

Walking unhurriedly towards the city centre, the weapon replaced in the messenger bag, left hand to his lapel, he whispered: "Elvis is leaving the building." He didn't look back. The white van drove past him, heading in the same direction.

On the opposite pavement, he dropped the messenger bag into a street cleaner's cart and continued without pause or acknowledgement. Turning right at the junction, he passed the 'Pig and Whistle' and walked calmly into a side street, softly announcing: "Elvis has left the building."

Thirty metres later, he stopped and selected another playlist, nonchalantly checking the street behind him before continuing.

The street cleaner closed the lid to his cart and trundled it off. Occasionally stopping to brush something up, he reached a quiet side street less than half a mile away. Within 30 seconds, both he and the cart had been loaded into the rear of a white van and driven away.

CHAPTER 4
3rd March 2014

Chalkie stood in the doorway to the DCI's office. "Sorry to interrupt, but the Control Room have just been on. There's been a shooting in the city, Fazackerley Street. Local CID reckon it's one for us. Looks like a professional hit. They're asking us to attend."

Thurstan glanced up from the paperwork he'd been discussing with DS Lizzie Johnson. "Do we know the victim yet?"

"Not confirmed at present," Chalkie replied, "but a vehicle at the scene is known to be used by Tony MacMahon, and a credit card on the body is in the name of one his companies."

Thurstan looked at his DS. "OK. Lizzie, we'll have to finish this another time. Grab some of the chaps and follow us down to the scene. We'll take it from there. Oh, and tell Derek where he's taking me."

Ten minutes later Degsy delivered him to the scene. They entered via Rumford Place and were instructed by a Traffic Officer engaged in the road closure to park up and walk to the inner cordon. Uniform had taped off the area. The Sergeant directing wore a high visibility yellow jacket, traditional foot officers' helmet and carried a signalling stick.

An older officer sporting a thick moustache, he recognized Thurstan as he approached the tape.

"Alright, Sir." He smiled then nodded at Degsy. "Alright, young Mr. Drayton. Nice to see you. Just getting some of the troops out to these buildings to round up any witnesses, get lists of occupants and

14

the like." Turning to a Probationer with a clipboard, he added: "Make sure you get their details on the log, young Bartlett."

The bobby looked at him quizzically. "But you know them, Sarge."

"I know I know them, Bartlett," the 'Sarge' said slowly and deliberately, "but I may be dead tomorrow and then where would we be?" He gave the Officer a chastising look.

"DS Nolan's over by the vehicle, Sir," the Sergeant said waving his signalling stick in the direction of a black BMW.

Thurstan and Degsy made their way over to a second taped area, the primary crime scene. "Hang on there, Boss!" Sammy Nolan called to them. "I'll come to you. It'll save you having to suit up."

The white suited detective ambled over and they shook hands. "Long time no see, Boss," he was grinning broadly. "Good to see you."

"And you Sammy!" Thurstan placed his left hand over Sammy's as they gave each other a firm extended handshake. "We really must stop meeting like this." They both laughed. "This is DS Derek Drayton, I don't know if you've met before."

"Don't think we have," Sammy replied. "I would have remembered someone more handsome than me, I'm sure." Degsy and Sammy shook hands.

"Right, what have we got?" asked Thurstan, taking in the scene. The body lay on its back now but he assumed it may have been turned over by either the officers first on the scene or the paramedics as they attempted to save life.

15

"Mark Anthony Stephen MacMahon, forty eight years old," Sammy recited, matter of factly. "Subject to formal identification of course, but the car's one we know he uses, the bank cards in his wallet belong to companies he owns and, anyway, I recognize him. Last locked him up eighteen months ago, when I was still on the Matrix. As you might expect, it didn't go anywhere. Surprising sudden lack of witnesses," he added sarcastically.

Thurstan wasn't surprised. Until now MacMahon had been the city's undisputed crime lord surviving many attempts to bring him to book, usually through witness intimidation.

Sammy detailed all he knew in respect of the current situation. The first officers on the scene thought they'd felt a pulse. The paramedics had turned him over to work on him, but provided 'confirmation of life extinct' practically immediately. He had a gunshot wound to the front right side of the head and one of the officers had found an empty shell casing roughly fifteen metres away, near the building line which she'd protected with a small cardboard box pending the arrival of the Crime Scene Investigators. The shell casing looked like a 9mm, the weapon most probably a semi-automatic pistol. As nobody heard a gunshot it was probably silenced, all still to be confirmed by forensics. The CSIs were nearly finished, the Coroner's Office had been informed, the body would be removed shortly and Sammy was ready for a cup of tea and a sandwich. Then as an afterthought, he told them the three workmen, who'd called the job in, were giving their details to the Matrix patrol in the big yellow van over by the Apartment Hotel.

"Thanks, Sammy, I'll come back to you in a minute if you'd delay that cup of tea for a bit. I just need to speak to my DS over there." Thurstan indicated back towards the first taped barrier where Lizzie Johnson and five other members of the MIT were gathered. He patted Sammy on the shoulder then he and Degsy walked off towards the barrier.

Constable Bartlett looked up from his clipboard and wondered if he was going to be on Youtube. He'd noticed the man on the balcony of the Apartment Hotel earlier on, and now he was back and looked like he was filming the scene on his phone. The Officer stared up at him and then he was gone, back into the room. "Come on young Bartlett," his Sergeant chided, "Don't be daydreaming. You've got a job to do."

Thurstan called the Sergeant over and together they discussed the options with Lizzie and Degsy. The Sergeant provided four Uniforms to team up with four of the DCI's detectives and Thurstan briefed the officers who then split into teams and began visiting the nearby buildings.

Thurstan looked at the three left. "Taff, you co-ordinate the 'house to house' such as it is. Derek, you and Lizzie go speak to the Matrix, over there. Find out what their witnesses can tell us and get some statements taken. I'm just going back for a quick word with Sammy Nolan."

"Got you, Boss," they replied almost in unison. Thurstan walked back towards the primary scene.

Lizzie and Degsy split up, collected leather document holders from their vehicles and met up at the Matrix van.

"Alright, Offs. DS Lizzie Johnson from MIT."

"Alright Sarge," replied the officer, shaking her hand, then nodded at Derek. "Degsy." He gave them a brief account of what the witnesses were saying.

"Me colleagues are takin' statements. One of 'em's in the carrier," he said, thumbing behind him to the yellow van with riot grills and the Matrix logo. "An' the other's in this place's reception." He pointed to the Apartment Hotel. "The other fella's behind the carrier havin' a smoke. I'd be takin' his statement, but we didn't have enough statement forms. If you can give me some, I'll go and take it now."

"Thanks for that," Lizzie smiled at him. "It's ok. I like to keep my hand in. I'll box him off."

"I thought you lot were all fully employed with the St.Helens job," Degsy said to the Matrix constable.

"We are, but we were warned for an all dayer at the Mags. The Buck eventually decided to throw his hand in, so we finished early an' thought… City centre patrol. You know how it is, Degs." He smiled broadly.

Degsy smiled back. Lizzie was walking the remaining workman towards her vehicle.

"I'll have to go and see if my colleague needs anything," he said apologetically, patting the constable on the upper arm: "Nice to see you, Tommo. Give us a ring and we'll go for a pint."

"Yeah, yeah. We must do lunch sometime," Tommo called back.

Later that evening, the staff gathered in the MIT office, sitting around on various desks and chairs, some standing. Thurstan stood before them, recapping the day.

"Right. Well, I think that's all we can say for now." The DCI looked around the room. "Where's Lizzie?"

"Here, Boss." She held her arm up.

"Ah! Sorry, Lizzie, I didn't see you come back in. Any news on Tommy Cole?"

Tommy Cole was MacMahon's second in command, now Liverpool's new crime lord, although they all doubted it would go undisputed. He'd handed himself in to his nearest Police Station having heard about MacMahon's demise on the local news. Not wanting to be caught unawares, he'd arranged for some 'housekeeping.' With the help of his solicitor, he employed a strategy designed to delay the inevitable search of his home and any other properties he owned. He knew if they'd arrested him at home they had the power to search without the nuisance of obtaining a written authorisation or relevant warrant.

"Degsy's gone down there with Devon and is still in interview at present, Boss. Cole turned up with his 'brief' and as far as I'm aware, he's not been arrested, yet."

"Thank you, Liz. Right! If no one's got anything else, those of you with completed H to H enquiry forms see Arthur and get them sorted and anyone with a statement that hasn't been handed in to DI White yet, please do so now. Otherwise you're in your own time." As they started to disperse he raised his voice above the hubbub. "And make sure you're fully aware of your new shifts."

"Phone call for you, Boss." one of the team called out. "It's the Press Office."

The conversation was brief. Despite his protestations they told him the Chief Constable had instructed it required a DCI. Thurstan put the phone down and looked at the officer. "Have to do a Press interview tomorrow." The Detective noticed the long face. Taking a tube of mints from his pocket, he said: "Polo, Boss?"

CHAPTER 5
March 2009

The Crows Nest was known for its fine selection of real ales and socially varied clientele. Nicks started to drink there after his wife died. Ovarian cancer. She was 47.

Despite their brave fight, Mary passed away, next to him, one morning 14 months after he'd retired and 13 months after they'd learnt the awful truth.

He'd been awake next to her; all that night she lay in a morphine 'sleep', her breathing heavy and laboured, clinging to life until she felt it safe to leave him.

He'd called the District Nurse who injected her with something to clear her lungs. They turned her on her side and he'd continued his vigil. Eventually, exhausted and unaware, he'd fallen asleep.

At 5.45 am he awoke suddenly in a fright. She was breathing normally and was peaceful. He saw a hint of a smile on her face. He'd tried to stay awake but drifted off again. He woke at 6.30. She'd left him, softly like the song.

It was what she wanted. She knew he'd have *begged* her to stay: one more day, one more hour. Her heart would have broken.

During the day he'd pretend she was at work and would be home as usual but, as 5pm approached, the fantasy would crumble. For that reason everyday at 4.30pm he could be found at the Crows Nest. And thus they found him.

It was a chilly dark evening and Nicks sat at a heavy wooden slatted table in the car park. He was alone and that's how he preferred it. People would come out for a smoke, remark how cold it was and stand chatting to each other. When finished, they'd disappear rapidly back into the warm interior of the snug, lounge or public bar according to their social loyalties. Others would come out alone and there'd be an exchange of small talk before they too fled to warmer climes. Nicks did his best to be pleasant.

With his fourth pint of the night, he sat down on the bench seat, took a mouthful of ale and lit a cigarette when the man approached him. He was wearing black trousers, shiny shoes and an expensive long black overcoat. Around his neck he wore a patterned scarf which Nicks thought was probably expensive too. His hair was thinning but brushed forward in an effort to disguise the fact. His broad and conspicuous nose sat above thin lips which, when he spoke or smiled, displayed teeth with a hint of prominence. It wasn't an unpleasant face but could never be described as handsome. Nicks decided he was most probably a solicitor and pondered whether or not the man recognized him from his days of evidence giving in the courts. He was, he concluded, definitely looking for him, or he was the world's most loneliest man.

"Do you mind if I sit here?" he said placing his pint on the table and sitting down, not waiting for a reply. "It's very chilly, isn't it?"

"Not if you're wearing the right clothes." Nicks was dressed in combat trousers, layers topped with a hoodie and a windproof softshell jacket.

"Yes, quite," the man nodded in agreement. "I should *really* have brought a hat."

He'd a refined voice with the plummy overtones of an English public school education. Nicks promoted him to a Barrister.

"It's Nicks, isn't it." It was more statement than question.

He was wary. "Sorry, do I know you?"

"No, Nicks, you don't, but I know you *or* should I say I know of you."

The man ignored the fact he'd received neither confirmation nor denial. He didn't need it. He sipped his beer. Nicks was intrigued but before he could say anything the man continued in measured tones:

"I've been receiving very good reports about you for a long, long time now Nicks and I'm here to offer you employment. But," he held up his left hand, two fingers extended as if giving a blessing, "before you say anything I must tell you it's a very challenging, exciting opportunity requiring the ability to work as a team whilst using one's own initiative in situations that could be, shall we say, quite fluid. It needs loyalty, courage, determination and a belief in justice and what's right. Things I believe you possess in abundance. If you accept, you'll be working in this country and perhaps occasionally on the continent."

It was almost as if he'd lifted it direct from a standard job description the Police were fond of using. The man sipped his beer again.

Nicks quietly said: "But I'm not looking for a job."

"No, I know you're not," the man replied matter of factly before adding: "And may I just say I'm very sorry about Mary, we all are, but

23

we're looking for you Nicks. Or should I say we're looking for who you were before you decided to try and drink yourself to death." He paused momentarily. "It takes a lot longer than you'd think," he said as if, for a split second, he was somewhere else. "You know *she* wouldn't approve of what you're doing, don't you?"

Nicks stared at his pint then took a mouthful, swallowed slowly and thoughtfully and said: "I know."

"I don't want an answer now but if you're interested just phone this." He proffered a plain business card divulging only a telephone number. "Just leave your name and mobile details and we'll text you with information in respect of where you and I can meet again to discuss this further." He took sip of his drink and declared: "Excellent beer."

Nicks took the card: "Is this a Government job?"

"Hmmm. The best I can tell you now, Nicks, is that it's not officially a Government job. I'll explain should you wish to meet again." Another sip then he rose from the table. "It would be nice if you didn't mention this to anyone."

"No problem," Nicks replied with a shrug.

"By the way, my name is Don."

Leaving his half filled glass on the table, he turned and walked away. Nicks looked at the business card and emptied his glass. When he looked up Don had already disappeared. He stared at the unfinished beer on the table. Picking it up, he drank it in several gulps then went inside for yet another.

Four days later he phoned the number on the card.

CHAPTER 6
November 2009

He'd taken the 3.30 pm from Liverpool Lime Street arriving in Inverness shortly past 11pm. Outside the station he saw the two men standing next to a dark grey Range Rover. One about 5 foot 7, the other slightly taller. They looked like seasoned professionals. Nicks guessed around sixty to sixty five years old. Something about them made him think they were probably ex SAS. He wasn't going to ask.

The taller of the two made the introductions. "Hi, Nicks. I'm Mick and this is Lofty. Give me your watch and any phones you've got." He'd a south eastern accent Nicks automatically associated with London. There were no handshakes. Nicks complied. "Right, stow your stuff in the boot and get in." He held the rear passenger door open as Lofty went to the back and opened the boot.

"How did you know who to look for?" Nicks asked Lofty, a Scot, as he threw his rucksack into the back.

"You don't have to be a fuckin' rocket scientist, son. Besides, we knew what you were wearing." This was the first hint Nicks had that he'd been watched during his journey. The accent was so thick Nicks assumed he was from Glasgow. He was amused he'd been called 'son'.

Sitting on the rear seat, he saw the windows were blacked out. Between him and 'them', a similarly glassed partition through which he could only just make out the back of the headrests in the front.

An intercom voice spoke. It was Mick, the Londoner. "You ok, in there? You'll find a couple of cans of fruit drink in the centre console. Don't drink too much because it's a bit of a drive and we won't be making any piss stops."

The intercom went off. He wasn't interested in replies. Some two hours later, in the middle of nowhere, they arrived at a small hunting lodge.

Nicks collected his gear and followed Lofty into the building where he was shown his accommodation. A small room with a wire sprung bed, plastic covered mattress, bedside cabinet, small table lamp, wardrobe and sink with a mirror over it. It was unmistakably Government surplus. On the bed an old army sleeping bag had been unfurled.

"Have you eaten?" Lofty asked brusquely.

"I had something earlier, on the train," Nicks replied, although he was feeling quite peckish.

"Good. You're not gettin' fuckin' fed 'til the morning anyway. Right! Leave your kit here, I'll show you the canteen."

Lofty turned and left the room. Nicks threw his rucksack on the bed and followed him.

In the canteen they told him to strip naked and searched through his clothing. When they'd finished, Lofty told him to bend over and spread his buttocks. That done, he was told to get dressed.

Mick grinned. "Right, go and get your head down and we'll see you in the morning." They hadn't told him what they were looking for but Nicks knew they were looking for a phone. Returning to his room, he found someone had emptied his rucksack onto the floor and been through every item.

The next morning, as the light began to creep over the hills, his door was flung open and he woke to a loud: "Ok, son, time to get up. Get a fuckin' move on! Come on!"

He rubbed his eyes in the harsh light from the unshaded bulb in the centre of the ceiling.

Lofty threw some clothing and a used pair of training shoes onto the floor.

"You'll need all of that. It's a wee bit chilly out there. If the trainers don't fit, tough shit! Come on! Move yourself! Outside in five!" He was gone.

Nicks extracted himself from the sleeping bag and got dressed: two pairs of tracksuit bottoms, two tops, one pair of socks and a beanie hat. The trainers, luckily, weren't a bad fit at all.

An hour later Mick and Lofty returned a mud spattered, soaking wet Nicks to the front of the Lodge, leaving him with the instruction to shower and be in the canteen in fifteen. A rushed fourteen and a half minutes later he sat down, watching Lofty and Mick, clean and refreshed in their DPM combats and green sweatshirts, serve the breakfast they'd just cooked; full English and a steaming mug of hot sweet tea.

Once done, Lofty declared: "Right son. Arse into gear. Time to get a fuckin' move on."

It was the same every day – run, breakfast, weapons training, specialist skills, evening meal at what Nicks thought might be 8pm, followed by testing on what he'd learnt. He'd no firm idea of the time. There were no clocks. He got up in the dark and he went to bed in the dark. That's all he really knew.

Late afternoon on the fifth day, as the light began to fade, he was taken to a small windowless room containing two chairs facing each other across a table. A single light bulb with a metal shade hung from the ceiling. They told him to take a seat and wait. He allowed the silence to envelop him.

The door opened. It was Don.

This time the pleasant manner was absent, his thin smiles at times both condescending and minacious. Nicks would be a Leveller. An executioner. His call sign, made up from the first letter of his title and three letters from the word 'eviscerate', was 'Elvis'. Nicks smiled inwardly.

Next came Alex: a bespectacled young man in his 30s whose physique gave away his liking of pies and cakes.

He spoke quickly and efficiently. Nicks' pay would be placed in a safety deposit box relevant to the centre of operations. His box number would always be S-179. Details of the appropriate bank would be sent to him by encrypted text.

A smile, then Alex delved into a large buff envelope and placed two swipe cards and a secure key on the table."In the meantime, you'll need these for access. Most bank secure keys work on a six figure random number, this generates eight. Initial set up? Press the green button and key in your chosen PIN, four to eight numbers. To confirm enter the PIN again and press the yellow button and it's done." He looked at Nicks for a sign of comprehension.

Satisfied, he resumed his instructions, "To get through the outer door of each location you swipe with the white card then key in the random number from the secure key. You'll then be in an 'airlock'. The next door will not open until the first door has closed securely. When it has, the device on the next door will show a green light. Now it's thumbprint recognition time. That's why you'll need this." He produced something resembling a very small condom from the envelope. "Despite what it looks like it *is* very robust," he said noticing the look on Nicks' face. "Slip it over your thumb making sure this bit is at the front and press it against the pad. When the door opens, another 'airlock', same again. Green light, swipe the black card and key in another random number and hey presto! You're in. There's no point me telling you anymore because the staff will talk you through the internal procedures." He sat back with a smug look on his face. "Any questions?"

"Yes," said Nicks. "CCTV?"

"There isn't any," Alex replied.

"There's no CCTV?" Nicks squinted back at him.

"Absolutely correct." He looked even smugger now. "There's no need. If you knew the levels of security in these places you'd understand. Besides, it's one of the selling points for the customers." He caught Nicks' frown.

"It's attractive to people with dodgy things to hide. They feel safe with our banking practice and entrust all sorts of interesting things to our care which we feel, on occasions, need to be shared with the right people, anonymously of course." He flashed a broad smile. "Anything else?"

Nicks thought for a moment, "Just out of interest really, what stops someone digging their way in or trashing the entrance doors?"

Alex looked at him questioningly. Nicks didn't need to know this but on the balance of things he saw no reason not to tell him.

"If you can dig your way through twenty feet of steel reinforced high quality concrete littered with tremor monitors or get through three doors of ballistic glass and steel reinforcement then you deserve at least a cup of tea in reception." There was that smile again. "Right, now for the comms gear."

Alex opened the briefcase on the table and produced two devices and a set of in-ear headphones.

"Look just like Smartphones. This one," he waved the black one, "is a phone and radio combined. Similar to the system the Police use, but better. Encrypted phone calls, texts and radio transmissions."

"Will it play music?" Nicks interrupted, smiling condescendingly.

"Yes, it will but we don't provide it. Load your own just as you would a normal smartphone. Music has the lowest priority so everything else will interrupt it." Alex, seemingly unfazed by both the question and the smile, continued without pause. "This one," he held up the blue phone, "is actually a tracking device …." and so passed the next hour as he took Nicks through a practical on the use and capabilities of the equipment, including battery life and care, after which came the inevitable. "Are there any *more* questions?"

Nicks shook his head.

Alex looked relieved.

"Finally, when we need to speak to you you'll receive a text saying: 'Aunty Dot misses you'. If you receive a text saying: 'Aunty Dot needs a visit' make immediate contact and get your arse on the next available flight." He handed Nicks the black smartphone.

"What about the tracker?" Nicks said placing the phone on the table with his other stuff.

Alex shook his head, "Your handler will give you that each time you do a relevant job. This one's an old version, the battery life isn't as good but the controls are the same."

They sat and looked at each other. Alex rose from the table and said, matter of factly: "Well then, I've got other things to do, so *if* there is anything else you want to know you'll have to ask one of the others." He smiled, picked up his things, they shook hands and he left the room.

Nicks sat there for five minutes examining the items he'd been given. He'd been told someone would come for him when they were ready. Suddenly the door opened and Lofty popped his head in.

"Right, stash that lot in your room and I'll see you in the canteen in ten."

At 8.30 that evening they dumped him at Inverness with a "Good luck, Nicks" and a "Take care, son" and drove off without waving. *'It's always sad when the Circus leaves town,'* Nicks thought as he trudged into the station.

CHAPTER 7

Born and raised on the Wirral Peninsular Thurstan Braxton Baddeley had a happy if unremarkable middle class childhood in the affluent village of Caldy.

At 19 years of age, fuelled by his enjoyment of the Army Cadets, he'd walked through the gates of the Army Selection Centre in Sutton Coldfield, fresh faced and eager.

Three days later, sporting confirmation Army barbers knew nothing of the real world, he walked back out carrying a bag of damp sandwiches, packet of stale crisps and a travel warrant for the Royal Military Police Training Centre in Chichester. The year was 1986.

On completion of his training, armed with one stripe, he was posted to West Germany where almost immediately he came into contact with members of the SIB; army detectives, civilian clothes, collar length hair, long sideburns and, more often than not, a moustache. As soon as he saw them he knew he *had* to join 'the Branch'.

After two years hard work, Corporal Baddeley and his new moustache were selected for the prized 6 months attachment with an active SIB Section.

He'd shone and promotion to Sergeant soon followed. The work was interesting and varied: thefts, burglaries, serious assaults, robberies, rapes and murders. He'd found a home.

When his father died of a heart attack at the age of sixty eight, his mother was left rattling around the large five bedroomed house with its views over the Dee estuary lost in her grief, something which pained him deeply to see. His new posting to Catterick didn't suit him, it was too sedate and, feeling he should be there for her, he reluctantly left the Army and returned home. Despite everything he tried to do for her, without the only man she'd ever loved, the man she'd adored, his mother struggled with daily life and during the course of a year, she slowly deteriorated until one night she slipped quietly away in her sleep.

Accepted by the local Police Force he'd explained his circumstances and they'd been very understanding but were now pressing him for a date he would turn up for training. There was no cause for him to delay any longer, she was gone, and he missed her *and* his father immensely, but it was time to re-enter the world. Selling the old home, he bought a smaller new build for cash, banked what remained and reported for duty.

During his first two years, he managed not only to distinguish himself amongst his peers but also attract the professional admiration of the local Detective Inspector who recommended him for the Trainee Investigators Programme.

He was a 'natural' and, confirmed as a member of the CID, was back in the land he loved.

There were two major differences between his former job and his current one however. Firstly, he no longer had a 'captive audience'. In the Military, apart from the occasional 'dawn swoop', all he had to do in places like Germany and Cyprus, once he'd identified his prey, was to contact their Unit and request the suspect's attendance at the SIB offices. Sometimes his suspect would have gone AWOL, in which case he'd wait until the uniformed Military Police personnel picked them up in a routine sweep of known haunts and visits to the homes of the bar girls to whom they seemed drawn like moths to a flame. The more serious offenders who were devious enough to have left town, were circulated to the relevant Police authorities. In civilian life he didn't have that hold over them and was often surprised any of them turned up at all. Mostly, they didn't and with a colleague or two he would have to go out and fetch them in, if they hadn't already been arrested by a Uniform for some other offence.

The second difference was the volume of work. It was a lot higher and seemingly ceaseless. It was his version of cocaine and he thought he'd never tire.

CHAPTER 8
4th March 2014

Officially designated the A57, the only remarkable thing about Dale Street, besides its history, was the Magistrates Courts. In an earlier life Nicks had spent many hours giving evidence there against some of Liverpool's finest toe rags.

That the Magistrates Courts were where the 'tourist trail' ended was a fair comment because unless you lived in Liverpool you were unlikely to venture beyond to the two unprepossessing pubs that lay at its north-eastern end. The second, the Ship and Mitre, was renowned for its fine selection of British real ales and beers from around the world. It had the ambience of a good old fashioned British pub in the front part, whilst the rear had a slightly more continental feel. In either part, it was beer heaven for the devoted.

Crossing the junction with Hatton Garden and walking past the Excelsior, the more attractive of the two pubs, he entered the drab looking Ship and Mitre by the door on North Street. Taking the few steps down to the short corridor connecting both bars, he turned left and entered the dimly lit rear lounge, spotting his Handler at the far end of the bar.

Simon was in his early forties, with a rounded face, glasses and a mop of fair hair. Carrying slightly more weight than he felt comfortable with, he knew what he *should* do about it, but at the moment the beer was winning. Nicks liked Simon.

"Been here long?" he enquired.

"Nope," Simon replied. "I'll get these in. What you having?"

"Cheers. I'll have a draught Fruli."

"Pint or half?" Simon enquired.

"Pint, of course. Silly not to really," Nicks replied casually.

"Yeah, SNTR," Simon smiled.

They stood in silence as the barman poured their drinks. Nicks surveyed the room. Two stood at the bar and two tables occupied on the raised seating area; a young couple in the corner and three young males who looked like students.

The barman presented Nicks with his pint. Whilst Simon waited, Nicks sipped his strawberry flavoured Fruli wondering if it would count towards his 'five a day'.

Simon received his Kriek, gave the barman 30p from his change, turned and lifted his pint. "All hail to the ale", he grinned.

"We sitting over there?" Nicks pointed to a circular table for two furthest away from the other occupants of the seating area. Walking up the steps he sat down with his back towards the wall so he could see the rest of the room. It was a habit he'd had for a very long time.

They took satisfying gulps of beer and had a brief discussion about the current Premiership situation. It was brief because Nicks would never win a prize as a conversationalist, and in any event he'd virtually lost interest in football since pay and performance had seemingly stopped being connected. As they talked he meticulously straightened the spare beer mats on the table. Satisfied, he took another mouthful of beer and wiped his lips. "So what have you got for me?"

Simon leant forward. "Abdul Azeez El-Hashem." He took out the removable hard drive from the pocket of his jacket draped over the back of his chair, sliding it across the table to Nicks. "It's all on there. You could say he's a 'very naughty boy'. Not a nice man at all."

"How good's the Intel?" Nicks asked, picking it up and placing it inside his jacket lying on the seat next to him.

"Excellent." Simon smiled. "It's first hand Humint."

Nicks sipped his beer. "So, go on, what does Hugh Mint tell us?"

"It tells us that Abdul Azeez El-Hashem was a frequent enthusiastic visitor to training camps and facilities in Afghanistan, Iraq and lately Syria. He's given shit loads of, shall we say, 'inspirational' talks on why 'infidels' *and* those providing them support should be killed wherever they may be and how to go about it. It's first hand stuff."

Nicks frowned. "So how come this El-Hashem got back into the country?"

Simon looked apologetic. "Look, it's taken ages to gather this stuff. It's not easy to get information out from these areas, you know. Some of it's from very well placed resources and some from captive sources. Suffice to say, he wasn't originally seen as a huge danger. However, the Security Service has an extremely reliable source providing, at great risk, up to the minute Intel showing beyond doubt El-Hashem is the power behind several cells currently tasked with planning and carrying out attacks within the UK."

"Why don't they arrest him?" Nicks interjected.

Simon frowned this time. "Come on, Nicks, you know the justice system here. Don't get me wrong, mate, I'm glad we have it, but it's going to be very difficult to make this stick; it's basically all intel and this source is just too valuable to risk. How long did it take our local finest to put away some of the biggest villains in Merseyside? 20 years or so, if not more, and then they couldn't do it without a ton of co-operation with Customs and Excise and an outside Force or two."

"Ok, ok, I get your point," Nicks acquiesced, adding: "So what about the cells?"

"Not our problem," Simon replied. "Our concern is solely El-Hashem. They've decided we're going to take him out. The only issue here is the Security Service has him under surveillance but ...." He paused and looked around before continuing. "Having surveilled the surveillers, we've noticed there may be one or two opportunities for a benign intervention. Once the official surveillance has been lost, we're looking for a window of opportunity."

Nicks looked kindly at Simon. "So in other words, plan A is a wing and a prayer?"

Simon grimaced. "Sort of." He took another mouthful of beer.

Nicks sipped his Fruli thoughtfully, "Is there a plan B at all?"

Simon drained his glass slowly and stood up. "Nope. Fancy another? Same again?"

Nicks laughed.

"Yep? Go on! SNTR!" Simon replied with a grin, adding as he walked away: "Don't worry, I'll be with you all the way on this one."

Nicks smiled back at him sarcastically. "Oh, that makes it so much better."

They stayed another half hour discussing the music scene and forthcoming festivals. Nicks, as usual, bemoaning the demise of bands his 'patronage' had apparently doomed. He and Simon had a mutual interest, although their tastes differed. Nicks preferred something melodic and lyrically interesting. Simon apparently had no such qualms.

Finishing their drinks they put their jackets on. Nicks checked his to make sure he still had the hard drive. "Oh, and I'm going to need more. The names are inside," he said, handing Simon an envelope.

Simon folded it casually into his coat pocket. Walking away he called back. "I'll text you soon, ok?"

Nicks left the way he'd entered, stopping at the gents toilets. Age was catching up with him.

Walking back along Dale Street, now busy with office workers making their way home or to the nearest bar, he saw a couple of 'bucks', loafing outside a pub. They seemed happy, drinking their pints and smoking a fragrant 'brand' of cigarettes.

He stopped, checked his watch and feigned looking for someone so he could briefly listen to their conversation. They bore all the hallmarks of a couple of 'pumpkin positives', the sort whose brains were so small that if you shone a penlight into their mouths their heads would light up.

"Got off with it mate," said the ugliest one, in his nasal accent, to his only slightly more handsome colleague. "Sixty quid dey dun me fuh."

"Sixty, yer divvy!" exclaimed Handsome.

"Fuck off," said Ugly, "I tort dey wuz gonna bang me fuh two undrud buh me woolyback breef torked 'em aht uv it."

"Go 'edd, nice one, mate," replied Handsome.

"Ting wuz," continued Ugly, "I 'ad tuh ang around all th'savvy 'cos it wuz chocka. Did me fuckin' 'edd in."

Nicks moved off, smiling to himself. The scouse 'bucks' ability to imply victory from defeat but somehow spoil it all always amused him.

CHAPTER 9

The removable hard drive taken from his inside pocket and placed on the pillow, he folded his jacket over the chair by the dresser. Opening the wardrobe, he punched in the safe's 4 digit code then removed the tablet and cable, checking the other contents were as he'd left them. Swapping the hard drives, he connected the tablet to a power source and turned it on. The password field finally appeared: two chances to get it right before the drive wiped itself clean. After a moment's thought he punched in 14 alpha numerical digits. For Nicks it was simple. There were only two types of human being – nice people and arseholes. Race, nationality, religion, sex, sexual orientation or position in a society didn't matter to him. If you were an arsehole and on his 'to do list' he'd kill you without remorse and Abdul Azeez El-Hashem was an arsehole; a racist and religious intolerant, a purveyor of hate.

He erased the hard drive using the inclusive data destruction software and replaced it with his own. Placing everything back in the safe he locked up and put his jacket on. He'd Skype Anca later. Right now, he needed something to eat.

CHAPTER 10

He lay on the bed watching the news. A DCI with an unusual name was giving an interview about the previous day's shooting of a 'local business man'. He came across well and, somehow, Nicks knew he was looking at a decent, dedicated but very determined man. The DCI, he noted, was wearing an SIB tie. As an ex Military Policeman himself, he knew the Investigators of the Army's Special Investigation Branch rarely gave up easily.

The problem for the Army was that when the SIB entered an establishment to investigate some offence or allegation, there was no telling where it all would end. As enquiries unfolded they would follow whatever they found, wherever it went. It was not unusual for them to enter a unit to investigate an assault and come out having uncovered significant fraud, organised thefts of equipment and clothing, minor fuel scams and potentially serious breaches of security. Many considered them an immense nuisance.

Yep, the fact the DCI was ex 'Branch' was disconcerting.

CHAPTER 11
5th March 2014

His mother answered the door. "Frank, get the shotgun there's a strange man on the step." She took his carrier bag and pinched his cheek.

"I'll make you a nice cup of tea, eh? Go and see your Dad, he's upstairs, on the computer. I'll stick these on a quick wash."

Nicks went upstairs and popped his head around the door.

Frank looked up from the computer with a big smile.

"Hi son. I've just got to finish off the seating plan for the Lodge's Ladies Night and I'll be with you soon. Go and get your Mum to show you what we've done in the front room."

Nicks went back downstairs and drank his tea. Mum showed him the bookcases the 'wonderful man I married' had made. He had to admit Mr. Wonderful had done a very good job.

Sat in the living room Nicks knew what was coming next. There was no stopping her. Family news. He found these sessions tedious, but knew he had to do it. He never remembered who was who. Apart from funerals, he didn't see them often so he frequently confused names and faces. Both his parents came from large families and were very family orientated. Nicks wasn't. He was an only child. As a general rule, he preferred his own company.

"Oooh!" said Mum, "I didn't mention, did I? Cousin Justin?"

"Who's cousin Justin?" Nicks replied.

"You know him!" Mum insisted.

"No, I don't know him, Mum. If I knew him, I wouldn't have said 'Who's cousin Justin?' would I?" he smiled.

"Yes, you do!" she countered. "You met him at Dora's birthday party."

"Who's Dora?"

"Oh, for goodness' sake! She's your cousin Melissa's mother-in-law."

"Cousin Melissa? I've never heard of her."

"Yes, you have! You met her at the reunion."

"I never went to a reunion. I swear to God you make this stuff up, Mum!"

"Don't be so obtuse," she scolded. "You were there! So, don't argue."

"Well, I still don't know who this Justin is," he said quietly, trying to bring her back on track.

"Justin?" she said quizzically. "Oh! Yes, cousin Justin. What was I going to tell you about him? Never mind, it'll come back. Now, your cousin Melissa…."

And so it went. He knew once she'd imparted all the news, the family genealogy would be next. She'd taken up that particular interest several years before, but somehow, it had mutated beyond immediate family into researching people only remotely related. This did nothing to prevent her from holding lengthy phone conversations with their descendants, in New Zealand, while Dad grimaced and tapped his watch, rubbing his thumb and fingers together to signify the cost. He knew he was wasting his time but felt he had to try. That was the thing about her. She could make connections with anyone. She'd once had a conversation with a woman on a pedestrian crossing. Ten years later, they were still exchanging Christmas cards. Nicks couldn't do it.

After the news and genealogy, she rose from the sofa and began the ritual of forcing him to eat something. He offered token resistance, then succumbed to a roast chicken dinner which, 'co-incidentally,' just happened to be already prepared. Afterwards they played the game of 'What do you want for dessert?' The 'rules' were simple; he'd tell her he was full and she'd ignore him. Today she'd decided he was having cake. How could he resist? He couldn't. Life wasn't long enough.

The tour of the garden followed and Nicks admired their gardening skills whilst they discussed their new neighbours, a welcome change from the previous occupant; a fan of loud music, drugs and verbal abuse.

Finally, in spite of attempts to delay him, dry clothes in a carrier bag, he left having decided to drink at the Lady of Man, on Dale Street, in the city. He could sit out in the courtyard. He didn't like crowded places preferring somewhere he could distance himself from others and, of course, have a smoke.

It was early evening but surprisingly the courtyard was quite full and it was only as he walked up the entrance steps to the bar to be greeted with "Nicks! Glad you could make it!" from a man ladened with pints, whom he vaguely recognized, that he realized he'd walked into a Police function of some sort.

CHAPTER 12
9th March 2014

Up at 6 o'clock, he watched the early morning news and had a light breakfast of poached egg on toast topped with mushrooms. Outside, he had a smoke and checked the weather situation while he drank his tea.

It was a crisp, bright March day. The sky was clear, no rain forecast. Nicks decided it was a nice day for it, whatever 'it' was. He took his time.

Back in the room he showered and put on a pair of grey cargo pants, walking boots, a 'T' shirt, microfleece and dark grey waterproof walking jacket. He shoved his black neck gaiter and beanie hat into his trouser side pockets and put the spray plaster and latex gloves into the front compartment of his National Trust day sack, adding one thin single use plastic carrier bag and one thicker one, both folded four inches square. He took a clean handkerchief and an unopened packet of chewing gum from his bedside cabinet, threaded the lead to the headphones into his left breast pocket and plugged them in the 'job's' smartphone, attaching the pressel switch and microphone assembly inside, close to the jacket collar. Opening the room safe he took out some money, stuffing it in the concealed pocket of his cargo pants, relocked the safe and put on the £8 'Limit' watch Mary had bought him in Llandudno. It still kept perfect time.

He picked up his sunglasses and rucksack then left the room. Seconds later he re-entered, touching all the drawers in the bedside cabinets and the dresser, making sure they were closed. Leaving the hotel he put on his shades, inserted the headphones in his ears and selected a playlist.

The text had simply said: "Albert Dock. Welcome Centre. 0830. Tomoz." He looked at his watch. Plenty of time. He'd have his coffee there.

Simon found Nicks sitting on a bench at the northern entrance to the Dock, one of Liverpool's main tourist attractions. He pulled into the empty taxi rank then reversed back until he was opposite, leaned across the passenger seat and waved. It wasn't needed, Nicks was already up and walking towards him.

"Morning, and how are you today?" Nicks enquired as he installed himself in the front passenger seat and closed the door.

"Not bad," Simon replied. "The El-Hashem job's on. When I say 'on', I mean they're going to try the 'benign' intervention so we've time to get sorted. All the stuff's in the back."

"Where're we off to now?" Nicks inquired. "I need to check the weapon."

Simon smiled. "No probs, got it sorted. Lifeboat Road in Formby. There's a spot where we can stop and quickly disappear into the woods for the test shoot. We can go through any other stuff in the car when we're there."

"Ok," Nicks replied, then looked at the music CD sticking out of the player on the dashboard. "Anything decent on it?"

Simon laughed. "You can try it."

Nicks pushed the CD into the player. After two songs he ejected it and stared at Simon intensely. "Si, how on earth do you listen to this shit?"

"It's good," Simon replied defensively. "It's different. You need to broaden your horizons, Nicks."

"Yeah, I'm sure I do, but not today, thanks." He bent down to pick up a litre bottle of mineral water that was three quarters full and annoying him as it rolled about his feet. "How old is this?"

"Fresh this morning," Simon threw him a glance. "Help yourself."

Nicks did, then chose another playlist from his smartphone, settled back listening to real music and watched some familiar sights go by.

Simon pulled over onto a section of hard-standing on the left hand side of Lifeboat Road. A small opening in the fence separated them from deciduous woods; on the opposite side were pine woods with an open aspect. The road was narrow and named because it once led to the long gone Formby Lifeboat boathouse, established as Britain's first between 1771 and 1776.

It wasn't a perfect position, but at this time of the day the road was quiet and they were beyond the last of the houses. It was enough.

Nicks applied the 'spray on plaster' to the ends of his fingers and thumbs then, when dry, he pulled on a pair of latex gloves as Simon 'popped' the boot from inside. He moved the 'junk' Simon had stored there and found the metal mechanic's case containing the weapon. It was pale grey and looked just like a large socket set. Inside under the soft cloth, a SIG-Sauer P226 DAK with raised sights, threaded for a suppressor, the suppressor itself, a loaded magazine and a box of spare

124 grain 9mm JSP ammunition. Simon joined him acting as both lookout and cover for his actions. Nicks quickly checked the weapon was safe by pulling back the slide, locking it in place with the locking lever and checking visually that the chamber was clear of ammunition.

Simon handed him the National Trust bag, already opened. With his left hand, Nicks removed the thicker of the two carrier bags, shook it out and placed the weapon in it. Then he stuffed it in the day sack along with the magazine and suppressor. He took the soft cloth from the 'gun case' and wrapped one round from the spares box in it, stuffing it in his pocket. As he did so, Simon took a quick glance around and said, "Yep, it's OK."

"Right. Bring the water," Nicks replied.

He walked through the gap in the fence and into the wood. After 30 metres he stopped, placed the bag on the ground, opened it and removed the weapon. He attached the suppressor, inserted the magazine and released the locking lever so the slide moved forward under the pressure of the spring, picking up a round from the magazine and loading it into the chamber. Unwrapping the spare round, he ejected the magazine and fed the round into it before sliding the mag back on the weapon.

He chose a spot roughly 20 metres away, behind which a fold in the ground rose gently several feet, and pointed. Simon, carrying the four litre bottle of water he'd taken from the boot, placed it down and returned to the car. Seeing him exit, Nicks raised the Sig, pausing momentarily as he breathed in, then gently squeezed the trigger. 'Klak'. The bottle reacted to the obvious hit. He recovered the ejected shell casing and walked over to check the result. He'd aimed at the centre of the white oval on the label. Satisfied, he wrapped the weapon in the soft cloth, put it back in the carrier bag and zipped up the day sack. Picking the bottle up by its carrying handle he threw it into the bushes.

Returning to Simon, he enquired, "Well?"

"Sounded like a twig snapping," Simon replied. He looked at Nicks. "You happy?"

"Very," Nicks grinned.

They got back in the car and Nicks placed the day sack carefully on the floor between his feet. Simon leant around dragging a small black rucksack off the back seat and placed it on his lap, opening it as he did so.

"Right, you might need this. It's a tracker," Simon informed him producing a small slim black object. "Simple device. As you can see, it looks like a smartphone. Press and hold this button firmly for 3 seconds. Let's call it button 'A'. It'll send out an encrypted signal which any colleague within a 5 mile radius will be able to pick up and then track you, right down to the last metre. Hold this button firmly for 3 seconds, let's call it button 'B', and the screen comes on. You can now do exactly the same as your colleagues, provided they've also activated their trackers, and it'll show you your own position relative to theirs. Touch screen, which can be magnified like any normal smartphone, and it'll track up to 5 people at any one time. Any questions?"

"Nope," answered Nicks laconically. Simon had been doing so well he didn't like to tell him he'd seen and used one before.

Simon threw the rucksack on to the back seat. "Right, let's go then. We'll have to turn around in the car park at the top." He started the engine and put it into gear, releasing the clutch. The vehicle jerked forward and stalled. "Fuck!" he exclaimed.

"Try taking the hand brake off at some point, Si. It might help."

"Fuck off!" Simon replied in mock indignation, starting the engine again.

"I suppose it's the wrong time to ask if we can stop somewhere for another bottle of water," Nicks tormented him.

"Yes, it fucking is," Simon retorted, struggling now to get the handbrake off. "For fuck's sake!"

"In your own time." Nicks smiled inwardly as he replaced his earphones.

CHAPTER 13

"Mornin', Timothy."

Pete Simmons threw his small rucksack onto the bed in the front bedroom of the little terraced house in Burnley. It was 4 am.

Tim Argent pulled his glasses off his nose, rubbed his eyes and yawned.

"Mornin', Peter."

Simmons peeled off his jacket and dropped it on top of his bag.

"Is there a brew on?"

"Yeah, Farooq's just making it." Tim replaced his glasses, stood up and stretched. "Nothing to report. The blue minibus is still there, hasn't moved all night and there's been no comings or goings," he said, yawning again.

"Fine," Pete replied, slipping into Tim's vacated seat. "You stopping for one or getting straight off?"

Tim lifted his jacket from the coat hook on the back of the bedroom door. "I'm out of here. Just want to get to my bed now." He gave Simmons a wan smile then made to leave the room, stepping back momentarily as Farooq Hussein entered carrying two steaming mugs. "See you later, Farooq," he said as he left the room.

"Yep. See you, Tim," Farooq replied absently, placing Pete's mug down on the desk in front of him before pulling up a chair and sipping his tea. He watched the three screens on the desk, images from miniature cameras in the eaves of the house, front and rear.

"Mover one….Silver clear to exit," the voice whispered from the encrypted radio Simmons held to his ear. "Silver, yes yes," Tim's voice replied.

Farooq sipped his tea again. It would be another hour before Ben, Simmons' colleague, arrived. Only then would he be able to get to his own bed. And so it'd been for the last month. Three days on: two mobile, one static, one day off. Four teams of two each. Under normal circumstances it might've been adequate, but El-Hashem was a savvy customer when it came to his anti-surveillance drills. They'd soon realised the inadequacies, requesting an increase almost from the start.

Having lost him a couple of times they'd decided to put a tracking 'lump' on his hire vehicle. It all seemed to be going quite well until a drive past of the vehicle, parked on double yellow lines in Bolton, found it empty. They'd watched it for an hour and a half when its position attracted the attention of a Police foot patrol. The Officer was obviously checking its details on the PNC when he was approached by a white male in his late forties. As they watched, the male gesticulated towards the inside of the driving compartment then opened the door taking something from behind the driver's sun visor and showed it to the Officer, along with a sheet of paper he'd taken from the pocket of his jeans.

Through their local Special Branch liaison officer they ascertained the white male was the hire company rep who'd been contacted by the hirer to recover the vehicle. *They* needed to recover the 'lump' and salvage something from the day. The vehicle was impounded.

So physical surveillance all the way it had to be, but that presented further problems. El-Hashem had started to employ a multiple vehicle, multiple driver strategy. Using a network of Muslim owned small hire companies they found they'd embarked upon a hit and miss intelligence gathering exercise. The fact that all the vehicles they followed used basic anti-surveillance drills such as frequent random turns, u-turns and multiple circulations of roundabouts hadn't helped at all. On some occasions they picked what they thought was the right vehicle only to find it contained a body double. Sometimes they were lucky and obtained usable photographic intelligence. Several times they'd been to the seaside on either side of the country and simply watched El-Hashem and others eat ice cream; on one occasion they'd watched him and Nazim go for a walk in the woods at Delamere.

It was obvious to them they were dealing with a man who'd a lot to hide but their requests for more people received the inexplicable answer that the situation did not warrant such a move. During the last week though, they'd been told more staff had been sanctioned but it couldn't take place until the following Monday.

Pete Simmons, as the overall Team Leader, understood the logic. He was the only member of the Team who knew of the existence of a 'mole' within El-Hashem's sphere of influence, although he didn't know their identity. His senior officer told him Abdul Azeez's arrogance had grown and he was speaking more openly to audiences throughout the North than he had before. Important information was being gathered. All Simmons had to do was keep the morale of the team up. Not the simplest of tasks in the circumstances.

Later that morning Ben and Pete were sitting watching their targets gather. The house was diagonally opposite, five doors down. Nazim and Hakim arrived first and were standing on the pavement talking. Next to arrive, Amir. All three were well known to the surveillance crew. The last had been Salim, an occasional visitor they considered a minor player. Pete watched the screens while Ben was taking photographs.

"Another day, another dollar," Ben said quietly.

"So it seems," Pete murmured. It wasn't unusual for there to be activity at this hour. Suddenly they heard footsteps on the stairs.

"I thought you'd be ready for something to eat and a cuppa." It was Noor. "I've done you both some fried egg sandwiches with tomato sauce and a mug of tea for you, Peter, and a coffee for you, Benjamin." Noor was not a fan of name shortening. She placed the tray on the desk in front of the screens. "I don't like those two. They've not got a pleasant reputation around here and that Nazim, I don't like the way he looks at me. Gives me the shivers."

Ben had known Sahid and Noor since university. It was Sahid who'd tipped him off when El-Hashem had come to live in the same street.

"If you need anything else, I'll be downstairs but I've just got to pop out later on for some shopping and Sahid'll be back at four."

Ben sat on the bed and ate his sandwich, taking occasional sips from his mug. Pete remained watching the monitors at the desk, tomato sauce dripping onto his plate as he munched away. They'd both just finished and were wiping their hands on the paper towels

55

when Pete leant forward peering at the screen and exclaimed: "Game on! They're off." He quickly picked up the handheld radio. "Eagle, Mover one."

"Mover one."

"Eagle, all five subjects now in the blue minibus. Standby..." he paused, writing down the time on his log sheet, 09.43 hrs, then: "Mobile now towards Burleigh Street."

"Mover one, yes yes."

Amir drove the minibus to the junction with Burleigh Street and turned left. At the junction with Brougham Street he turned right, carefully easing his way past the large bin lorry that was stationary on double yellow lines outside the hairdresser's, before continuing on towards the B6434 at the end of the street. Mover one pulled away from the kerb reaching the junction within ten seconds.

"I have the eyeball. He's right, right, right, onto Brougham towards the B6434. Shit!"

The white, two axled, box truck pulled out of the street opposite and stopped with a jerk, at an angle to the waste management vehicle. The driver started to shout and gesticulate at the occupants who returned the compliments.

"Mover one, I'm blocked Brougham Street. Lost the eyeball." He knew where Mover two and three were positioned; effectively prevented from taking over. "Mover one, Mover four?"

"Mover four, yes yes, at the Asda. I'll pick him up at the roundabout."

Amir arrived at the small roundabout next to which stood the Asda parking area and supermarket. He drove around it twice before taking the exit into Rectory Road which served a small industrial estate and two rows of houses running parallel to the main carriageway.

"Mover four, I have the eyeball, twice round the roundabout now taking a left, left, left into Rectory Road."

Mover 4 left the Asda service road and took the same exit. Meanwhile the two truck drivers were face to face in the middle of Brougham Street. Fisticuffs were imminent.

"Mover four, he's taken the exit from Rectory onto the B6434. Fuck me!" the operator said, slamming on his brakes, as an articulated truck and trailer emerged from the side road to the industrial units and stopped at the junction blocking his path. "I'm blocked on Rectory Road. A fucking artic. Temporary loss." He banged on the horn and shouted out of his window. "Move, you fucker, come on!" The truck driver looked back at him and shrugged his shoulders. Mover 4 threw the vehicle into reverse gaining enough space to mount the grass verge to his right.

Selecting first gear, he started to drive over the grass hoping to circumvent the truck, but as he did so, it slowly pulled out onto the main road blocking him, taking up both lanes. He waited for it to straighten up, but it didn't, by which time he now had three vehicles in the outside lane impeding his access to the grassed central reservation, waiting for the same thing. Several more vehicles joined the queue. He was screwed. He banged the steering wheel several times, shouting "Fuck! Fuck! Fuck!" then over the radio, "Mover four, lost the eyeball. Last seen towards the motorway."

After what seemed like eternity but was in reality no more than three minutes the lorry, after much grinding of gears, started to move, slowly, straightening up jerkily. Nobody seemed to feel the need to let Mover 4 out into the outside lane, so it was only when he'd reached the roundabout he made any progress.

Amir took the M65 motorway; east to Nelson, the next town. Somewhere, in the anonymous traffic behind him, a calm quiet voice: "Whisky three with the eyeball."

They left the minibus in Forest Street, boarding a waiting people carrier. Rejoining the M65, Amir headed west towards Preston and the M6 motorway. He didn't know it yet, but they were on their way to Delamere Forest. Mover 4 flashed past them on the opposite carriageway.

Meanwhile at the other end of Stoneyholme, the driver of an articulated lorry parked in Monk Hall Street, close to its junction with Danehouse Road, heard: "India one and two clearing." He picked up his radio and said: "India four yes yes," then drove the vehicle right onto Danehouse in the direction of Nelson. It was a tight turn which held up the traffic but he managed it.

CHAPTER 14

Following Nazim's instructions, Amir had taken the M6 south, the M56 and the A56 to Frodsham, where they took a left turn at the traffic lights into Church Lane.

The motorcyclist behind them said: "Whisky six, left, left, left at the lights. The B5152 towards Delamere."

"Whisky one, yes yes. Looks like the forest again. Anyone take the car parks?"

"Whisky seven, taking Whitefield."

Two other call signs volunteered; a motorcyclist and two saloon cars sped up the long slow incline of Fluin Lane, Frodsham, towards its eventual junction with the B5152.

"Whisky six, I can take the Ashton Road car park if someone takes the eyeball."

"Whisky five I have the eyeball."

Seeing an opportunity for an overtake, the motorcyclist Whisky six pulled out and shot past the people carrier leaving it in her wake.

"Whisky five. Subjects blocked by traffic entering the car park at the shopping parade." Thirty seconds later: "Whisky five, mobile now towards Delamere, thirty miles an hour."

Whisky seven reached Whitefield car park with ease and parked centrally towards the far end. The occupants, a couple in their sixties, stood at the open boot of their car and were donning drab coloured walking jackets when Amir, giving them only a casual glance, drove the people carrier containing El-Hashem and the others passed. A Jack Russell Terrier scuttled back and forth around the couple's feet.

Amir parked the vehicle in the north-east corner, reversing into position. Other than themselves and the couple with their dog, the car park contained only five other vehicles. They remained seated.

Whisky seven's occupants now stood on opposite sides of their car as the 'husband' poured some tea from a thermos flask and passed it to his 'wife'. To an onlooker they were just talking and enjoying a quick drink before taking their dog for a well earned walk.

Abdul Azeez El-Hashem sat in the front passenger seat of the people carrier. "The English and their dogs," he laughed, then looked at his watch and said to his driver: "Amir, we seem to be early. You stay here and wait for our friends."

"How will I know them?" Amir looked quizzically at him.

Abdul Azeez smiled benignly. "They will find you."

He turned around in his seat and declared to the others: "It is a nice day. Come with me for a walk. I have something to discuss with you."

He turned back, opened the door and got out. They stood outside putting their jackets on, then Abdul Azeez said: "I seem to remember this is a pleasant walk," indicating the footpath fifteen metres away. He strode off, the others obediently following.

Whisky seven's crew observed the movements within the vehicle and reacted to the doors opening by calmly packing up the thermos and cups into their car. A quick call brought the dog running to the female, who having leashed him said quietly into her concealed microphone, "Seven one...four subjects on foot to north east pathway into woods. Subject four remains with vehicle...subjects into woods now. Keeping the eyeball." Her call sign indicated she was now on foot.

"Whisky one, yes yes."

She and her partner set off at a brisk pace along a trail leading east into the trees. As they walked she reported: "Seven one. Subject one now wearing blue jacket with fur hood."

Within thirty metres of entering the tree line they reached a junction with a track running north. Out of view of Amir in the people carrier the male set off at a jog northwards. His partner continued to broadcast the descriptions of the others, slowing her pace to a stroll until she found herself in a position to monitor the people carrier and its occupant through the trees. The dog sniffed around then urinated briefly on the nearest tree trunk.

Nicks exited the car just before the entrance to the car park. At a fast jog, he took the path leading along its northern edge. As he ran he activated the tracking device and replaced it in the right chest pocket of his waterproof jacket.

"Elvis on plot. Talk me in," he gasped into the microphone.

"Seven two, yes yes" replied the male operative. "Tracking now. Slow down but stay on that line. Temporary loss."

Nicks wasn't complaining. He'd overlooked the fact he hadn't even run for a bus recently and had set off too quickly. He slowed to a manageable jog, concentrating on getting his breathing regulated. He could now see the people carrier parked at the top end of the car park so knew he'd have to veer further to the left if he was to remain

61

unseen by its occupant. Ahead he could see the junction of two paths. He broke into a brisk walk taking the left one which he saw opened out onto a field after approximately seventy metres. He checked behind him to his right and saw his view of the people carrier was obscured by the trees.

"Seven two … Elvis"

"Elvis, go 'head."

"Seven two. Eyeball regained." He was out of breath and whispering. "Keep on that track. When you get to the end where it enters the field you need to turn right and come along the tree line for two hundred metres then stop. Subjects temporarily halted in a small clearing sixty metres from that location."

"Elvis, yes yes."

Following the instructions, he picked his way along the edge of the field, still happy he couldn't be noticed from the car park. After what he estimated to be two hundred metres, he used the undergrowth for cover.

"Seven two… Elvis"

"Elvis. Go 'head."

"Seven two. Interesting development." He'd got his breath back now, but was still whispering. "Subject one directing matters. Subjects two and three have jumped five and now have him tied up kneeling on the ground. Subject one not happy. Repeatedly slapping five about the head and face."

"Elvis, yes yes. Wait... wait," Nicks replied, taking out the tracker device and holding down button 'B' firmly whilst counting to three. The screen sprang into life. "I'm tracking you now."

"Seven two, yes yes. You need to go another fifteen metres further, then turn to face me. They'll be directly in front of you, sixty five metres away."

"Elvis, yes yes."

He moved slowly and carefully along the tree line until he heard "Seven two. Elvis. Stop. Subjects in a direct line towards my location, sixty five metres from your position." Nicks checked his tracker then replaced it in his chest pocket, acknowledging the call. Concealed by the undergrowth, he pulled up his neck gaiter to cover the lower part of his face, took his beanie hat from his leg pocket and pulled it over his head: the combination left only his eyes exposed. Removing his day sack, he took the P226 from its coverings, briefly checked the magazine and suppressor were secure, zipped the bag up and put it back on. A deep breath then he moved stealthily forward, through the trees and sparse undergrowth.

"Seven two, Elvis."

"Elvis. Go 'head," Nicks whispered.

"Seven two. Subject one has left the group. He's walking up a mound that separates the group from you and... wait.... wait... he's over it now and out of my view heading in your direction."

Nicks stopped. "Yes, yes ... What about the others?"

"Seven two, I think they're going to top him. One of them's filming while the other one's waving a big fuck off knife about and looks like he's giving some sort of speech."

A whispered: "Yes yes ... Elvis has entered the building."

He moved swiftly through the trees in a crouch, suddenly seeing his target walking away from the incline over which remained the rest of the group. El-Hashem turned to his left and after a few paces stopped, taking up the unmistakeable stance of a man about to relieve himself of body fluids. Nicks slowed but continued forward, carefully placing his feet so as not to break anything underfoot that would attract El-Hashem's attention. The Target, undisturbed, unleashed a stream of urine onto the forest floor.

Nicks, now less than fifteen metres from him, raised the weapon. Pausing momentarily, he squeezed the trigger. 'Klak'. El-Hashem collapsed instantly. As he hit the ground, his face slapped against the urine soaked dirt and debris of the forest floor.

Abdul Azeez El-Hashem's last thought was fairly mundane. It was simply: "I wonder how far I can piss."

As quickly as stealth permitted, Nicks moved to the base of the incline then began to crawl rapidly up it, making sure he didn't gain his viewpoint at the same place El-Hashem had left the group. On reaching the top of the mound, he slowly, carefully, peered over it and saw them. One was blindfolded and kneeling on the ground facing away from him, his hands clearly fastened behind his back, his head bowed. Alongside him, and nearest to Nicks, stood another, holding the kneeling man by his hair whilst gesticulating with a large knife in

64

his right hand. The third male stood facing them, filming the event on a small hand held camera. The man with the knife began proclaiming: "Allahu Akbar. Allahu Akbar." Nicks raised the P226, sighted and exhaled.

"Allahu Akbar. Allahu Akbar," Nazim said to the camera, his voice raised in passion. With a final flourish of the knife, he stepped quickly behind the kneeling Salim, pulled his head up so his neck was exposed and was about to draw the knife across his victim's throat when he suddenly collapsed as if his strings had been cut. He didn't even register the 'Klak' the 226 made as it sent him on his final journey.

Hakim, who was filming, heard the 'Klak' but didn't understand its importance or meaning. He was still struggling to comprehend what had happened to Nazim when the next two rounds slammed into the top of his chest and throat. He dropped the camera and, clutching his neck, sank to his knees before collapsing onto his right side.

Nicks scrambled up from his firing position making his way down the incline. He didn't bother checking Nazim. He knew he didn't have to. He was more interested in Hakim. The headshot hadn't been on because of the way he'd held the camera so he'd opted for two to the top of the chest. As he approached Salim he said: "Don't say a fucking word! If you say anything I'll kill you." He walked calmly past him, noting his ankles were cable tied, and went to Hakim. Standing over him, it was obvious he was still alive. He was making gurgling noises and moving his left leg as if to gain a position from which he might be able to stand up or at least make it to a crawl position. He had no fight, but Nicks could see his flight response was still partially intact. He rolled him onto his back. From Hakim's eyes he saw he was still taking things in. Nicks leaned into his field of vision, unmasked his face, smiled and softly said: "God is indeed great" then, pulling the neck gaiter back over his nose, he stood up and shot Hakim in the head. Bending down again, he picked up the camera that lay between Hakim's now lifeless legs, and pressed 'stop', then 'rewind'.

"Stay exactly where you are. I'm watching you," he said to Salim before pressing the camera's 'play' button followed by 'fast forward'. Satisfied he didn't appear on the footage, he dropped the camera back on the ground between Hakim's legs and went to Salim. "You understand me, don't you?"

"Yes," sobbed Salim, the tension and relief followed by returning tension proving too much for him.

"I'm going to leave you now. I want you to count slowly to six hundred. If I hear you shouting before that time has passed, I *will* come back and kill you. Do you understand?"

"Yes, I understand you," whimpered Salim.

Nicks leant close to his ear: "You know that little voice in the depths of your head, the one asking you if you're doing the right thing? Who do you think that is?" He waved the weapon casually around. "This lot, they're just a random selection of knobheads venting *their own* anger. God's not speaking to them, he doesn't want to speak to knobheads but he's talking to *you*. Listen for fuck's sake!" He stood up, looked down at the sobbing Salim then leant down again whispering in his ear: "I was sent to save you. Fucking earn it."

With that he was gone. Up and over the mound, past the body of Abdul Azeez El-Hashem, or whoever he really was.

CHAPTER 15

At the tree line he crouched down and placed the day sack on the ground. He made the weapon safe: removed the magazine, ejected the live round from the breach, visually checked the chamber then released the working parts. The ejected round placed back in the magazine, he reloaded, wrapped the Sig in the soft cloth, turned off the tracker, dropped them both in the plastic bag which he stuffed in the day sack. Zipped up, he put it back on. Neck gaiter off, hands in pockets, he walked along the small track that led to the car park entrance where Simon would meet him. He took out the smartphone radio, selected 'Music', brought his left hand up to the pressel switch as if adjusting his collar and said: "Elvis has left the building." Mr Blue Sky filled his ears.

A couple walked towards him on the track. In their early seventies, they had a black and white springer spaniel, off the leash. The dog roamed back and forth in the field; the woman shouting in a high pitched voice: "Rebel! Come! Come, Rebel!" Rebel was living up to his name. They looked typical upper middle class country types. That wasn't what concerned Nicks though. It was the dog.

He nodded politely to them as they passed, quickening his pace. He didn't want to be in view if Rebel decided to go walkabout in the trees behind him. No expert, he *knew* this sort of sporting dog was good at finding things that had just been shot.

Skirting the car park, he looked to his left as the people carrier came into view through the trees. The driver was standing in front, pacing up and down using his mobile phone. On the home stretch, he saw Simon pull into the funnel shaped entrance and swing the car around in readiness to leave. Nicks veered off the path and walked through the scrubby undergrowth, stepping over the low wooden barrier onto the dirt track.

Halfway across, he briefly stopped as Whisky 7 coasted past him and turned left onto the main road. Throwing the day sack in the passenger well, he sank into the seat and ripped the headphones from his ears, closing the door behind him.

Simon moved off from the fence line, checking for oncoming traffic before turning right.

"How'd it go?"

"Fine," Nicks replied casually. "The body count got a bit high though."

"What do you mean?" Simon had a serious frown. "I lost comms there for a while."

Nicks bent down, opened the day sack and removed the magazine from the P226, laying it carefully next to the still suppressed weapon. It was now unloaded and completely safe but returning it to an operational state would take mere seconds.

"Well," he said eventually, "they were going to saw a blokes head off with a fucking big knife so I didn't really have a choice."

"Fuck!" Simon exclaimed, "How many are we talking about?"

"Just the three," Nicks replied. He turned to look at Simon and said: "What?" inviting a response.

Simon quickly looked back at him. "Nothing. If it had to be done, it had to be done. What happened to the victim?"

"I left him there, still blindfolded and cable tied," Nicks replied. "Someone will find him soon, if they haven't already."

"Ok, so be it. Everything ready to go?" Simon looked at him again. Nicks nodded in reply.

"Right, stuff it all in the little black rucksack on the back seat," he said.

Taking the plastic bag from his day sack he transferred it to the black bag which already contained the gun case and the box of ammunition. Removing his latex gloves he put them into the thinner plastic bag then stuffed it all into the map pocket of his jacket before bending down to recover the new water bottle from the footwell.

Winding down the window, he held his hands outside and poured water over them to remove any powder residue left by the gloves. The window wound back up, he took several gulps of water and dropped the bottle back by his feet.

They reached Beech Lane, a narrow road where two way traffic was just about possible with adept use of several gated entrances. Simon pulled into one, as close to the gate as possible, and turned off the engine.

Within minutes, the small blue van pulled up at an angle in front of them. The writing on its side indicated that the blue overalled driver, an equally small man of middle eastern extraction, was a mobile mechanic. He got out of the van carrying a small black rucksack.

Simon tugged the bonnet release, pulled the rucksack from the back seat and got out. They put their bags down and Simon lifted the bonnet. The mechanic stuck his head under for a few seconds then walked around the vehicle before lying on his back and tussling with something near a wheel arch. Eventually declaring satisfaction, he got up, the bonnet went down, they picked up the rucksacks and parted ways.

"What was all that about?" Nicks asked, as they continued their journey. "Why didn't you just give him the bag?"

Simon glanced at him before replying. "We had to get the tracker taken off. The type you've got is no good for vehicles. It hasn't got the range and the body of the car interferes with the signal."

They drove back to Liverpool, stopping briefly in Runcorn where Nicks dumped the carrier bag containing the gloves in a bin.

He was glad to get back to the hotel. Putting the smartphone radio on charge, he stripped off, placed his clothes and National Trust day sack in a bin bag then stuffed them into his large rucksack. He'd take them to his parents tomorrow for a 'special Mum clean'. After a shower and fresh clothes, he decided to eat later because right now he was going to the appropriately named 'Slaughter House' next door, for a pint. Probably more.

CHAPTER 16

Salim knelt and counted through the tears, the man's words tumbling around his head. In the distance a high pitched voice called: "Rebel! Come, Rebel!" Suddenly, a mobile phone rang. It was close; it must have been Nazim's. Eventually it stopped. He kept counting.

Amir was worried. They'd been gone for what seemed like an age. He wondered what they were talking about. He decided to phone Abdul Azeez. Getting out of the vehicle he paced up and down in front of it as he made the call. The phone was off. He phoned Nazim. No answer.

He could hear a dog barking. Instinctively, he made his way along the track and through the trees towards the sound. Coming upon the clearing he froze, momentarily, then dropped down on one knee behind a tree.

Two bodies lay on the ground. Salim knelt, blindfolded, between the bodies, his arms behind his back. A dog stood on a mound barking towards something out of Amir's sight. Panic started to grip him. The dog, still barking, ran down the mound towards Salim.

Amir ran back towards the track leading to the car park. By the time he reached the people carrier and saw Abdul Azeez hadn't returned, he knew it was time to leave. He'd go to the other car park and wait. Maybe Abdul Azeez would call him and he could pick him up somewhere. Yes, that's it, that's what he'd do.

Driving to Delamere Railway Station, he reversed into a space and turned the engine off. Thinking clearer now he took out his mobile phone, found the number and tapped 'call'.

"Pizza Napoli, Luigi speaking. What would you like?"

"Luigi, we have a problem," Amir said to his MI5 Handler.

CHAPTER 17

Finding something interesting, Rebel lost all inclination to obey his owner's calls. The elderly couple walked into the woods to find their wayward dog. The husband told his wife to remain and save her legs whilst he went to fetch the springer; stubbornly barking 30 metres away. Closing on the dog, he saw the body. He gingerly checked for signs of life. There were none. Returning to his wife he told her to phone the Police.

Rebel continued to bark then suddenly ran up the mound, stopping at the top where he looked intently back at them then at something beyond their view. He barked again then disappeared. The man swore under his breath and began walking up the slope.

CHAPTER 18
11th March 2014

At the bottom of an anonymous set of steps in Sweeting Street, lay the unprepossessing basement office of Granger, Harland and Sackville, Solicitors.

It may have been thought that Rupert Sackville had outlived his partners, but in reality they'd never existed. An invention, solely to give his practice more gravitas.

He represented many people, but in truth had only one actual client. Mark Anthony Stephen MacMahon, whom he referred to as Anthony, pronouncing the 'th', as was intended by MacMahon's parents when they named him. It could be said he was the 'family' solicitor, for he represented all the members of MacMahon's criminal gang except for one. Tommy Cole insisted on having his own. They'd never been on friendly terms. In fact, he knew Tommy despised him. For his part, he didn't despise Tommy Cole. He just feared him.

Now Anthony was dead, Rupert Sackville feared Tommy Cole even more. He'd lost his protector, his friend and the man he'd secretly loved. He'd been 'Brian Epstein' to MacMahon's 'John Lennon', having fallen for his presence and good looks the first time he'd represented him as Duty Solicitor at the Mags Courts, all those years ago. Anthony had been only twenty years old and he'd been thirty five. Last week had been the worst week of his life.

He knew Cole would replace him. It wasn't a matter of loss of income that worried him. He'd been very careful with the money he'd earned. Anthony had been very generous, but then again he *had* worked hard to earn that generosity and had done things that hadn't been in his career plan prior to their first meeting. True, he lived well, as did his mother with whom he shared his home on Allerton Road. They'd wanted for nothing, and Anthony had always treated his mother with the utmost respect. She in turn had treated him like another son. No, it wasn't the money. He just didn't believe Tommy Cole would let him walk away.

He looked at the clock on the wall. Seven o'clock. He needed to get home. Mother would be worrying. He'd had no idea she knew about his feelings for MacMahon. She'd never said anything. But now, with his passing, she'd told her son she'd known from the first moment he'd brought him home. Then she'd held him as tightly as her frail form could, as he broke down and cried in her arms. She said he should take some time off, but he'd gone to the office hoping it would make things easier. It hadn't.

Putting on his thick, warm overcoat he set the alarm, turned off the lights and locked the entrance door. Then he climbed the anonymous steps to the narrow open gateway bounded by a building line one side, black wrought iron railings on the other. It was only as he neared the top and his security light went out that he realised the normally lit street was in darkness. Stumbling on the top step he steadied himself with a hand on the railings and stepped out onto street level.

He didn't see where the man came from. He just felt himself being swung by his coat lapels against the metal security shutters of the office next door. He grunted involuntarily as his head hit them hard, then again as a punch to his diaphragm left him breathless. He felt the grip on his throat as his head was banged against the brickwork.

His assailant let go. He collapsed onto his backside, heard the click, saw something glint. A coarse scouse voice said: "Yuz 'av brung dis on yerself, yer fucking snide, yer fuckin' mummy's boy. Tony's not 'ere tuh fuckin' save yuz anymore, or yer fuckin' Ma."

By the front of his coat, he was pulled to his feet. "Please! No! Please! I've done nothing wrong. I've done nothing!" His hands were waving wildly in an attempt to fend off the attack. He held the arm that held the knife, but knew he couldn't hold it long. His assailant was too strong, *he* was too weak. He felt the punches to his head, the warm urine flooding his groin. He was going to die. "Oh, Mother! Mother!" he heard himself call. He sobbed as the last of his strength ebbed from his grip.

"Ay! Ay! Pack it in, Lad!" A nearby shout. "Leave him alone! I'm callin' the Bizzies!"

The assailant slid his arm free of Rupert's exhausted hands. "Yuz won't be so fuckin' lucky next time," he snarled then ran off along the alley towards Dale Street.

Seconds later, a man was standing over him, helping Rupert up, supporting him against the security shutter. "Are you ok, mate?" he said with a softer scouse accent. "Do you want me to call the Bizzies?"

"No, no..." Rupert struggled to get the words out. "I'm... I'm alright... I think I'm alright." He wiped his eyes.

"Can you walk?" asked his saviour. "We need to get out on to the main road. It'll be safer. He might come back."

"I think I can..."

Rupert took a few faltering steps. "Yes, I think I can manage it."

His rescuer steadied him as they walked slowly towards Castle Street and the bright lights. "Av you been robbed, mate?" he asked. "You need to report it, you know."

"No. No, it was just a disgruntled client. There's no need for the Police." He was feeling better, more in control of himself now. "I'm fine. Thank you so *very* much for helping me. I don't know what I would have done otherwise. Silly of me to work so late."

As he spoke he checked himself. His head was throbbing and he had a few lumps on his scalp. His hands had several superficial cuts to his palms and knuckles.

"You should put somethin' on them when you get home," the man suggested. "Listen, I think you should get a taxi. Here's one now." They'd emerged onto Castle Street and turned towards the Town Hall. Without waiting for a reply, the saviour hailed a black Hackney which swung into the marked loading bays nearby.

Rupert clambered into the back of the cab. Sitting down he turned to his 'hero'.

"I cannot thank you enough. I haven't got any money to give you. I think I've just got enough to get home."

"Not a problem, mate," the 'hero' smiled back at him. "I never dun it for money. I dun it 'cos you needed help."

Rupert handed him a business card. "Look, I know it's not much, but please take this. If you ever need a Solicitor, I'd be more than happy to provide my services free."

Hero took the card. "Thanks, mate. You never know in Liverpool, do yuh? Take care." The man shut the door and was gone. Rupert couldn't turn around to see him walk away; his neck was now suddenly very sore and stiff.

He gave the taxi driver his address and sat back in the seat, acutely aware that his trousers were very wet. He examined his hands which were still trembling. He'd been lucky. If his rescuer hadn't intervened, he would be dead by now.

During the journey he phoned the Police and told them he was calling on behalf of his elderly mother who'd seen an intruder in the back garden. He then spoke to *her*, telling her the Police would be there soon, so she should 'play along' until he got home.

"Is this all about Anthony and his friends, dear?" she'd asked.

"Yes, Mother," he replied.

"You can trust me," she'd said simply.

The fear within him began to turn to anger. Never give them a second chance, Tony had taught him. If Tommy Cole expected him just to roll over and take it, he could think again. He knew all about MacMahon's safety deposit box. It had been him who'd suggested it. He'd even placed things in there himself when Anthony was too busy to make a 'deposit'. He knew most of its secrets, particularly Anthony's 'insurance policy' against Tommy Cole.

When he arrived home, a Police car was outside and two Officers were sat in the kitchen with his mother, enjoying a cup of tea.

CHAPTER 19

Three minutes after Rupert Sackville's taxi left Castle Street, two workmen strolled into Sweeting Street. Hi-visibility orange jackets and blue hard hats, they carried a toolbox and a short lightweight metal ladder. Opposite Sackville's office, one took a few steps up then opened the electrical box mounted on the wall. His colleague handed him a small screwdriver. A couple of turns and the lights glowed into life.

CHAPTER 20

He turned the corner and walked, unhurriedly, out onto Dale Street; hands in pockets, heading towards the Ship and Mitre. Without pausing, he dropped the flick knife into the first litter bin and disposed of the latex gloves at the next, spraying his hands with sanitizer.

He was receiving his half pint of Fruli when Simon entered.

"Pint or half ?"

"Just a half," Simon replied.

He ordered then looked at Simon over the top of his glass as he savoured the taste. "How'd it go?"

"Fine. He was pretty shaken up and he'd pissed himself. Left a little puddle on the floor. Oh, and he had some cuts on his hands, on the palms and across his knuckles." Simon thanked the barman and took a satisfying sip of Kriek.

"Wasn't intentional." Nicks leant back on the bar. "He was waving his arms about like a crazy fucker. He kept grabbing the blade. Anyway, it was your fault. What took you so long?"

"Someone asked me directions." He calmly took another sip then noticed the look on Nicks' face. "What? I got there, didn't I?"

"Fucks' sake!" Nicks exclaimed quietly. "What are you like?"

"It would have been impolite."

Nicks shook his head in disbelief.

"I take it he didn't want to phone the Police?"

"No. As expected," Simon replied, absent-mindedly, as he counted the change he'd taken from his pocket. "Listen, I haven't got enough money for another round. Can you sub me a tenner?"

Nicks pulled a face that said 'not again' and laughed. "Yeah, no probs." He took the note out and handed it to Simon.

"Ta." He held it up to the light. "You can't be too sure can you? Same again?"

Nicks nodded.

Simon grinned. "Great, enough left for a kebab."

CHAPTER 21
14th March 2014

DCI Baddeley entered the main office, signed in and glanced up at the TV screen above him as it reported the local news; footage of a helicopter landing in a field, civilians in suits and barbour jackets emerging whilst the newscaster said details of a large counter terrorism exercise, held in Delamere Forest at the weekend, had just been released; shots of Police road closures, tantalising glimpses, taken at some distance, of balaclavered, armed, black clad people loading heavy bags into a military helicopter.

"Sorry I'm late," Thurstan said as he entered his office where Chalkie, Lizzie and Degsy sat drinking their coffees. "Collision in the Tunnel. Tunnel Police had it down to one lane." He unbuttoned his coat and stuck his head out the office door, catching the attention of a passing Detective. "Taff, any chance you could get me a coffee, please? Milk and one sugar. My mug's on the tray by the kettle."

"Not a problem, Boss. Just give me two minutes to get rid of this stuff," Taff raised the pile of papers he was carrying.

It'd been ten days of intense activity for everyone in MIT. Another naked body had been found out in St.Helens, and Thurstan's team had been working practically around the clock. Assisted by other specialist units and patrol officers, they'd arrested MacMahon's rivals and 'friends'. Every power of search the Police and Criminal Evidence Act provided them was utilised and when not possible, they used search warrants from the Magistrates Courts. Organised crime came to a standstill, temporarily. They'd wanted to send out a message: there would be no repeat of the armed conflicts that'd once invaded the streets of Liverpool.

Thurstan looked enquiringly at the three of them. "Ok, where are we up to at the moment?"

Chalkie looked at Lizzie. "Go on Liz, your stuff first."

She put her cup down. "Right. Well, we've no outstanding warrants left and everyone on the 'circulations' list has been arrested. All interviewed. Fred and Devon finished the last one just before midnight down in Thames Valley somewhere. They've not long gone off duty. I've debriefed all the interviews first thing this morning, making sure at least one from every interviewing team was on shift. Nothing. No hard info. The overall feeling was the 'bucks' are clueless. They just don't know who's responsible. Any new DNA and fingerprints are going through the system now." She smiled and picked up her cup.

"Ok, thanks Liz," Thurstan smiled back. She had a lovely smile. "What have we got from the 'walk ins', Derek?"

Those were the few higher placed criminals like Tommy Cole who'd presented themselves, with their 'briefs', at various Police Stations throughout the county. Knowing at some point they'd be receiving the inevitable visit, they felt their 'business interests' were best safeguarded if they co-operated.

"All more than adequately alibied," Degsy replied, "particularly Tommy Cole, who was at a wedding in Cheshire. I've spoken to the venue. They provided the photographer and I've seen the photos. He was definitely there all day."

Thurstan gingerly sipped from a steaming mug. "Chalkie?"

"As you know, the searches were quite productive – couple of cannabis factories, a counterfeiting press and a good selection of firearms and ammunition. All being dealt with by the Matrix. Nothing for us though. Overall, the word from the street is it's not local, probably 'out of towners', although no one's got a clue who. I think we need to look at MacMahon's wider business interests, something intel's not aware of, maybe." Chalkie picked up his mug, saw it was empty and replaced it on the table. "One interesting thing is the unaccounted fingerprints in his car belong to one Monica Jean Masterson a.k.a Monique Masterson, previous for shoplifting, nothing recent though. I'd guess she was his 'bit on the side'. We're still trying to find her at the moment."

"Ok, so that means we've no outstanding DNA or fingerprints from the car. What about the white van that stopped next to the workmen?" Thurstan shot a glance at them all in quick succession, not sure who had the enquiry.

Lizzie chipped in. "Nothing, Boss. Been back onto them, but none of them can remember anything about the registration number. However, one of them now remembers seeing a bin man. You know, the sort with his own cart?"

"And we've made enquiries with the Council who tell us?" The DCI interjected.

"They tell us they didn't have anyone in that part of the city and, before you ask, all their carts were accounted for anyway. Some sort of audit was going on." Lizzie smiled sweetly at Thurstan. It was, ostensibly, a victory smile.

"Thank you, Lizzie, don't let it go to your head!" He smiled back. "Where did we get with the CCTV? I know the stuff from around the scene all seems to have a temporary fault, which, though unusual, is not unheard of but what about anything from Chapel Street, Old Hall Street, etcetera?"

This time it was Degsy. "I've been looking at that one, Boss. I know it's taken a while, but with everything else going on, it was difficult to co-ordinate. I had to resort to getting some of the local bobbies to make the enquiries and get us copies, some of which got stuffed in a bobby's locker while he went on rest day. So, I apologise for the delay."

The DCI nodded his appreciation. Degsy continued, "I've had a composite made up by the technical fellas and I've set it up to view in the quiet room, it's easier to see the screen in there. The thing is every sequence recovered from Old Hall Street, through the primary scene and onto Chapel Street and Tithebarn has sections that are totally unviewable."

"Was that a localised issue, or was there some sort of 'city wide' problem?" Thurstan ventured.

"It was localised, Boss. I took the opportunity to get some stuff from a selection of premises within a quarter of a mile. The problem only seemed to occur within one hundred and fifty metres of the outer area of Old Hall, Chapel and Tithebarn. It's best to take a look at the composite." Degsy sat back with a resigned look on his face.

86

Thurstan pursed his lips and thought for a few moments.

"Ok. What about the ballistics? Chalkie?"

The DI searched through the papers on his lap, producing three sheets of A4 which he passed to the others. "Well, as you can see, the forensics on the bullet, or what was left of it, together with the analysis of the shell case recovered, has produced a list of weapons that would produce similar characteristics namely a right hand one in ten rifling twist with six rifling grooves. What we're looking for is, to put it simply, a semi-automatic pistol. It's not a huge list, but it's not a small one either. We can rule out certain makes of pistol, basically those with polygonal rifling which is completely different from what we're looking at, that's why you won't see old favourites like Glock and Heckler Koch on there. Forensics put Sig-Sauer and Beretta at the top because they reckon they're the popular models and therefore more likely."

Thurstan sat, elbows on desk with his hands clasped, fingers interlaced underneath his chin. "Ok, thanks for that." He let out a short sigh. "Now what about house-to-house, such as it is? You, I believe, Derek?"

"Nothing at present, Boss. Nobody saw anything, it appears, but we've still got a couple of guests from the Apartment Hotel to speak to. Most of them were out for the day sightseeing, only two couples hadn't left the hotel and were in their rooms." He desperately stifled a yawn. It had been a busy time. To top it all, the twins hadn't been sleeping well recently, consequently neither had he and his wife.

Thurstan noticed. He was well aware of the strain affecting everyone but was particularly concerned about the two DSs who were shouldering a lot of responsibility organising and managing the teams.

"Right then!" he said, tapping his hands lightly on his desk. "Let's take a break. Go and get a drink or something to eat from the canteen. The fresh air will do you good and I'll see you both in the quiet room, in...," he looked at the wall clock, remembering he'd forgotten to get someone to find him a fresh battery. He glanced at his watch. "Let's say twenty five minutes."

Chalkie remained seated as Lizzie and Degsy left the room.

"Sackville?"

Thurstan nodded. "Just close the door, Chalkie, please."

Rupert Sackville had requested contact with a Matrix senior officer who'd visited him at home the evening of his attack. He'd told the Matrix DCI everything he knew about Tony MacMahon's safety deposit box in return for Police protection.

"The Matrix want it kept well under wraps at the moment. As you know, we recovered the contents of MacMahon's safety deposit box yesterday. It was interesting. Some sort of accounts ledger, an events diary and some photos of Tommy Cole executing someone in Oglet Lane, Speke, two years ago. It's written on the back. It was taken using an image intensifier and, I should think, quite a powerful lens. So, what we need now, Chalkie, is for you to liaise with the Matrix in respect of *anything* in the ledger and events diary that may provide us with any leads, particularly to MacMahon's wider business interests. See who he's upset elsewhere in the country."

Chalkie stood up. "Ok. Not a problem. What about Tommy Cole's photo?"

"I'll get Arthur to dig us out some info on that. He'll probably be able to tell us all about it off the top of his head anyway." Thurstan smiled. "Oh, and the Matrix and the National Crime Agency are putting together an operation based on what was found so we should see some developments in the next week or so."

He pulled a business card from his inside jacket pocket. "Speak to this fella at the NCA, they might have something that can help us." He handed it to Chalkie who glanced at the card.

"I know him. Ex Met. I'll get it sorted."

Thurstan stood at his office window overlooking the car park for a few moments, deep in thought. Returning to his desk he picked up the phone and dialled an extension. "Ah! Arthur. It's Thurstan. Do you know anything about a murder two years ago, Oglet lane, Speke?" There was a pause. "Yes? Wonderful! You do that, and I'll see you shortly in my office." Another pause. "Yes, I would actually! Milk and one sugar."

CHAPTER 22

DS Drayton was looking forward to eating undisturbed. He walked back into the main office, carrying his ham salad sandwich and 'latte to go'.

"Sarge! Phone call for *you*. Sergeant Tranter, St. Anne Street." The Foetus held his arm up. Degsy strolled over to him, took the handset and said:

"Sarge, nice to see you the other day. How've you been?"

"I've been fine, young Derek," the 'Sarge' replied, "and it's Bill. We're both the same rank now. About time you got used to it."

"Well, old habits die hard, Bill. What can I do for you?" Degsy took a mouthful of coffee.

Those who incurred his displeasure knew Sgt Tranter as 'Billy Tarantula'. A sobriquet he was not unpleased with. Sometimes lessons had to be learned the hard way, and if Bill Tranter thought it necessary, then that's how you learned them. Once, after parading for duty on 'mornings', Degsy had engaged in idle chat with a member of the section going off duty and was late getting to the front desk to collect the radio he needed for patrol. Bill was waiting for him and saw through his feeble excuse in an instant. "Well, if you can't be arsed to collect your radio, then I can't be arsed to give you one. Now go on, 'fuck off' onto your beat. You've got a whistle."

As Degsy trudged miserably out of the station, Bill called after him. "And be at Broadway shops at nine. I'll peg you there." Degsy was, and Bill had signed his notebook then handed him a radio with a brief: "Lesson learned, I hope."

If you did your job he was no problem. If you were a shirker, heaven help you.

"I've sent a young bobby across to see you," Bill said. "He should be there any minute. Young Mike Bartlett, he's a good lad. He's got some information to tell you about the MacMahon job. You might know already, but then again you might not. It's been bothering him for a while, so I'll let him explain when he gets there, but go easy on him. As I said, he's a good lad, keen as mustard. Reminds me of you, when you were a probationer."

Degsy laughed. "He must be amazing then! Ok, I'll be nice to him. Mike Bartlett, you say?"

"Yes, and don't be telling him what I said. I need to keep him on his toes. Can't be having him getting *over*confident at this stage of his career. Look what happened to you." It was Bill's turn to laugh now. "No, if he turns out half as good as you, Derek, he'll still be a good un."

"I won't let him know there's a soft heart in there somewhere, Bill. Your secret's safe with me," Degsy replied, smiling broadly.

"You'd better not, Derek. I know where you live." They both laughed then said their farewells.

Derek finished his coffee as he ate his sandwich in the quiet room. He'd just polished off the last mouthful of ham and salad, and was brushing the crumbs off his trousers when The Foetus leaned through

91

the doorway and said: "Apparently I've been mistaken for the receptionist. There's a bobby here to see you, Sarge."

He looked up as Constable Bartlett entered the room. A smart looking young officer; apprehension and awe for the 'big boys' of the MIT marking him out as a probationer. Sitting him down Degsy listened as Bartlett recounted his seeing the guest at the Apartment Hotel filming with his mobile phone.

"I'm sorry, I didn't think much of it at the time but it just kept bothering me and Sergeant Tranter must have noticed and, well, here I am. I just thought what if he'd been on the balcony filming at the time of the murder, but hadn't realised what went on? The Sarge said it was better late than never."

Degsy smiled at him, "No, that's great. We haven't been able to make contact with a couple of the guests yet. Fourth floor balcony you say?" The Officer nodded.

Thurstan walked in. "Right, are we all here?" he said as he entered. "Sorry, Derek, am I interrupting anything?"

"No, Boss, we're finished." Degsy stood up taking a pace sideways. "This is Constable Mike Bartlett from St. Anne Street. He's just given me some really good info about seeing a guest at the Apartment Hotel doing some filming of the scene when we turned up there. He thinks it's possible he might have recorded something earlier on."

Mike Bartlett stood up. Being unsure whether, in the presence of a Senior Officer, he should put his helmet on or not he decided he would just fumble with it instead.

Thurstan advanced upon him, hand outstretched. "DCI Baddeley," he said. Bartlett shook his hand. Thurstan continued, "Well, that's good. Nice to see someone using their initiative. You're one of Sergeant Tranter's section, aren't you? Make sure you listen carefully to what he has to tell you. Knows his stuff, your Sergeant, excellent man." He glanced around the room. "Are we ready to view the videos, Derek?"

"Yes, Boss," Degsy replied.

"Right. Well, let's not detain the Officer any longer. I'm sure he's itching to get back out on the street." He smiled. "Thanks again for letting us know. I think it could be very significant."

Degsy escorted the Officer to the main office exit, chatting as they walked. As Mike Bartlett disappeared along the corridor Lizzie came in. "Sorry, Degs, I *had* to go to the loo and then the cleaner got chatting. I thought I was never going to get away."

When they'd run through the composite of the CCTV from the area of the scene, Thurstan said: "Just play that again Derek. The bit two or three clips back. But this time can we slow it right down?"

Lizzie sat forward on her chair. "Yeah, I thought I saw something right at the end of it, just before the camera position changed."

Degsy replayed the section but now in slow, slow time.

"What's that? Re-run it." Thurstan screwed up his eyes and pointed to the screen. "That's it! Stop!"

They all peered at the screen which now showed a colour still picture. It was slightly blurry, but it was unmistakably the image of a street cleaner pushing a cart.

CHAPTER 23
13th March 2014

Nicks entered the India Building from the Water Street entrance and strolled along the ornate shopping arcade admiring its coffered barrel-vaulted ceiling, pendant lights and shops with their decorative bronze fronts. It was one of Liverpool's hidden gems.

He stopped now and then to look into one or two of the shop windows: he had time to spare before heading for his appointment at the safety deposit bank.

He'd just turned from the sweet shop when he saw them. Four suits entering the Brunswick Street entrance. Two looked like 'bosses', one in particular he felt he'd seen before. The third, with slightly dishevelled elegance, was Rupert Sackville. But it was the fourth who'd caught his attention most. He'd worked with him briefly on a couple of firearms jobs. The last Nicks heard he'd done a bodyguard course.

They'd stopped at the entrance to the alcove where the lifts were situated, discussing something. The bodyguard wasn't interested. He was too busy eyeballing his immediate surroundings, standing passively with his hands crossed over each other at trouser belt level. The position of his hands told Nicks he was right-handed.

Too far away to register as a threat, a couple of paces took him further as he feigned interest in something in the window. Another quick glance, this time through the glass entrance doors behind them; a people carrier, another suit, younger, sunglasses, left hander.

They moved into the alcove; he knew where they were going. Walking back towards the Water Street entrance, he took his phone out, pressed the speed dial and after a few seconds said: "Hi, I've got an appointment for ten thirty this morning. I'm afraid I'm going to have to cancel. Certainly, my name's Ian Hughes. Yes, would the day after tomorrow be ok? Eleven o'clock? That'll be great. Have a nice day."

CHAPTER 24

After an early life of car theft, during which he'd been fortunate enough to meet Rupert Sackville, Tony MacMahon graduated to armed robbery. He drove for the 'big boys' and made decent money which he didn't splash around. Sackville had taught him that, as well as suggesting some very useful investments.

He'd known Rupert was gay from the start; it hadn't been a concern for him. The man was damned good at his job. With his wisely chosen barristers for Tony's sporadic Crown Court appearances, he'd kept him free from convictions. He knew Rupert was 'fond' of him, he'd been careful to nurture that 'fondness' whilst making it plain where his own preferences lay.

With Rupert's counselling, he'd seen the writing on the wall. The Police had bought themselves a shiny new helicopter and he knew it would catch him sooner rather than later, so he'd bought himself a small local vehicle recovery concern and by way of 'aggressive marketing' built it up to be the flagship of its kind within the county. A lucrative contract with several insurance companies followed. A small clothing shop was purchased for his wife Lisa.

They both had a natural ability for the wheeling and dealing required for success and had gone from strength to strength. He'd acquired several more legitimate companies. They actually turned over excellent profits and had been doing so for years. Meanwhile Lisa's clothing store expanded into all the Northwest's major towns and cities. Even the Taxman was happy, he was getting his share, albeit not as large as it should have been.

He was a good businessman, but he found being legal just *too* easy. Missing the 'buzz' of criminal activity and 'life on the edge', he went into the import/export business. Importing drugs and exporting violence.

Tony MacMahon had, in reality, always fancied himself as 'The Godfather' and that's exactly what he'd become to some. Ruthless and benevolent in equal measure, he'd beat someone with a baseball bat, or have them beaten, then pay for them to be privately treated in the best hospitals available.

Silence ensured a return to the fold, at a lower position of responsibility. Those who failed to see sense would find themselves and their families physically and mentally intimidated until they did. Then, he'd be generous. Occasionally though, he'd had Tommy Cole despatch them to a better place. Not necessarily better for them, just better for him and Tommy.

He'd cash financed other things; two transport companies, two property developers, a travel agency and, of course, there was the funeral directors. His involvement was untraceable. He didn't appear on the list of directors or anything else connecting him to any of them but he took a cut of the legal profits and the lion's share of the illegal ones. The Funeral Directors didn't generate any illegal earnings but it'd been very useful on several occasions.

He'd money and property all over the place. True, based on the money the Sunday Times *thought* he had, he hadn't made their Rich

List, but what did they know. With regards to where his money actually was, Lisa knew only half the story. Only he and Rupert Sackville knew the full picture.

But now it was time, he'd thought, to sit back and think about enjoying it. No point in pushing his luck. He'd take the entire family, parents and all, somewhere warm and nice to live. Spain seemed favourite. They *all* enjoyed Spain.

Unfortunately, Tony hadn't been able to concentrate on setting a date yet. He'd a little problem. She was 5′4″ and called Monique. He loved his wife. More than anything else he loved his kids. But, he also loved the thrill of 'playing away from home' and he'd had a string of mistresses over the years.

Lisa was a formidable woman, still attractive at forty five and hard as nails. She'd told him a long time ago; if she ever found out he was cheating on her she would take his kids and make sure the only time he *ever* saw them would be in a burger bar, one Sunday a month; if he was lucky. He knew she'd do it.

Monique had been fun, twenty eight years old, vibrant and carefree but sadly naïve enough to believe he loved her. When he'd tried to end what was for him just another affair she'd threatened to tell Lisa everything. He couldn't understand what her problem was. He'd set her up in her own apartment on the docks, bought her a nice car, jewellery and lined her bank account with enough cash to keep her comfortable for quite a while, all untraceable to him, but she just wouldn't let it lie. Insisting he loved her, she *kept* saying Lisa should know her marriage to him was history. He couldn't, under any circumstances, let that happen. She was a ticking time bomb. She *had* to go.

His meeting with the intermediary had gone well. The guy seemed to know his stuff and he'd come highly recommended from 'out of town' contacts. Tony paid 50% up front with the rest to follow within days of completion. He was surprised but pleased the plan was ready to be actioned that very evening, the intermediary having two 'experienced' Birmingham associates in Liverpool ready and waiting for the word, which Tony readily gave.

But there'd also been 'that weasel Kehoe' to deal with. His police source earned his money with that one. He'd known they'd a 'snitch' somewhere in the business, but hadn't thought it would be Kehoe. Alfie reminded him of himself from the very early days and he'd actually liked the little fuck. It was unforgiveable. Tommy would sort him. He knew Tommy enjoyed dealing out a bit of long slow torture with the offer of forgiveness being followed by savage realisation.

He and Tommy had a long history together, it went back to the old days of the vehicle recovery firm, but Tony was aware he'd become increasingly ambitious. He'd started conducting his own business on the back of 'the firm' and the realisation he shouldn't have taken him into his confidence so early about his retirement thoughts had now sunk in. It had given Tommy too much time to think and thinking wasn't Tommy's greatest strength. Tony knew he would screw it up.

Ostensibly, nothing in their relationship had changed but it was there. He could feel it. He'd always relied on him, but he'd never trusted him completely. That's why he'd got his 'little insurance policy', the photos from Oglet Lane, where Tommy had done his bidding. It had cost him a pretty penny, but the ex Special Forces guys, whose motto was 'who pays wins', had done a great job.

Tommy was planning an early change of management, he felt sure. He knew he wouldn't have the patience to wait. No point in stalling any longer. He had to sort Tommy before Tommy sorted him. Well, that had been the plan.

CHAPTER 25
15th March 2014

Simon watched Nicks arrange the bank notes in his wallet in denomination order, Queen's head facing forward. They were in the cafe of the Merseyside Maritime Museum.

"So how many do you need?" he eventually asked him.

"Two," Nicks replied, replacing his wallet in the side pocket of his combat pants, satisfied with his work. "I've written the names down on the back and here's the old IDs. I still need one set for the next hotel."

He slid a small white envelope containing three debit cards and driving licences across the table to Simon, who glanced at the names Nicks had written before placing it in his pocket with a smile. "Ok, I'll get them onto it straight away."

It was normal practice. Nicks would supply them beforehand with identities he felt comfortable with, and they'd produce standard packages of a debit or credit card and driving licence in each name. Out of boredom, he started to throw in the occasional name that made up a phrase or could be amusing if written in the right form. No one appeared to notice, which served only to entertain him even more. Recent efforts included: Richard Spring, Jack Goff and Michael Hunt.

"Oh, and I'll remind them to put the cancellation in for just after ten o'clock tomorrow, if that's ok?" Simon looked at him for confirmation.

"Fine," Nicks replied. "I'll have a coffee and an almond slice while I'm waiting for the text."

It was simple. A booking would be made and later cancelled, taking advantage of hotel cancellation policies. Nicks would receive confirmation then walk in off the street asking if they had a room free. Seemingly by chance they always did. He'd produce a debit card as 'security' and the driving licence as his ID, should it be required. If the hotel photocopied his ID for their records, it mattered not because the photo driving licences were produced with an in built transparent layer acting in a similar way to number plates designed to thwart traffic cameras. It was the same with any photo ID he used. Hotel staff very rarely took much notice of photocopies showing a photo too dark to be of any significant use as long as the personal details were visible. If they did comment on it Nicks would apologise and state it was all he had. Faced with losing business over such a triviality the toner always got blamed.

All the bankcards would withstand scrutiny and related to accounts inserted into the relevant banks' computer systems, complete with a record of payments in and out. Normally he paid in cash but if he had to 'bug out' before settling the bill the charged card would always pay out. No names were used twice and all accounts would subsequently be deleted.

"You having another one?" Nicks asked, sipping his latte whilst considering whether to finish it or make it last.

"No, I need to get back to work, they'll be wondering where I am," Simon replied as his phone buzzed in his jacket pocket. Reading it he frowned.

"You're going to need to hang around a bit longer than expected," he said apologetically.

"Why?"

Simon shrugged. "Not sure at the moment. It just said to put you on hold and they'd get back to me within a couple of days."

Nicks sighed. "You'd better give me two more IDs."

He scribbled another two names on the back of the envelope. Standing up and putting on his coat, Simon replaced the envelope in his pocket. "I'll get these sorted. Text you when they're ready."

CHAPTER 26
18th March 2014

DCI Baddeley and DI White stood in front of the team gathered in the main office. Chalkie called everyone to order then Thurstan stepped forward and began the briefing.

"Good morning everybody. Sorry for the early start, but we need all the time we can get. The body found in Potter's Wood, close to the junction of Crank Road with Abbey Road, St. Helen's, has been confirmed to be that of Monica Jean Masterson, also known as Monique Masterson. She'd been strangled, stripped, rolled up in an old carpet and *dumped* just inside the fence line."

Thurstan selected his words with care. He'd emphasised the word 'dumped', using it as much to convey his contempt for the person or persons who'd taken Monica's life as to describe the reality of the situation in which her body had been left. Believing she deserved respect he would avoid referring to her as 'the deceased', 'the body' or 'the victim' wherever possible. She had been, and was, Monica Jean.

He continued in a measured manner. "It's evident whoever was responsible hoped to make it look like the work of our St. Helens killer. However, she'd not been sexually assaulted, her breasts and genitalia were intact, and therefore due to this, and one or two other matters, our colleagues on the St.Helens investigation team are satisfied this is not the work of their killer. This one is down to us now." He paused for effect. "It appears whoever murdered Monica Jean lifted her over the low fence and dropped her into the undergrowth. There's no indication the perpetrator climbed in to straighten things up so we believe at least two people were involved in the placing of her body.

"From the roadway she couldn't be readily seen and initially anyone who did approach the fence close enough to notice would've simply seen an old rolled up carpet and, I believe, think it to be the work of fly tippers. From the condition of the body, it's estimated she'd been there for around ten days before she was found, which puts her death roughly around the same day as Tony MacMahon's.

"Her car was found, parked and secure, in the car park at Calderstones Park. It's a Fiat 500 Gucci model, light blue, which she's owned for three months and paid £17,000 cash for, apparently. Not something she could easily afford, so, *that* and the fact her fingerprints were found in MacMahon's car give rise to a strong suspicion she was a mistress of MacMahon's, but this has still to be absolutely confirmed. A local night patrol checked the car two days before her body was found and as there were no reports on it and, not surprisingly, Monica couldn't be contacted, the patrol placed an information marker on the Command and Control system.

"Forensically, we've gained nothing from it except her mobile phone on which there's a text message from an unattributed phone saying 'Meet me at the usual place 1 am. Good news.' The car park itself, as you know, is well used during the day so any external evidence that may have been there is now, unfortunately, well gone. The St.Helens enquiry team are releasing some of the Matrix Disruption who'll be conducting House to House enquiries from

Allerton Police Station." He turned to Arthur. "Their Supervision will be controlling that aspect, Arthur, and of course any searches we need doing, so it's business as usual for you." He paused surveying the room. "We don't believe Monica Jean's death is mere coincidence *but* the contrast in the modus operandi in respect of MacMahon's killing would tend to suggest our killers are not the same, although we need to keep an open mind on this.

"DI White will be running the enquiry, assisted by DS Johnson, and they'll now let you know who's working which enquiry and brief you accordingly *so*, unless there are any questions you feel can't wait until they brief you further, that's all there is from me." He paused again. The room was silent. "Oh and local CID are providing extra personnel. I asked for five so we'll probably get three." He turned to his DI and added with a weak smile: "It's all yours, Chalkie. We'll speak later when you're ready."

Catching Degsy's eye, Thurstan pointed to his watch flashing the five digits of his right hand and pointed to his office with his thumb. Degsy nodded.

"Right, Derek, what have you got for me?" he said waving him towards a seat, five minutes later.

The DS shook his head, declining the offer. "We need to view this, Boss." he said, placing a CD on Thurstan's desk. "As you know, Sparky and Sandeep went down to Hertfordshire and picked up the witness footage from the guy on the balcony. Sandy downloaded the original file and we've had it copied."

"So we're off to the quiet room to view it?" Thurstan asked.

106

"No, Boss. I had the IT Department put a player on your PC last night so we can view it here." Degsy moved around Thurstan's desk so he could access the computer. "Is it ok if I sit here?" he asked, indicating Thurstan's chair. "It'll just be easier to sort stuff out."

"Help yourself," Thurstan pulled up a small chair and sat next to him.

"Right, here we go," Degsy said clicking 'play'. "I looked at it last night. It's not great and, as you'll hear, he's being distracted by his wife, which accounts for it being all over the place, but there's two bits of interest."

They sat in silence watching a disjointed account of room, balcony, street, brick walls, pavement, road and sky with the odd fleeting glimpse of a human being.

When it finished, before Thurstan could make any comments, Degsy said: "The bits where we actually saw someone I've had isolated and…" He made several quick clicks through the disc menu. "This first one shows the front of MacMahon's BMW, then sweeps across the roadway and we see the figure… now, then it's gone. OK, the second sequence; slightly longer, figure again, see the hand movement? I'll play it again. I thought he was maybe talking into a microphone or something, so I got it blown up, but it's hard to tell. It's too blurred."

Thurstan watched the replay with interest. "Just stop it there Derek."

Degsy paused the footage.

"It's not good, but it looks to me like he's got a beard, what do you think? Looks a bit middle eastern?" Thurstan ventured.

"Yeah, what I thought, Boss," Degsy replied.

"And you're right; he could be talking into a hand held mike. Just play it again."

The Boss stared intently at the screen.

"Hmmm, it's hard to tell, Derek. He could just be rubbing his nose and that bit looks like the thing people with beards tend to do. Have you ever noticed? They sort of run their hand around their mouth and chin. Or it could be he's just doing that to cover his use of a microphone, who knows. Can't we get a better enhancement?"

"I've asked, Boss. Apparently it's the original resolution that's the problem. His phone was only a cheapie. Can't put pixels where pixels don't exist, I was told," Degsy replied apologetically.

"Not your fault, Derek. Tell you what; let's look at the first clip again."

CHAPTER 27
18th March 2014

"What would you like?" asked the barmaid at Ma Boyles in the grandly named Tower Gardens, in reality not much more than a large alley.

"Two pints of Guinness, please, if you've got any left?" Simon replied, smiling, leaning on the bar. He nodded to the bar's other patrons. The two men nodded back. He looked around the room. It was empty. He checked his watch. Maybe Don had been held up.

"Busy yesterday?" he asked the barmaid. It had been St. Patricks Day, or Paddy's Day as Scousers preferred to call it. The barmaid rolled her eyes and the men chuckled.

"Did you get me a Guinness?" Nicks manoeuvred the bar stool and nodded to the two men as they tacitly helped Simon prevent any possibility of the bar counter collapsing. They nodded back.

"Yeah. You sort them out?" Simon answered. He was referring to the three Japanese tourists who'd asked them for directions as they'd been about to enter the bar.

"Yep. No guarantee they won't still be wandering around at midnight though." Nicks surveyed the room. "You checked downstairs?"

Simon looked up from inspecting the wooden bar top. "I thought it was only the toilets down there?"

"No, there's another room," Nicks replied, picking up the pint the barmaid had just placed on the counter and taking a mouthful.

"Have you come to meet the posh fellah, love?" the barmaid enquired. Before either of them could answer she continued. "He's downstairs waiting for you. He said he'll pay for these." She looked at the other pint of Guinness she was pulling. "It takes a while to settle. I'll bring it down to you."

Thanking her, they descended the stairs into a dimly lit room where they found Don the only occupant, sitting at a table at the far end beside the ornate but closed bar, sipping what looked like a sherry.

"Thanks for coming, chaps," Don smiled, his usual pleasant façade. He didn't get up but just waved his hand indicating where they should sit.

"Right, Nicks. Sorry to have delayed your departure, but we have something that you may feel you could action whilst you're here," Don continued in measured tones. "Unfortunately the window of opportunity has closed temporarily, but I thought I'd brief you anyway, knowing what your position is regarding matters you might view as political. Now, whilst there is a political aspect to this, I think you need to consider the finer detail." He lifted his head as he saw the barmaid approaching with Simon's Guinness and paused, holding his palm up to alert the others to the need for silence. Simon turned, received his drink and thanked her.

"If you need anything else just let me know," she said pleasantly. "I'll make sure you're not disturbed." She reserved a special smile for Don. She liked men who were cultured.

They sat in silence until she'd started to climb the stairs when Nicks said, "Ok, I'm listening."

Don took a deep breath and his normal cordial manner slipped away into the darkness of the room. He lowered his voice, leaning forward on the table. "The person subject of the proposed next action is a local ex-councillor who's enjoyed high level protection over the last thirty years. Not a prominent figure, I *certainly* had never heard of him, but a man who ingratiated himself with many highly placed people with shared predilections for young boys, especially those aged eight to twelve years of age. He's been able to secure his protection for so long because he had intimate knowledge and photographic evidence not just of sexual abuse, if that's not bad enough, but also of sexually motivated murder *and* because he was, and still is, 'their' procurement manager. He's the provider of their dreams," he said matter-of-factly, taking a sip of sherry. "All this has been covered up using the excuse of 'National Security'. These 'things' would have brought Governments down, whatever party they were. In fact, it *probably* still would. That's the political aspect, but it's not our major concern. Our concern is he's still active, as are several of his protectors. For *this*, and every other Government, it's been, very much, the elephant in the room, but we can't allow it to continue. If we do, then we are as guilty as the perpetrators."

Nicks sipped his beer, unconvinced as to 'their' prime concern.

"Now, our chap had arranged for the procurement of a young boy specifically of the age of ten, preferably from a care home or other turbulent background without proper family ties. He wants this child for sexual pleasure which, *we know*, is to end in his death at the hands of a man who has, over the years, become increasingly sadistic. We

111

know this because we've an extremely well placed informant. Admittedly, the informant has their own agenda and unfortunately we *are* having to pander to this person for the greater good for the time being. We also know our chap has the evidence I mentioned earlier because he'd squirreled it away for many years to prevent the Security Service, or those purporting to be acting for them, from obtaining it. However, over the last few years, several people close to him have died, people to whom he'd entrusted relevant material, to be released in the event of his death, including his lawyer; traffic accidents, the odd suicide, that sort of thing. It spooked him into lodging them bit by bit with several high security safety deposit banks. Unfortunately for him, they're all controlled by ourselves. Now we have it all." He sipped his drink thoughtfully. "It was a very complex operation."

"I assume you didn't arrange a similar 'accident' for the Councillor because you couldn't control the release of information? So what's stopping you now?" Nicks looked Don squarely in the eyes.

Don flashed a wan smile and seemed to squirm, momentarily. "Look," he said eventually, "we had to be able to control those files because there are people that have made 'silly' mistakes in their lives. Nothing on the scale of the main players, I hasten to add but still things that could bring them down. We *need* these people, Nicks, at least in the short term. A sad fact of political life but it *is* essential, I assure you."

"But why the need for what amounts to a public execution? Why not just another accident?" Simon asked.

112

Nicks butted in, but was looking at Don. "Because, Si, 'just another accident' is not headline news. Now, a 'public execution' will be. Mystery and intrigue. Maximum exposure?"

Don was looking a little flustered and delivered his answer with a slight exasperation. "Well, it sends out a very clear message to those in the 'know', Nicks. Hopefully, the pack of cards will start to topple even before we have to exert pressure or release further details concerning *those* hard faced enough to try to cling on to their power or position. Once our man is dead, we'll begin feeding the evidence out into the public domain through selected journalists and publications."

"What about the D notices the Government slap on the papers to prevent them disclosing information against the 'national interest'? Isn't that going to just close this whole idea down?" Nicks flashed him a quizzical look.

Don smiled condescendingly. "The Government can have as many of what are now called DA-Notices issued as they want. It's not going to matter this time. There are certain members of parliament very keen to get their hands on this information and anyway," Don concluded tetchily, "the notices themselves can't be enforced. It's a voluntary thing between the newspapers and the Government. We have journalists and publications who'll simply just not comply anymore."

It was obvious Don was not comfortable with the direction their questions were taking him. They all knew this was slightly more political than moral so Nicks changed the course of the conversation. "You said earlier he '*had* arranged' for a ten year old boy. What happened? Is that the reason for the delay?"

Don nodded.

"Yes. The boy to be procured got himself run over, nothing *too* serious, I'm glad to say, but he's currently in Alder Hey Hospital and will be for some time so our councillor is having to get a replacement. You'll have an updated intel package shortly." He sat back from the table brushing some imaginary fluff from his trousers, feeling he'd regained control of the conversation. "As soon as we have it we'll get it to Simon and, of course, he'll supply you with any further documentation you need." He flashed Nicks a slick smile, stood up and edged his way from behind the table whilst buttoning up his overcoat. "I can see you need time to consider the proposal, Nicks. Just read the intel and briefing carefully. In the meantime, have yourself a little holiday in the city, visit a few museums, but make sure you're available in any event. We *are* paying you after all. Don't forget, we *do* have a young child's life in our hands." There was that smile again.

He started to walk away but suddenly stopped and called back: "Try the Walker Art Gallery. There's an exhibition of Walter Sickert's paintings there. I know you like Sickert. Jack the Ripper and all that." Without another word he turned and left.

Simon and Nicks sat in silence for a while and finished their pints. Eventually Simon said, "Fancy another?"

Nicks looked into his glass, swirling the dregs around thoughtfully. "Yeah, somewhere else though. It feels a bit *dark* in here now."

CHAPTER 28

The letter had been tucked between the pages of the *Teach Yourself Italian* book she'd kept in the drawer of her bedside table and which she'd bought in preparation for the holiday she didn't survive to take. It was addressed to 'My beautiful and wonderful husband'.

It was some time before he was able to open the envelope. When he did, his weeping made it impossible for him to see what was written. Finally, sat on the kitchen floor, his face drawn and tear stained he'd managed to read it.

She told him how much she loved him; how she'd adored him from their first meeting, how he'd been the answer to her prayer. She'd cherished their life together and whilst he might think the last year had been the worst, it had somehow also been the best. He was too young to be on his own for the rest of his life. She wanted him to find someone who could give him the love she knew he needed and to whom he could give all his love, as he'd given her. Finally, she told him he would always be able to feel her love and if there *was* 'something' after this life, then she would be there for him.

Tears flowing down his cheeks, he remembered how he'd taken her to the bathroom and helped her wash; how she'd sat naked, looking up at him as he held her hand and stroked her hair.

"I'm scared," she'd suddenly said. He knew instinctively what she meant. She wasn't afraid of death; it was the manner, and what came next.

He'd told her she'd just go to sleep one evening and not wake up again, that there was either nothing or something and if there was nothing she'd nothing to worry about but if there was something, it would be nice.

It had taken all his strength to keep the tears at bay that moment: it was not what she needed to see. Taking his hand, she'd kissed it gently, smiling up at him. All was well. She was happy.

CHAPTER 29
24th March 2014

"Boss, can I have a word?" Degsy stood in the doorway to the DCI's office looking perturbed.

"Certainly, Derek, grab a seat," Thurstan replied, looking up from the file on his desk. "What's the problem? Family issues?"

"No, Boss, just something's been bothering me since we viewed the 'Balcony Man' footage.

"I didn't come to you earlier because, quite frankly, I thought you'd think it ridiculous. I thought it ridiculous, but I did some digging. It may still be ridiculous, but it's not as ridiculous as it first seemed."

"Derek," Thurstan interrupted him, "is this some sort of variation on the house-to-house game of trying to see how many times a certain word can be introduced into a conversation? Because if it is, I'll tell you now, you're the winner." He smiled, but Degsy could detect a hint of impatience.

"No, Boss. I know I'm not explaining myself very well. The 'Balcony Man' video. You remember the movement the blurred figure made in the close up?" He didn't wait for a response. "Thumbs his nose and strokes his top lip and chin with his right hand. Well, I couldn't shake the feeling I'd seen it before. *Exact* same thing. It's been nagging at me. Then, I suddenly remembered. I went to a 'do' at the Lady of Man, Dickie Trimble's retirement bash – do you know him?"

Thurstan shook his head, "No. I think I would remember a name like that. Go on," he said dryly.

"Well, I saw a guy there who did the same thing, several times during the evening. *Exactly* like the clip. He had a beard, close cut like our guy appears to have and it made him look a little bit Middle Eastern, again like our man.

"I didn't know him, but I know a couple of the blokes who spoke to him so I engineered a meeting with one of them and casually enquired as to who he was; said I thought I recognised him but couldn't remember the name. Turns out he's ex Job, always worked from the City and retired ten years ago. I should have left it there but I just had this… this thing… bugging me. So, I did some background checks on him and that's where it got interesting."

Thurstan reclined in the tall backed swivel chair he'd inherited from his predecessor, hands clasped under his chin with his two index fingers pressed to his lips like a miniature church spire. "Go on, Derek, I'm listening."

Degsy took a deep breath. "He's ex Firearms so I went to the Training Unit and managed to speak to one of the instructors who, as it happened, knew him. He let me see the old records." He paused for effect. "This guy, Boss, was apparently shit hot. Top scores every time. The Instructor said he was a natural shot. The handguns they were using then were the Sig 226. It's on our list of possibles from forensic, Boss." Degsy looked for a reaction but received only:

"Go on."

"Well, I checked our pension provider, to get his current whereabouts. They gave me his next of kin details and the account they pay his Police pension into." Thurstan looked at him quizzically. "You were at a meeting, Boss, so I got DI White to sign the authorisation," Degsy offered as explanation for his DCIs lack of knowledge of the enquiry. "Anyway, his account is in Crosby which is the same as his last known address and it's where his parents live as well. I did a voters check which came up negative for him, but confirmed his parents are still there. So I did some online research and found he bought his house in 2002 but sold it again five years ago. I found the Estate Agent who dealt with it and confirmed."

"So where is he now? Do we know?" Thurstan inquired thoughtfully.

"Not *exactly*, Boss. The colleague who gave me the initial info said he'd been told he was living in Berlin."

He was silent for a few seconds. Thurstan could see there was something else he wanted to say so said nothing, silently inviting him to fill the conversational gap. Degsy cleared his throat.

"And I had a little look at his Bank Account."

Getting up from his desk Thurstan slowly wandered over to the window overlooking headquarters car park. He stood gazing out of it. Degsy adjusted his tie and brushed some fluff from his trousers.

"Did we *get* a court order to access his account?" Thurstan eventually said.

"Well...Umm..."

Thurstan turned and looked at him, his eyebrows raised in a question Degsy knew said: *"Please tell me you did."*

He shifted uncomfortably in his seat. This was the bit he hadn't been looking forward to. Thurstan's expression changed to one that clearly conveyed the message *"You twat."*

"I'm sorry, Boss. I really am," Degsy mumbled.

"Then why did you do it? What on earth possessed you?" Thurstan asked calmly.

Degsy shrugged his shoulders. "I know. I just thought there wasn't enough to ... and anyway I know someone who works at the bank. They owed me a favour."

"I hope we're not adding blackmail to the list now, Derek?"

He shook his head. "No, Boss, it's not that sort of favour. They're a good friend. They just took a little look for me and it seems the guy's never withdrawn any cash outside the UK using their cards, *but* he does make a sizeable monthly payment to another card provider. Sometimes as much as £3000."

Thurstan shrugged. "So he's using another card to make cash withdrawals. So what?"

"But my contact has a mate who works for the other provider and... well... it appears there's something odd about the way he's withdrawing it. He said they couldn't tell me anything else without the right paperwork, more than their jobs are worth." The errant DS gave him a sheepish grin.

"Oh, I'm *so* glad I'm not the only one who thinks it's important." Thurstan scolded him. He looked out of the window again and sighed.

"Ok, I want it done *properly* though. No shortcuts. No circumventing procedures. Let's *get* court orders and see what the banks can tell us about him. We've no other leads at present so it would be foolish not to." He returned to his desk, picked up his mug, swilled its contents around and took a mouthful of cold coffee.

"So what's his name, Derek?"

"It's Chris Nickson, Boss. Christopher Peter Francis Nickson."

CHAPTER 30

After 5 years on the beat he became one of his Division's responses to incidents involving guns. There weren't many in those days and he'd carried a revolver on just two occasions. The only time he took the weapon out of the holster was to put it back in the station gun safe.

Later, he was posted to a specialist unit. It provided house to house enquiry teams for major crimes: murders, rapes, serious assaults and teams to search through dustbins and rubbish tips; grubby excrement littered alley ways, woodland and open spaces. He'd escorted dangerous prisoners and nuclear loads, been part of armed containment teams and, ahead of VIP visits, he'd searched for bombs. The unit was the Force's first responder to any incident involving large scale public disorder, a term much preferred by the Police hierarchy in place of the word riot which, once declared, made the Force liable under the Riot Damages Act to pay compensation for any damage to businesses caused by failure to efficiently quell the disturbance. The unit's riot tactics were consequently innovative and very 'robust'.

Performing both uniform and plain clothes crime patrols and unencumbered by routine calls for Police involvement, it concentrated on locating and outwitting car thieves, burglars, muggers, robbers, drug dealers, pickpockets and 'ram' raiders. Such people were cunning and resourceful, but not cunning enough to evade the attention of the circling shark that was an OSD patrol. That needed a criminal genius and they were few and far between. Unloved by the local criminal 'fraternity' they were relentless and successful; without fear or favour.

Promoted to Sergeant, he was sent to the suburbs, responsible for supervising street patrols and it was there, one evening, a 'chance' encounter led to his becoming an SFO.

The training was intensive. Becoming proficient in numerous weapons, raiding techniques, methods of entry and rescuing hostages, he joined another specialist unit. This one had two distinct groups. The Snipers, seldom seen by the public due to their predilection for dressing as the occasional tree, bush or lump of grass; and the Entry Teams, who were the 'glamour boys'; black clad, balaclavered, bristling with weapons. Nicks bought a pair of shades.

On a 'call out' system for live operations whether they were performing normal duties, training or resting, permanently attached to a pager, forbidden alcohol, the effects of the call out system were *any time, any day*, no matter what they were doing. If the pager said 'job on', they went. Jobs could last from several hours to twenty four.

No aspect of personal life was safe from interruption and the job wasn't quite as attractive as his recruiter or the 'posters' made out; a 'stakeout' in the back of a van with eight other guys who'd all been on a curry 'fest' the night before was nowhere near as pleasant as it sounded.

CHAPTER 31
28th March 2014

Thurstan sat himself down in Chalkie's Office.

"Mervyn! How's things going?"

"Who told you?"

"Well, it's a long story but I met your sister in Sainsbury's." Thurstan smiled.

Chalkie sighed. "That woman just can't stop gabbing."

"Does your wife call you Mervyn?" Thurstan was feeling playful.

"No, we met in the Army so she's always called me Chalkie." He caught the enquiring look. "It's my mum's fault. She was very fond of her great uncle back in Jamaica so I got stuck with it."

"Never thought of a name change?"

"I did once but the wife thought Dash Riprock was a bit over the top." He smiled. "What about you... Stan?"

Thurstan grimaced. "Oooh, below the belt but point taken. Back to business. Where are we up to?"

"Well, we've had a bit of a breakthrough," Chalkie, magnanimous in victory, pointed at his cup with an enquiring look. The DCI shook his head. "House-to-house came up with a report of a black BMW seen in the early hours of the morning. It was stationary on Crank Road opposite the no entry signs to Abbey Road. The witness is a local man cycling home from work. Didn't get a registration number. Just thought it odd. He *can* say there were only two on board, but he didn't get a great look at them. Just said he thought they were *both* men and the driver looked foreign."

"Looked foreign? In what way?" Thurstan looked quizzical.

"Can't say." Chalkie paused and looked apologetic before continuing. "It was just an impression. Anyway, we trawled the systems for anything involving a black BMW and Camera Enforcement came up with the image of one bursting the lights on the East Lancs junction with Rainford bypass. We checked the number plate and it now shows up as stolen."

Chalkie lifted his hand to halt Thurstan who was about to interrupt. "There's more. The PNC has a marker on it showing the vehicle was recovered by West Mids from a scrap yard they raided as part of a Forcewide operation later that day. Seems it was about to be crushed. No reports on it at the time and it took them two weeks to locate the owner because he was out of the country on business.

"Meanwhile, the DI in charge wasn't happy, so he had forensic give it the once over straight away. They retrieved a few samples and we've now run them against those we took from Monica." He paused for effect. "There's no doubt, Thurstan. She *was* in the boot of that car."

The DCI put his 'I'm impressed' face on. "Good news, Chalkie. I take it they have someone in custody?"

"Yep." He leant back in his chair twiddling a pen. "Several, but the main interest to us is the owner of the scrap yard and a Lithuanian worker. Their fingerprints are the only ones from the workers there found in and on the vehicle. Not quite damning evidence, given the nature of the place, but it gives us something to target. I've sent Lizzie and Fred down to do a first interview."

"Good cop, bad cop?" Thurstan chuckled.

Chalkie smiled back. "You could say that. Not sure which is which. They're both good at this sort of thing. Fred just adds a little touch of physical street cred, I always think."

"I'm sure he does. What other enquiries are you making? Routes back? Probably motorway would be a first port of call."

"We're all over it." The DI drained his coffee and grimaced. "Ikky and the Strolling Bone are doing Lymm Services to Crewe inclusive, and the Foetus and Spud are doing Keele to Hilton Park. From the location of the scrap yard, our suspects would have come off the motorway just after Hilton Park. That's it really, except to say Lizzie and Fred are obviously going to liaise with West Mids and access their intel system."

"Great!" Thurstan rose from the chair. "At least I'll have some good news to tell the Chief this afternoon. I'd best get something to eat, he's brought the meeting forward to one o'clock. You ready for anything?"

Chalkie nodded, stood up and dragged his jacket off the back of the chair.

Thurstan stared out of the window. "Shame nothing actionable came back from the NCA regarding MacMahon."

Chalkie shrugged. "Yeah, but my mate's pretty certain it's not an outside crew. Says their contacts are impeccable. Suggests we either look again 'in house' or we look out of the box."

Signing out, they walked along the main corridor towards the lifts. Behind them Arthur pressed the remote and the office telly sprang to life; the national news main story was the multiple raids carried out in various parts of the country by the 'Anti- Terror' Police and Specialist Firearms Officers. Arms and explosives had been recovered and fifteen suspects were in custody.

CHAPTER 32

With time on his hands, Nicks embarked on a series of visits to Museums and Art Galleries, his favourite being the Walker in William Brown Street, opposite the magnificent St.George's Hall.

He and Anca had met each other for the first time there. Staring at a Walter Sickert painting in fascination, he'd become aware of someone standing behind him. He'd turned, briefly, and she'd smiled at him saying: "It's interesting, isn't it? Do you know the story of the artist?" and so began a conversation that led to Nicks buying her a coffee in the café downstairs and eventually to their life together in Romania.

He broke up the intensity of his cultural activity with a couple of trips out. The Lake District, staying at the Sun in Coniston from where he trekked up the Old Man and Helvellyn and then on to North Wales where from Penmaenpool he 'climbed' Cadair Idris, on the pony trail from Tŷ Nant farm and spent a pleasant fifteen minutes at the top, chatting with another loner whilst drinking sweet tea from the man's flask. Now with only the Museum of Liverpool left on his 'bucket list' he'd run out of ideas. There should have been a badge for this sort of thing.

CHAPTER 33
p.m. 28th March 2014

Thurstan took off his jacket and was hanging it on the stand when Degsy tapped on the open door. "Got a moment, Boss? Just want to update you on some stuff."

The DCI turned beckoning him in. "Yes, please do. Just been doing the same for the Chief at the weekly conference."

Degsy sat down, sorting through the papers he'd brought with him. "How did it go?" he said absently.

"Hmmm, could have been better. Despite the breakthrough in the Masterson job, he wasn't impressed when I told him we still had no suspects for MacMahon," Thurstan threw his mobile in the top drawer, closed it and sat down at his desk.

"So you didn't mention Nickson then, Boss?"

"No, Derek, I didn't. Best kept to ourselves, for now. I looked a big enough twat as it was." Thurstan stacked the files on his desk into a neater pile, lifted the thinnest one off the top and dropped it on his blotter placing the rest on the floor to the side.

"Before you start," he said opening the file, "I made some quick enquiries myself. Just for anything unusual in and around his parent's and former address. The only thing of note is his parent's neighbour died, February 2012. Nothing so unusual about that we might think. People die all the time except this neighbour was a right pain in the arse, drug dealer and all round little shit. I've had a good look through the file. Local CID investigated, and it seems he fell down the stairs

129

and broke his neck during an alcohol and drug binge one man party. I can't find anything to contradict the findings but it just makes me wonder though. Idle speculation at the moment. Anyway, it's there." He dropped the file on the front of his desk. "Take a look at it later and tell me what you think." He leant forward expectantly, his elbows on the desk, hands clasped together supporting his chin. "Right! What have you got? *Please* tell me you've got something."

Degsy handed him a sheaf of papers. "These are the printouts of his bank account and credit card transactions since he retired. I've seen the previous stuff, nothing interesting there. The thing is, in the year after retirement he's paid off his mortgage, taken quite a few holidays and generally spent what's left of his pension payout. This was the time his wife was being treated for ovarian cancer. Note he's only using the credit card for holidays and internet payments. She dies in 2007 and everything becomes more mundane, just everyday stuff. He appears to have hit the booze though, judging by his credit card use in off licences all over Crosby. Understandable, in the circumstances."

"Yeah, and I'd say he was trying to hide the fact, publicly, by spreading his purchases around," Thurstan murmured thoughtfully.

Degsy continued. "2009 he gets another credit card, from another provider. This one's best used abroad, gives the best exchange rates and charges. Early 2010 we start seeing withdrawals from the Berlin cashpoints. Seems normal but suddenly he starts taking out maximum amounts in blocks. Four, five day period usually but not always every month." He paused. "This one's interesting, though." He stood up and leaned over Thurstan's desk, sorting through the papers, pointing to an entry three quarters of the way down the page. "April 2013. Three withdrawals in Berlin followed by one in Budapest. It's the only break in his usual routine." He sat down again.

Thurstan rescanned the pages. "Hmmm ... interesting. A little slip up perhaps? He's like a squirrel hoarding nuts to get him through winter until he can get to the tree again. Thing is there's no shortage of these particular trees in Germany and particularly not in Berlin. Smells like he's trying to cover something up." He paused thoughtfully. "I think he wants people to believe he lives in Berlin, certainly that he lives in Germany. Odd though. I might have believed elsewhere in Germany but *Budapest*? That's intriguing. Find out what's near the 'man in the wall' he used there, travel links, that sort of thing." He shuffled through the papers again as Degsy sat silently making some notes. "I see he's still using the credit cards online. He's going to leave a trace there, Derek. Have you done anything about tracing his IP address?"

Degsy felt a little smug and hoped it didn't show. "Yeah, Boss. Gandalph took a look at that for me. Nickson's using IP addresses all over the place. It seems he's using Tor."

"What's that?" Thurstan's face screwed up.

"It's a software program you load onto your computer, like a browser, and it hides your IP address every time you send or request data on the Internet. It's heavy-duty encrypted and bounces everything through a shit load of servers all around the world. It's never the same route because it uses up to 6,000 different relays to send the stuff." Degsy sat back and looked apologetic.

131

Thurstan chuckled inwardly when he saw Degsy's slightly dejected look. "Not your fault, Derek. I'd like to think the Security Service would be able to do something about that, but it'd probably need some pretty high level clearance and we're a long way off at the moment. No, let's see what some good 'old fashioned' police work can do before we head down *that* thorny path," he said smiling benignly. "Incidentally, if he's buying stuff on the Internet, where's he having it delivered?"

"Parents' address, ever since he sold his house. If you look at the sheets with the results of the Border Agency enquiry, you'll see it shows every time he's been in and out of the country. Generally tallys with his online purchases. If you turn the page over you'll see I've highlighted that he's not left yet, he's still here and..." He paused. "There's a ten month period 2011 into 2012 with February right in the middle when he wasn't in the country."

Thurstan was pensive. He rubbed his chin with his hand and made a little sucking sound from the side of his mouth then exhaled deeply. Never one to give up easily, he finally said, "Well, not as far as we can tell, Derek. He may've entered and left at some stage using false identification. If he *is* our shooter I certainly wouldn't discount it." He slouched back in his chair, elbows on the armrests, hands clasped in front of him with his forefingers pressed against his lips, eyes closed.

Degsy sat silently watching him.

After several minutes Thurstan got up and closed the office door. Sitting down again he said:

"This isn't just about this Nickson chap and the little oddities that seem to surround him. I'll be honest with you, Derek. Throwing 'coincidence' out the window for the time being, this MacMahon job has a level of organisation and, dare I say, sophistication that disturbs me. The CCTV interference, the mystery street cleaner, the 'convenient' white van." He paused and let out a slow, thoughtful sigh. "It's too much, I think, for organised crime. It smells of something much bigger." He paused again. "I went for a drink the other night, with an old Army friend who's now in Cheshire SB. He told me something interesting. Did you see the news the other day? The item about the anti-terrorist exercise in Delamere Forest?"

Degsy nodded. "Yeah, I did, Boss, and I see there's just been a load of arrests. Connected?"

"I think so," Thurstan replied then leaned forward and spoke quietly, "I'm telling you this, Derek, in the strictest confidence and it's not to be taken beyond these four walls."

Degsy looked back at him seriously. "I understand, Boss. You can rely on me."

Thurstan looked him intently in the eyes. "I know I can, Derek. I wouldn't be telling you otherwise. Well," he continued in a subdued tone, "we were discussing jobs and cases, as you do, and got to speaking about the MacMahon job when my friend remarked about the 'old silenced headshot' making a popular return. I asked him what he meant and he looked a bit sheepish, as if he'd given something away he shouldn't have. Naturally, I pressed him on the matter, but he wasn't having it so I plied him with several more drinks until he'd

133

'relaxed' somewhat, well, quite a lot actually." He smiled before continuing, "Well, it seems it wasn't an exercise at Delamere. They had an incident there that left three Islamic fundamentalists dead, apparently surprised whilst recording an attempt to cut another Muslim's head off. To keep it to the point, Derek, headshots, semi-automatic pistol, witnesses nearby who should have heard something but didn't." He paused shaking his head. "To me, that means it was probably a suppressed weapon. Furthermore, it seems MI5 had them under surveillance but when they went mobile a number of 'traffic situations', as my friend put it, occurred which resulted in a loss. Coincidence? I think not. That's organisation and sophistication, Derek. Anyway, MI5 locked it down and it's theirs and SB 'eyes only' now."

He took a deep breath. "And I didn't tell you before, but I think you should know now, Matrix and the NCA wouldn't be making so much progress cracking open MacMahon's little empire without the information and documents Sackville, provided to them. I'm quite sure our Rupert would never have given this stuff up voluntarily unless someone had put him in fear of his life and I think that fear was instilled in him, not by Tommy Cole as he thinks, but by someone masquerading as a messenger from Tommy Cole."

The DCI slowly shook his head. "No, Cole wouldn't have sent a messenger round. It's not his style. It may have been MacMahon's, but it's not Tommy's. He'd have gone himself and turned the screws all night until Rupert had to tell him. He may have sent some thugs round to his mum's place as leverage, but that's as sophisticated as Tommy

134

gets. Meanwhile, he's obviously happy to believe Sackville's legged it to Spain. From his point of view, it keeps him out of our clutches. No, it wasn't Cole threatening him and I think it'll be quite some time before Tommy figures out Matrix have Rupert and his mother in a safe house in darkest Cheshire."

Degsy allowed himself a little smile. "Nice one", he said tilting his head in appreciation before adding, "I know Tommy Cole isn't the sharpest tool in the shed, but didn't he bother to check the airport at least?"

"Oh, he did, and the neighbours. Matrix had someone insert the holiday flights into the airport systems and they even had Sackville prime next door," Thurstan replied.

"So where does this take us, Boss?" Degsy was intrigued and a little confused.

Thurstan leant back, rubbed his eyes and then ran a hand through his hair. "What we have here, I believe, are two well organised and co-ordinated assassinations 'coincidentally' followed by intense Police activity leading to some very positive results after probably months or years of the subject being in the 'too hard to solve box'. No, I don't think that's a coincidence."

Degsy contemplated the information then said: "So you think the killer is the same person or at the very least the same 'crew'?"

"In a nutshell, Derek, yes," Thurstan said bluntly.

"And they're doing it so…?"

"They're doing it, I think, so the Police and MI5 *have* to do something. It's like standing at the edge of a swimming pool when you can't swim, or at least you're not a confident swimmer, and the instructor or someone just nudges you off balance into the water. You have to do something. Most people swim." The DCI looked pleased with his explanation.

"What if they drown?" Degsy replied with an apologetic half smile.

Thurstan frowned. "They won't drown, Derek, because there's always someone there to save them. Just like now."

"But... *Nickson*? He's... he's ex-job, Boss." Degsy shook his head. "It's not easy to believe."

They looked at each other in silence which Thurstan broke first. "I definitely think these jobs are connected. As for Nickson... Well, he appears to have the skills and he appears to be up to something." He leant back in his chair and discarded the pencil he'd been twiddling. "Anyway, you were the one who flagged him up in the first place."

Degsy managed to return a look combining doubt, determination and apology all at the same time. "I know, Boss, but I only did it because it was nagging at me and I just wanted to get it off my chest, *just in case*. You know how it is? I mean, a 'one off' for revenge I could understand, but this is a whole different thing."

Again silence then Degsy continued, "I admit, he *has* got an odd life map at present so I feel a little better about it, but I think the possibilities have just hit me. I mean ... we're talking ..." He paused, struggling for words, shaking his head again. "It's like ...I don't know....the dark side."

A flicker of a smile wandered across Thurstan's mouth. "I know what you mean," he said. "I knew people when I was in Northern

136

Ireland who you'd never have thought it of but they ended up working for shadowy organisations, often never officially recognised."

Thurstan rested his chin on his clasped hands. "Now, I've no idea who these people are, Derek. I don't know if we could be dealing with MI5, MI6 or some other Agency we know nothing whatsoever about. I don't know if it's rogues in the system or something entirely different. I'm clueless. I'm fairly certain though, the connection between our job and this job out in Delamere is *who* organised it. If Tony MacMahon had any Security Service or terrorist connections of any sort, I'm sure they'd have shut us down by now." He stared at his DS for several moments before saying quietly, "I think we need to tread very carefully, Derek, and I thought you needed to know." He flashed him a look of apology, encouragement and invitation. "Well, are you still game?"

Degsy looked back at him and shrugged. "Yeah. I'm in."

"Ok, so be it." Thurstan stretched his arms and stood up. "I think we could both do with some fresh air. A quick 'comfort break' and a drink then I think it's time we gave Nickson's parents a little visit. See what happens if we shake the tree. We'll work out our 'story' on the way." He grinned. "Time to go fishing."

CHAPTER 34

From the stone seating outside the Museum of Liverpool at the Pier Head, Nicks watched a couple eating ice cream being dive bombed by two seagulls. After days of the 'Tourist Trail' and Museums, he was just about full. His phone rang.

"Hi, Mum. How's things?"

"Oh, it's you, Christopher!" she exclaimed. "We thought you'd been kidnapped by pirates."

"And why on earth would you think that, Mum?"

He knew what was coming next.

"Well, it's been so long since we've seen you, or heard from you for that matter, anything could have happened. Why don't you pop up for tea tonight? I've got some lovely lamb shanks in the oven on slow. It would be no trouble to pop another in there with them," she ended hopefully.

"Firstly, Mum, I was there last week." He looked at the date on his watch. "In fact, only five days ago. Secondly, I might have to work tonight. I'm expecting a call later so don't put anything in for me. I'll give you a call before nine, if I *can* make it, but I probably won't be there." He tilted the phone from his mouth as he sighed and rolled his eyes.

"Alright, love. I'll pop the other lamb shank in, just in case, and if you can't make it, I know someone who will have it for his supper. Oh! I almost forgot. Your father needs to talk to you about the two very nice Policemen who called for you this afternoon." She made it sound as if they were two school friends calling to see if he could come out to play. Before he could ask her for more information, she was gone and he could hear her calling: "Frank, I've got our Chris on the phone!"

He waited, listening to the sound of his father approaching. He'd probably been in the garden.

"Hi son. Everything OK?"

"Yeah, Dad. Couldn't be better," he lied. He could have been in Romania, with Anca. "What's Mum on about two Policemen?"

"Oh, we had a visit from two detectives. They said you may have witnessed some incident in the city centre the other day and they needed to speak to you about it. Are you sure everything's alright?" He couldn't hide the genuine concern in his voice.

It didn't go unnoticed on Nicks. "Yeah. It's fine, Dad. Nothing for you to worry over. I know what it's about. Did they leave a contact number at all?" He pulled the small notebook with its little pencil out of the leg pocket of his combat pants.

"I'll just get the business card the older one gave me, hang on." Frank put the phone down and Nicks could hear the semi-comedic conversation between his parents as they did their 'where did we put it' routine. Suddenly, the phone was picked up and Nicks began noting down the details he was being given. DCI Thurstan Baddeley. Why was he not surprised?

"Are you sure there isn't anything wrong, son? It's just that the younger one asked if he could use the toilet, so we let them in and your mother took him upstairs to show him where it is while I had the other one wait in the living room. I had to go and sort out your mum's cup of tea in the kitchen, you know she doesn't like it stewed, and I saw the older one through the hatch, using his phone to take a picture of that photo of you when you were in the Firearms Team. You know the one? It's on the nest of tables in the corner. Then they asked about the neighbour, the one that died."

Nicks forced a laugh. "Stop worrying, Dad. Even I can't recognise myself from that photo." He wanted to dispel any fears they had, but had to ask, "What did they say about the neighbour?"

"They just said they knew about him, what he must have been like and it couldn't have been nice living next door to him. Of course I said it wasn't. Then the older one, that's the Baddeley chap, said it must have been very difficult for you, knowing we were having to put up with all his behaviour."

"And what did you tell him, Dad?" Nicks took slow a sip of his vanilla latte.

"I said we'd never told you because it would have upset you. Was that the right thing to say?"

Nicks smiled. "Yeah, Dad. That was the right thing to say. Anything else?"

"Well, they tried to make it sound like inconsequential chat, but they asked about our cruise and if we'd enjoyed it, whether you had stayed whilst we were away and if you had been staying recently."

"And you said... what?" Nicks lit a cigarette and blew out the smoke.

"I told them what you told us, you were working away, and in any case you always stayed in hotels because you like your own space." Frank paused as he accepted the cup of tea Anne had made him. Nicks heard him whisper "Thanks, love" then he continued: "They asked if we'd seen you recently or were likely to and where you lived, then, when they were leaving, the older chap asked what you did for a living. I said you lived somewhere in Berlin but we don't know where because we do all the Christmas and birthday stuff by email and occasionally Skype and then I told him what you told us to say, that you were a freelance personal security consultant." Frank sipped his tea. "Look, I know you can't say what it is you're up to, Official Secrets Act and everything, but are you in any trouble?"

"No, Dad," Nicks laughed. "It's much ado about nothing. I told you everything is fine. I'll give them a ring and get it sorted. In the meantime I might not be able to pop round again."

There was silence, then: "You didn't have anything to do with what happened to the bloke next door, did you, Chris? I mean, you paying for the cruise and then him dying while we were away. I know it was probably a coincidence, but I have to ask, son."

Nicks laughed again. "You need to stop watching all those murder mysteries, Dad. He was responsible for what happened. He managed to do that all by himself. Just put it down to a happy coincidence, that's all."

"Ok, Son. I'm glad." Nicks could hear the relief in his Dad's voice. "Try and give us a call before you have to go back though. For your Mum."

"I will. And Dad, make sure you're careful what you say on the landline. I just don't want to compromise anything. The 'powers that be' wouldn't be happy. Keep the mobile handy and I'll call you. Enjoy your lamb shanks."

"I'm sure I will, son. Speak to you soon." Frank put the phone down. Anne was shouting for him from the garden, something about 'that damned cat'.

Nicks finished his coffee leaving a mouthful of liquid in the bottom, thoughtfully toying with the container. He took another drag of his cigarette, dropped it in the cup and discarded it in the nearby waste bin.

He'd been right to have a bad feeling about Mr. Baddeley.

CHAPTER 35

Degsy pulled away from the kerb as Thurstan clicked his seat belt into place.

"Back to the Office Derek, I think."

Looking idly out of his window as the world slipped past he eventually said: "Well? Anything?"

The DS stole a glance at him. "No. Nothing in the bathroom to indicate he's staying there and when she went back downstairs I took a quick look through the rooms." He paused as he negotiated his way around the vehicles in front. "He may well have stayed there at some time, but I couldn't see anything to make me feel he's there now." He accelerated hard and slid the gears from second to fourth. "No photos out either."

"There was an old photo of him in the living room from when he was in the firearms team. I managed to get it on my phone. Must've been taken almost twenty years ago now." Thurstan hesitated. "I think we need to get his passport and driving licence pics. Probably the most recent photos we're going to get at the moment. When was his passport issued?"

Degsy was silent as he checked his mirror, signalled and overtook several cars. "Six years ago now, and he used it on his DL when he renewed it last year."

"Parent's address as usual I take it?" Thurstan looked at his colleague for confirmation. Degsy just nodded then said: "What do you think of the parents, Boss?"

Thurstan took out a battered half packet of chewing gum from the inside pocket of his jacket, picked off a piece of fluff and briefly offered the packet to Degsy who felt it safer to decline. He popped a piece into his mouth and started chewing.

"I don't know. They seem decent enough people. I think broadly speaking they're telling us the truth, or what they believe to be the truth, but Nickson seems to be very cautious for someone who's a simple 'personal security consultant'. I can't help feeling there's something they're not telling us though."

They sat in silence for the rest of the journey; Thurstan deep in thought. He'd been through the file on the Nickson's neighbour in great detail. His criminal record, the case file on his death, neighbours' witness statements, Coroner's, the lot. There were no unaccounted fingerprints, DNA or unusual fibres. Nothing. The Pathologist's report concluded the cause of death was wholly consistent with the Police evidence that, whilst heavily under the influence of cannabis and alcohol, he'd fallen down the stairs after tripping on his undone shoelace.

He'd obtained Nick's service record with minimum paperwork by exploiting an SIB friend, who now worked at the Service Police Crime Bureau. There was nothing in it to indicate Nicks had any military training which would have provided him with the skills to break a man's neck. It was a fairly unremarkable record. Three years regular

144

service in West Germany, 11 with a TA Provost Company in Manchester followed by 5 years with the TA SIB unit. *That* single piece of information was of interest. He knew it gave Nicks an insight into his head. No, he'd gained nothing from the visit to take him further forward, but it *had* filled in one or two blanks in his knowledge. Maybe the neighbour's death was a coincidence, these things happen. From what the Police files had told him, it was on the cards sooner or later, given his unreliable track record with his associates in the local criminal 'fraternity'.

What troubled him was if *his* parents had been in a similar situation, he'd have wanted to do something. Obviously, he wouldn't murder someone – well, he didn't think he would – but he'd have done *something*. He didn't buy it that Nickson didn't know but all he had was a gut feeling. No evidence. Not a glimmer. Time to put this one to bed, he thought.

Degsy had a good idea of what his DCI would say, when he was ready to say it. It wasn't something he looked forward to, and he knew the other team members on the MacMahon enquiry would be similarly 'thrilled' when he delegated the matter downwards.

Driving along New Quay then The Strand, they turned into Liver Street and Police Headquarters. "Drop me off at reception please, Derek," Thurstan said on passing through the security post. Degsy drove up the ramp, headed for the far left hand corner of HQ's open air car park and came to a smooth halt near to the entrance.

Thurstan got out, but held the door open as he bent down into the vehicle and said, "I know you're not looking forward to this, Derek, but we need to go through *every* hotel and 'bed and breakfast' in Liverpool. I want guest lists. I want one week before MacMahon's death right up *to date*. And I want them as soon as possible. When I say as soon as possible, Derek, I mean, of course, Monday afternoon would be good." He let a sad smile escape, closed the door and walked casually into reception. Degsy had the brief thought that should he look in the rear view mirror he would see the elephant, on the back seat, shrug its shoulders apologetically.

CHAPTER 36
February 2012

Torchlight softly bathed the loft space: partly boarded floor, insulation, double socket, large oblong of chipboard. A naked light bulb hung from its cord.

After several minutes crouched down, listening intently, he edged through the breach in the brickwork and began patiently and silently brushing the entire floor space.

Much later, he removed all evidence of his visit, the large oblong of chipboard was pulled over the gap in the dividing wall and the brickwork repaired.

Standing on his parents' landing, he closed the hatch and pulled his boots back on.

If anyone *even bothered* to look in the loft space, he doubted very much they would investigate any further.

He'd smiled.

CHAPTER 37
28th March 2014

Gambier Terrace sits overlooking Liverpool's Anglican Cathedral. Numbers 1 to 10, at the northernmost end of the terrace are Grade II Listed Buildings, designated to be of special architectural interest. The plans for the entire row to be built in the same Regency style were halted in the slump of 1837. Number 10 became the last of the original build; the remainder constructed later to a different, cheaper design and specification. Its best known occupants were probably John Lennon and his friend the artist Stuart Sutcliffe, who'd lived in a flat at number 3 during 1960.

The house Nicks entered hadn't been turned into flats. It'd been modernised but retained many of its original regency features, giving it an air of quirky modernity and style. The front door was answered by a woman in her early forties. Pretty in an unconventional way, she wore a light grey, below the knee, pencil skirt with a crisp white blouse. Her short hair was almost white and, when he introduced himself, she flashed him a dazzlingly pleasant smile.

"I've been expecting you, Mister Lees," she said, closing the door behind him.

The fairly wide hallway was narrowed considerably by the inclusion of a wildly overused set of coat hooks and a pile of assorted wellington boots and children's shoes against which Nicks attempted to balance himself. Opposite him stood a large, ancient radiator. Smiling again, she squeezed herself between him and the radiator

CHAPTER 37
28th March 2014

saying: "Follow me, please," and walked off along the corridor and up the nearby stairs.

On the first floor she crossed the landing and knocked on a door. Without waiting for an invite, she entered and announced to the two occupants: "Mister Lees." Nicks thanked her and she dazzled him again.

Two figures stood at the far end of the large wood floored room, highlighted by an angle poise lamp on a grand piano. The rest of the room was unfurnished. Floor to ceiling windows let in the last of the day's cold light. The Anglican Cathedral stood majestically beyond.

"Ahh, Phillip, I'm glad you could make it," Don strode out from behind the piano, smiling, and shook his hand.

"Let me introduce you to Mister Kovács." He turned to the other man in the room and said: "István, this is our Mister Lees." Stepping forward Kovács shook Nicks's hand.

In his late sixties, a profusion of dark grey hair almost touched his shoulders. Nicks thought he should've been carrying a violin.

"So glad to meet you, Mister Lees. You have come highly recommended," he said warmly. "I'm hoping you can resolve an issue for us. Let's not waste any time. Come." He indicated towards the piano upon which Nicks could now see a thin folder. "I will explain everything." He spoke English easily, with just a hint of an accent.

Don, still smiling said: "I'll go and arrange some coffee. I won't be long."

Outside, the light had quickly slithered away and through the windows Nicks could see the city being slowly devoured by a thick

149

mist. Three quarters of an hour later, after a comprehensive briefing, Kovács said:

"And now I must apologise, but it is necessary for me to show you something so you know the man you will be dealing with."

He opened the folder on the piano and removed seven A4 sized photographs. Nicks re-adjusted the angle poise lamp so he could see them clearly. They were pictures of the naked body of a young woman.

The first four were taken from various angles and showed the girl's torso which had been subjected to a sustained, violent attack. Her left breast had been cut away and she had multiple stab wounds: chest, arms, thighs, neck and sides. Her intestines spilled out of her stomach. The fifth showed the location in which she had been discarded, her body in the distance; a derelict courtyard, piles of rubbish everywhere. She was just another. The sixth; the left side of her face, black and blue from a clearly vicious beating.

The last was what she'd looked like on a happier day, a dead likeness to a picture of Anca at 17; the shape of her face and lips, her eyes, the colour of her hair, the same joy and exuberance.

Kovács noticed a change in his manner. "Are you alright, Mister Lees?" he asked, clearly concerned. Nicks gave him a weak smile. "Yeah... yeah, I'm ok."

CHAPTER 38

He stepped out into the cold night air, heavy mist shrouding the city. Pausing on the entrance steps he zipped up his jacket and pulled his woollen hat over his ears. The Anglican Cathedral had been stolen.

He walked through the wrought iron access gate onto Hope Street and its junction with Canning and Upper Duke. The streets were silent. Had it not been for the 20mph speed limit sign on the Victorian lamp post, he might've thought he'd travelled back in time.

In nearby Rice Street at The Crack, a onetime popular haunt of Lennon and Sutcliffe in their Liverpool College of Art and Gambier Terrace days, he found himself a seat in a secluded corner and sat quietly drinking three pints of real ale before returning to his hotel, through the fog.

The following night, in a quiet backstreet in the Liverpool district of Wavertree, Nicks dispassionately shot dead a former Liverpool Councillor whilst the man searched for the keys to a house in which he lived alone.

CHAPTER 39
29th March 2014

The more Tommy Cole thought about it the less it made sense and he'd thought about it a lot. He just couldn't see Tony MacMahon walking away from his 'empire' despite what he'd said. No, it was bollocks. If Tony thought he was going to swan off to Spain then pull his strings from afar, he was fucking off his head. Tommy wanted it all. He'd worked for it. It hadn't been Tony dirtying his hands with the killings, it had been him. Ok, he'd enjoyed it, but that wasn't the point. Enough was enough.

He'd been genuinely shocked at the news of Tony's death. Yes, he'd seen it coming, but only because he'd been planning it. Mainly, it was because he'd thought it was the start of a takeover by one of the other Liverpool crime gangs. Until then he hadn't thought *any* of them had the balls to do it. In the days following, he'd discovered none of them had. They'd been quick to let him know it was nothing to do with them and they were keen to keep it 'business as usual'. He'd no problems with that. Whoever it'd been, they'd done him a favour.

As usual in these cases, for two weeks the Police had been all over them. Nothing was getting done, but he could feel their enthusiasm fading away. It was time to start afresh. In a perfect world, he'd have given it a bit longer, but the arrangements had been made well before Tony got himself shot.

The drugs were coming in tomorrow night and he had to be there to oversee things, to make sure he wasn't being ripped off; he hadn't

CHAPTER 39
29th March 2014

dealt with these particular people before. They'd been vouched for by others with whom he *had* done business but it was best to be certain. He was a 'hands on' sort of guy and always had been, not like Tony who'd liked to keep a respectable distance.

Then there was Sackville. He had to 'speak' to him. He wanted the rest of Tony's assets and Sackville was the key. The problem was the little shit had disappeared. At first he thought he may have thrown his hand in with the Police, but then dismissed it, partly because he'd deliberately left him alone; send him the false message all was well and there was nothing to fear.

He'd had someone visit Sackville's house just over a week after the shooting. The neighbour told his man Sackville and his mother had gone to Spain for three weeks following the death of a close friend. Apparently it'd been the mother's idea. She'd thought it would help them get over it. Well, it might take Rupert and the old crone three weeks to get over it, but he was well over it already. Some people were so weak.

Just to be sure, Tommy's contact at JLA checked the passenger lists. Rupert and Necia Sackville were listed for both an outgoing and a return flight. He could have done without the delay, but he'd get a grip of Rupert 'La-di-dah' fucking Sackville soon enough.

But now he was off to Alnwick: a nice secluded beach nearby, just off the main road, close to where the River Aln met the sea. Tomorrow night he would be there to supervise the crew receiving drugs which would make him a very rich man. It'd been Tony's plan and he saw no reason to change it. Alfie Kehoe could wait.

153

CHAPTER 40

Despite the blustery overcast weather, the Ironmen of Anthony Gormley's Another Place stood silently and stoically watching container ships leave Liverpool behind.

In the public car park next to Crosby's Coastguard Station the occupants of the unmarked police vehicle had no idea if the tide was coming in or going out. Neither did they care.

"Here y'are, Alfie."

The hoodie wearing officer from the Matrix Covert unit handed Alfie 'that weasel' Kehoe, a bundle of money wrapped in a plastic carrier bag.

"Ow cum ahm gettin' it now? Yuz sed yer'd giz it wen everythin' wuz sorted?"

"Well, there's grateful," the Officer said, as he offered Alfie a notebook and pen. "Sign there."

"Ahm not sayin' like, ahm not yuh know, buh… yuh know wha' a mean like, Carlo?" Alfie signed the notebook with a flourish.

"Let's just say Crimbo's cum early an' things 'ave moved on," Carlo replied, shaking his head as he saw Alfie's scribble now obscuring several of his earlier entries.

"Giz a bit more time, an maybe ah can find out wear exactly it's gonna 'appen, like," Alfie offered.

"Alfie, lad, yer dedication is commendable, buh, as I said, things 'ave moved on." Carlo looked out of his side window as a seagull attempted a landing on the wing mirror. "Look, I busted me gut to get yuh this, so listen very carefully. Don't ask me how I know, buh yuh definitely need to take a little holiday right now an' I mean *now*. If yuh stay in Liverpool yer gonna encounter some life changin' health issues, know wha' I mean? If yuh look in the bag yer'll find directions to a place in Skegness. It's a B n B run by me cousin. Be there *tonight*!"

Alfie shifted uneasily in his seat. "Buh wha' bout me dog?"

Carlo exhaled sharply. "Yuh can't take the fuckin' dog 'e doesn't do fuckin' animals! Get yer Ma to look after it, she's dunnit before. Yuh never took the fuckin' dog to Teneriffe did yuh!"

"Ah know, buh – "

"Look, don't tell anyone where yer goin'. That includes yer Ma, yer bird, the fuckin' dog. *Anyone!* An' don't go back to yours. If yuh need any gear, an' I'm talkin' toiletries here, toothpaste, soap and so on, then get 'em at a petrol station or motorway services. If yuh need any clothes, Danny, me cousin, will tell yuh where's best in Skegness."

"That's gonna cost a bit tho'. Ar yuz payin' me expenses?" Alfie thought it was worth a try.

"Alfie, are yuh taking the piss, lad!? *I'm* doin' *you* a favour. If yuh don't go buyin' designer crap yer'll 'ave more than enough." He glanced at the seagull shit on the wing mirror. "Now yuh'd best do one an' give me a bell when yuh get there. Alright?"

"Yeah, ok." Alfie put the package inside his jacket and started to get out of the car.

Carlo turned in his seat and took hold of Alfie's arm. "Trust me, Alfie, don't fuckin' tell *anyone* where yer goin'. Don't come back to Liverpool until we've spoken an' *I've* told yuh it's ok." Then he added, as an afterthought: "An' get rid of that 'skunk' factory yer building in the loft at yours in Tuebrook before the local bizzies clock it."

Alfie tried to look unknowledgeable. "Wha'? Dunno wha' yuz on about."

Carlo looked back at him disdainfully. Alfie surrendered and said, "How d'yer know?"

"*I know* a lot of things, Alfie. Yer sudden interest in fuckin' hydroponics for one thing. There's only so much I can ignore. So, get shut of it *when* I've said yuh can come back. OK?"

Alfie nodded. Carlo looked at him. "Take care."

"Yeah, an' youse." He closed the door, pulled his hoodie up and walked back to his Ford Fiesta, two cars away.

CHAPTER 41
30th March 2014

Thurstan stood looking over a plump, damp body which lay on its back, both arms splayed out to the sides, the right leg bent at the knee. Had it not been for the neat bullet hole in the centre of the forehead and the pool of congealed blood cradling the head, he may have been forgiven for thinking the deceased had been attempting some sort of 'twirly' pirouette before succumbing to gravity and a heart attack.

It was 6.10 a.m. There was a slight but persistent drizzle and somewhere out there, beyond the clouds, the sun had risen.

"Time of death?" Thurstan asked the Forensic Medical Examiner, who'd just stood up from inspecting the body.

"As far as I'm concerned, the indications are that death occurred sometime around midnight, give or take. We'll know more after the post mortem." He hesitated. "Unless you need anything else, I'm off to my bed."

"As good a plan as any," Thurstan told him with a smile. They shook hands and the FME nodded to Degsy.

When he'd gone Thurstan said, "Interesting graffiti," pointing towards the word 'Pedo' sprayed in large red letters over the white painted front of the Georgian terraced house on whose pathway the body lay. He took in the scene as he slowly walked up and down. "Judging from where the spent case was found, I'd say the shooter stood about there." He pointed to an area about ten feet into the garden from the front gate. "What did you say he did for a living?"

"Dead man? He was an ex City councillor, retired several years ago now." Degsy thumbed through his notes. "Drank in the pub down the road on a regular basis. Lived here all his life; initially with his parents and when they died thirty years ago, on his own."

"Well, *I've* never heard of him," Thurstan replied absently. He was eyeing the graffiti again. "Who found him, Derek?"

"The milkman, Boss. Around quarter to five this morning." He briefly studied Thurstan's expression. "Are you wondering how long that's been there? According to his neighbour, it wasn't there when she came round to push a birthday card through his door at 10.30 last night. There's a security light, over there, that clear globe, see it? Comes on automatically and lights up the entrance steps and the door, so she says she'd have seen it, had it been there. Thing is, the light's not working now. The bulb was unscrewed. Looks ok, but it's not connected. One of the Bobbies discovered it. No prints on the cover or bulb, just smears. Probably wearing gloves."

Thurstan beckoned over the CSI who had just bagged the spent shell case.

"I just need to look at that a moment," he said pleasantly. Taking the small plastic bag he quickly examined the contents from several angles and handed it back. "Thanks, you can carry on."

They walked back up the path in silence and into the street. Thurstan had a good look around taking in the various styles of houses, their locations, possible views and probable occupants. "We need to get a house-to-house up and running as soon as possible, Derek," he said eventually.

"It's being sorted, Boss. Arthur will have a team out here within an hour so we can capture some of these people before they disappear for work but, at the moment, the closest neighbours didn't see or hear a thing."

Thurstan was silent for a while, deep in thought, then announced quietly: "So Derek, we have a seriously accurate shooter using a nine milly semi–automatic pistol, unheard *and* unseen. Sound familiar?" Thurstan shot Degsy an inquisitive look.

"I get the point, Boss. Can you be certain though, without forensics, that it's a nine millimetre? You're going to tell me it's your military training, aren't you?"

The DCI, nodding an acknowledgement to a passing Officer, replied in a low voice: "No, Derek. I'm going to tell you it was written on the base of the empty case."

Turning, he patted Degsy gently on the arm. "Come on, we need to speak to the Crime Scene Manager just to firm things up. Go and grab him, will you – he's over there." Thurstan pointed to the rear of a vehicle bearing the logo 'Scientific Support'. "I've just got to do something." And with that the DCI walked back to the body which was now covered and awaiting removal under the direction of the attending Coroner's Officer. He stood before it, thoughtfully, then murmured: "Happy fucking birthday, Councillor."

CHAPTER 42
30th March 2014

Two Range Rover Discoverys and a Freelander headed towards the beach down the unlit dirt track that led from the A1068. The small town of Alnmouth lay one kilometre away.

In total darkness, the flick of a switch disconnecting the brake lights, the drivers relied on their night vision goggles. There was no moon or stars. From the main road there was absolutely nothing to see. The countryside behind them was pancake flat. In front of them the sand dunes rose up from the seashore.

They were met by a woman in her forties who showed them the path they needed to follow to the sea. Her partner was already on the shore telling her, via a mobile, it was safe to proceed. They all knew they had to move fast to beat the incoming spring tide.

The vehicles were positioned for a quick getaway. The crews, dressed in dark clothing and balaclavas, stood in the shadows of the dunes sheltering from the south-westerly wind, peering out to sea. Tommy Cole held a military right angled torch aloft, sending out five brief flashes of red light then waited, scanning and re-scanning the sea with his thermal imaging binoculars.

Two inflatable zodiac boats suddenly hit the sandy beach and everyone, apart from Tommy, began rapidly unloading their cargo into the rear compartments of the vehicles. Satisfied, he handed the crew of the zodiacs two large briefcases each. They were gone as quickly and quietly as they arrived.

Mounting up, engines purred into life. In single file, they trundled between the dunes to join the 'beach watchers' in their Fiesta; heading carefully back to the main road. In the gloom of the shore, a camouflaged figure rose from his hiding place. Concealed on the land side, another CROPS man watched the convoy's progress and whispered into the ether.

At the main road the lights came on. The Freelander and one Discovery turned left, the others right. Within a hundred metres the Freelander turned onto a narrow tarmac road towards the village of Shilbottle and the A1 which would lead them, via the A69, to the M6 and Liverpool. The Discovery carried straight on to Newcastle. The others headed for Alnwick where they would part ways.

When the vehicles had disappeared the CROPS men, who knelt silently in the marram grass, shouldered their packs and walked back along the coastal path to their vehicle parked in the caravan park at Birling Carrs Rocks. Meanwhile at three separate locations approximately two and half kilometres from the 'beach road' armed Police and NCA Agents had moved into position. High in the sky a police helicopter monitored everything from a stand-off position downwind, several kilometres away.

Inside the Freelander Tommy Cole was feeling very pleased with himself. So far all had gone to plan and he saw no reason why it shouldn't continue. He checked with the others on his mobile. Apart from having difficulty hearing them clearly against the loud music they were playing, everything was just fine. He took a cigar from the top pocket of his barbour jacket, sniffing it before shoving it in his mouth, and patted himself down in search of his lighter.

As they rounded the bend on the approach to the junction with the Shilbottle and Low Buston Road, he saw a large box truck parked on the track in the field to his right; exhaust fumes spewed into the cold night air. He didn't have time to fully digest its significance.

"What the fuck?" His driver braked hard. In front of them an HGV was slewed across the junction. At that same moment, behind them, the box truck raced from the field blocking their rear. Unseen, a figure dressed from head to foot in black stood up in the ditch to their right, the large pack on his back weighing him down as he discharged a stubby black weapon at the engine compartment of the Freelander which shuddered to a halt.

"What the fuck are you doin'?" Tommy shouted at his driver, danger flooding his head.

"It won't start, it won't fuckin start!" the driver yelled back as he desperately tried to restart the engine.

"We're fuckin' blocked behind!" they wailed from the back seat.

He had no time to think about assessing that particular problem: multiple flash bangs exploded beneath the vehicle, windows disintegrated, glass everywhere, jarring muzzle strikes to his arms and head, pain amid the strident cries of "Armed Police! Armed Police! Show your hands! Show your *fucking* hands!"

Almost simultaneously to the south, just before Warkworth, and north, just beyond Lesbury on the road to Alnwick, similar actions took place. Pre-planned, well timed road closures by local uniformed

Officers at selected locations prevented members of the public 'wandering' into the strike zones.

The Discovery heading for Newcastle passed through Birling towards the crossing on the River Coquet. Behind it another large box truck and two marked armoured Land Rover Defenders spilled out from the works access, no lights, sprinting after it. Round the bend, at Station Road, an articulated lorry pulled out across the carriageway. Bounded by the high stone walls and embankments either side there was nowhere to go but back. The Discovery braked hard to a standstill, the lead Police Defender struck its front offside tyre, the second rammed it squarely from behind, the box van sealed them in. Armed Police swarmed the vehicle; flash bangs, shattered glass, raucous shouts and cries of pain.

At the railway bridge just beyond Lesbury another HGV and the screech of brakes. Vehicles appeared from nowhere blocking the rear. An NCA agent; heavy back pack, stubby black weapon. The concentrated electromagnetic pulse brought immediate engine failure. More flashes, more bangs, more glass, more shouts, more cries of pain.

Seventy metres back down the road the Ford Fiesta casually executed a three point turn and drove back towards Lesbury. No one pursued it. There was no need. The armed Officers at the road closure north of the roundabout would deal with it.

CHAPTER 43

Tony MacMahon's internet research of the area, when planning the operation, had told him RAF Boulmer, near Alnwick, was the home of some sort of air monitoring system, an Aerospace Battle Management school and an RAF Search and Rescue helicopter. The official RAF site was just gobbledygook to him so he sent some people up to the Alnwick area to make discreet enquiries. This they did, several times with several locals at several pubs over several pints. They were able to confirm there was nothing else at the base he needed to be concerned about. As he wasn't flying anything into the area and had no intentions of needing to be rescued from the sea, he reasoned it could affect nothing. It was written into the plan as a point of interest to be noted.

The skipper of the 324 gross tonnage stern trawler Melissa had noted the point and was tuned to the SAR frequencies, so he was not alarmed when he monitored the dispatch of SAR's 'A' Flight to the aid of a seriously ill seaman on a container ship behind him in the North Sea shipping lanes. Cross checking his radar against the information he was receiving, he quickly identified the vessel in question.

Had he known it was simply a ruse to cover the launch of the Merlin HC3a Special Forces helicopter and that HMS Tyne, lying in the shadow of the container ship, was co-ordinating his and his crew's arrest, he would have been far more concerned.

164

Watching the SAR aircraft's progress from Boulmer out across the sea, he tracked its navigation lights until he could barely see them, not knowing that just beyond it, in total darkness, the Merlin had peeled off and taken up its standby position downwind of his ship. The SAR transmissions dispelled any lingering doubts he may have held.

Things were going well. The two Zodiacs had been loaded and deployed from the stern, and now the last Zodiac was being hauled up the ramp, the cash already safely stowed. It was time to get under way and the Skipper felt a small celebration would be in order. He sent the second mate to break open a few beers.

At that moment, the Merlin tore across the waves in a final dash, banked sharply and hovered above the Melissa's rear deck, bathing the bridge and superstructure in light. Ropes were thrown down, clear of the rear gantry, followed quickly by the black clad members of the SBS fast roping onto the deck.

Simultaneously, the ship was dappled in light from the powerful handheld searchlights being used by one of the two Halmatic Pacific 22 rigid inflatable boats, with their complement of Royal Marine Commandos. They bounced across the waves and began circling the stricken trawler. Deployed from beyond the headland, they'd used the outline of Coquet Island to mask their approach from the Melissa's radar and lookouts. Having broken its cover, HMS Tyne moved swiftly towards the scene.

Resistance was futile and most of the crew of the Melissa knew it. Those that didn't quickly found out why.

As the bulk of the crew were being secured, one of the SBS members tapped a forlorn figure on the shoulder and said: "Stevie? Stevie Middleton?"

The man looked back at him with sad eyes, a resigned look on his face. "What? Oh, hi Davy," he said quietly.

The SBS man kept his hand on his shoulder and said: "What the fuck are you doin' here, man?"

Stevie raised a pale wisp of a smile, shook his head slowly, sadly and replied: "Hard times, Davy. Hard times."

CHAPTER 44
31st March 2014

The woman stepped out of the lift. When the doors closed, leaving Thurstan alone, he took the opportunity to check his tongue in the mirror then brushed his hair with his hand and inspected his eyeballs. He stepped back for the big picture and thought he detected some thinning of his hair at the front. Overall, he decided he looked pretty good for his age. His hair *was* greying a little though. Wondering how he would describe it, he settled for distinguished. Nope, all in all he was doing ok even if he needed to lose a few pounds from what he imagined was a paunch. Maybe he'd cut back a bit on the whiskies.

He felt the lift slowing and turned swiftly, straightening his jacket and adjusting his tie. The doors hissed open and Thurstan stepped out of the lift to find a worried DS waiting for him.

"I'm glad I caught you, Boss." Degsy's relief was tangible. "We can't access yesterday's job on the system. All of us are locked out."

He would have said more, but he was interrupted. "The system will have just crashed or something, Derek. It's not a problem." Thurstan tried to reassure him and encouraged him to 'walk and talk' with a hand on his shoulder.

Degsy wasn't having it. "No, it's not that simple, Boss," he insisted. "We're definitely locked out and there's a Superintendent from SB in your office with a couple of suits. Judging from the testosterone levels in there, I'd say they were the secret squirrel squad."

Thurstan stood silent for a moment then said: "Ok. Can we still get into the MacMahon job?"

"I don't know, Boss. I never asked anyone." He was apologetic but also annoyed with himself for not having checked.

"Right, go and get someone to do that now and don't make it obvious. I'll waste a couple of minutes then I'll make an appearance." Thurstan turned back to the lift and pressed the call button. The doors opened almost immediately and the sole occupant, a uniformed Policewoman, said: "Going up?" He nodded. "Why not."

Several minutes later, he made his entrance. As he signed in, Arthur sidled up to him and murmured: "I think there's an ambush waiting for you in your office." The DCI looked across the room and saw the SB Superintendent sat in his swivel chair whilst the two 'suits' amused themselves, one idly inspecting the memorabilia Thurstan kept on his filing cabinet, the other picking imaginary fluff from his lapels. He smiled and said: "So I see. What great joy." He walked away but then turned and called back, "Oh, and if you see Derek tell him to come and see me please, Arthur."

As he entered his office, the SB Superintendent nonchalantly got up from Thurstan's chair and, smiling in a sickly manner, said: "Ah, Detective Chief Inspector! So nice to see you've been able to get here."

"Superintendent," Thurstan replied, reservedly.

"It's Acting Chief Superintendent, actually," the SB man said as he inspected the fingernails on his left hand. Satisfied, he looked up. "But let's not dwell on that. I have some good news for you, but first let me introduce my two colleagues. They're from the Security Service."

They didn't like each other and never had. Thurstan thought the Superintendent was a climber of the 'greasy pole' who had been promoted beyond his own mediocrity, over the heads of some far more capable and worthy people. For his part the Superintendent thought Thurstan was a sanctimonious little shit.

Thurstan extended his hand to the nearest suit and said, "And you are?" The suit ignored the gesture and replied quietly. "Our names are of no consequence, Detective Chief Inspector. We're here to collect all your documentation and evidence, forensic or otherwise, concerning yesterday's unfortunate murder."

Thurstan withdrew his hand and looked back at the SB man. "And the good news is?"

"That *is* the good news," the SB man replied. "The matter is now being investigated by Special Branch." He waved a gracious hand towards the suits. "Under, of course the direction of the Security Service. Matters of National Security are involved and that's all *you* need to know. You should be pleased. Reduces your workload at this very busy time." The sickly smile again before he continued. "Have your people box it all up. There's a couple of my people coming to help take it downstairs. Oh, and I think you're probably already aware that access on the system has been restricted to SB only." Another smile. It was a smile of triumph. "We'll wait here." He sat down in Thurstan's chair and added with false pleasantry: "If you don't mind."

Thurstan was about to mind very much when Degsy appeared in the doorway. "Did you want to see me, Boss?"

He held his tongue, smiled pleasantly and, with a hint of sarcasm, said: "Yes, Derek. We'll speak more later, but for now have some of *'our people'* box up everything we have on the Councillor's murder and take it down to the SB offices. SB will be sending some of *'their people'* up to assist."

"OK, Boss, I'll get it sorted." He half turned to walk away but stopped and said: "Oh, and that other matter we spoke about? It's fine now."

Thurstan waited for Degsy to disappear back into the main office and was about to tell the SB Superintendent what he thought of his idea of where they should wait when his work mobile rang.

"Excuse me, I need to answer this," he said with as gracious a smile as his inner fuming would permit. "DCI Baddeley."

"Hello, Boss, it's Taffy. We've found an interesting CCTV. Well, two to be exact. One from a house on South Drive, just around the corner, as it were, from the scene, and the other in a little pizza kebab place at the end of Grove Street and Wavertree High Street. Just wanted to let you know we'll be bringing them in shortly."

Thurstan's brain was now racing, all thought of verbal revenge gone. If he left the office to continue the conversation, it might look suspicious. But if he stayed he needed to manage it cleverly and, he hoped, with style.

"I'll have an egg mayonnaise, Taff," he found himself blurting out, "and if they haven't got that, I'll have tuna." He took the phone from

170

his ear and shook his head dolefully at his audience. "I knew I shouldn't have sent a Welshman," he told them before speaking into the phone again. "Ok, listen carefully, Taffy. You stay where you are and I'll come down and sort it out myself." With that he cancelled the call, turned to the clearly uninterested suits and his SB temporary nemesis and said: "Well, you seem to have this all under control. Make yourselves comfortable, won't you. I may see you later but I really have to go and sort out my lunch. If you need anything else speak to DS Drayton." And with that he turned on his heels and left.

As he made his way out through the main office he caught Degsy's arm and hissed, "Give them anything they need. Try and keep them occupied and away from the windows and get them out of here as soon as you can. I have to go. You can get me on my mobile." Then he was gone.

Once out of the lift on the ground floor he called Taffy's mobile, striding out into the parking area. By the time the call was answered he'd already started his car.

"DC Blevins," Taffy said as he swallowed the last mouthful of his chicken kebab.

"Taffy, it's the Boss. Sorry about that before. I'll explain later. Where are you now?"

"We're on the High Street just near to Grove Street, Boss," Taffy replied.

"Are you eating?" Thurstan queried. "Are you in Sperry's?"

"Well, as it happens … yes," Taffy reluctantly admitted, "but this is where we've got one of the CCTVs from, Boss, so I just thought, you know, seeing as we're here…"

"I'm not interested in that, Taff. Just stay there," Thurstan interrupted him, then as an afterthought, he added, "Are you parked on the double yellows?"

"Well –"

"You bloody are, aren't you!" Thurstan interrupted again. "For goodness sake, don't get a ticket. I'll be with you in 10 to15 minutes and don't speak to anyone at the Office." He hung up as he drove down the ramp and left Police HQ.

CHAPTER 45

He pulled up in front of the unmarked Police car parked outside Sperry's on the High Street. Sandy was standing on the pavement waiting for him.

"Where's Taff, Sandeep?" Thurstan asked as he drew his jacket around himself. "That wind's bloody nippy, isn't it?"

Sandy smiled from within his faux fur lined hood. "It is a bit, Boss. You should get yourself one of these," he replied as he patted the front of his padded jacket. "Taffy's inside. I'll mind the motors." With that he walked to the entrance door and called to the man behind the counter. "This is the Boss. Ok for him to go through?" The man beckoned him in. "First door on the right."

He found Taffy in the small office, sat at a battered table filling in his Police pocket notebook. "Hello Boss," Taffy said folding up the PNB and returning it to his jacket. "I've downloaded what we need, but grab a seat and I'll show you what it is." Thurstan pulled up the only other chair in the office as Taffy prepared the playback.

"Right, we were doing some house visits and it wasn't looking good until we found this place in South Drive, just around the corner from the scene, only a minute's walk away. No one around there had any CCTV but this guy's had some anti-social behaviour issues with local bucks. He's from Manchester, you know what they're like, calling him 'the Mancs' and throwing eggs at his windows, so he had it installed. Watch this. According to the clock, it's twenty three forty yesterday."

The screen showed a darkened street lit only by sparse sodium light. After several seconds, headlights lit up the road as a car turned right and drove directly towards the camera. "It's come out of North Drive, and from the junction it's only about a hundred metres to Sandown Lane. From there the scene's within fifty metres, I'd say. All this is happening in the road just behind us." He indicated over his back with his thumb.

The vehicle followed the road around, passing in front of the camera at a 90 degree angle. The house security lighting suddenly came on, illuminating it briefly before it disappeared from view.

"Now I know you can't see the occupants clearly, but the driver is wearing a light coloured top or jacket and I'd say that's a Ford Focus. *I think* it's silver. On top of that, if we play it back … to here, you can see the front offside headlamp is misaligned slightly." He let the footage run until the security light came on, then said: "And in case you were wondering, it was the cat. Just there." He pointed to a small object caught entering the driveway. "The whole point of this, Boss, is what's on the *next* one taken here."

The screen kicked into life again to show a view of the inside of the shop. Visible through the front window, the pavement and part of the roadway. After several seconds, the bonnet and headlights of a car came into view as it halted next to the kerb outside. The headlight on the driver's side was noticeably misaligned. A figure walked past the bonnet and into the shop. The man was wearing dark clothing and his woolly hat and beard had the effect of making him look eastern European or of Middle East origin. Once at the counter, he made a quick glance upwards adjusting his position so that for the rest of his transaction he stood side on with his back mostly towards the camera.

On exiting the shop he turned left, towards the car and out of view. Seconds later the headlights came on again and the car drove off, heading into the city. The driver, seen briefly, was wearing a light coloured top or jacket.

"Well, what do you think, Boss? Taffy asked. "The clock says twenty three forty five, which fits in with the previous footage. We have the headlight, it's a Ford Focus and I'm pretty sure it's silver *and* there's the driver's clothing. It's the same car. It's got to be!"

Thurstan stood up, placed his chair back where he'd found it and patted Taffy on the shoulder. "Good work Taff," he grinned. "Incidentally, what on earth led you here?"

Taffy looked a bit sheepish."Well, to be honest, Boss, I was a bit peckish and this is one of my regular eating places. I know the owner fairly well now. He asked me if I was working on the murder. One thing led to another and he mentioned his new CCTV and did I want to have a look. Well, I thought it would be foolish not to and here we are."

"Good stuff," Thurstan patted his arm again. "What did you have?"

"What?" Taff was momentarily perplexed. "Oh! I had a chicken kebab."

"Any good?" Thurstan asked.

"It was lush, Boss. Always is, that's why I come here," Taffy responded with a grin.

Leaving the office they thanked the owner and wandered out onto the pavement where they joined Sandy.

"Well done, Sandeep. Good day's work," Thurstan said. "Listen, both of you, you're probably not aware but the SB descended upon us this morning and have taken this job over. I don't know exactly why, but I think we can all guess. They don't know about this stuff and that's the way I want it to stay, at least for the time being. Don't mention it to anyone, apart from DS Drayton. The less anyone in the office knows then the better it is for them. Ok?"

Sandy and Taff looked at each other, nodded, then as one replied, "OK, Boss."

They stood in silence as the DCI looked up and down the street. "What about these other premises?" he said eventually.

Sandy shook his head. "No CCTV, Boss. Inside only, and they weren't open, of course. That one over there ..." He pointed to a building across the road. "Only had it fitted this morning whilst we were here and that one," he pointed to a shop further along the street, "is a dummy."

Thurstan rubbed his chin thoughtfully. "Ok, I'll take the downloads and you two do whatever it is you need to do and I'll see you back at the office when you're finished."

Back in his car he sat with the engine running and the heater on full blast. When he'd warmed up sufficiently he turned on the car radio and manoeuvred into the city bound traffic. The local news was reporting a serious assault in the south end, the arrest of a man and woman as they attempted to abduct a 10 year old boy from a street in nearby Bootle and the fact that it was going to be a warmer day tomorrow.

CHAPTER 46

He spent the afternoon at a Senior Officers meeting listening to a 'management consultant' talk drivel then tried to look interested as they later discussed the 'burning issues'. He hadn't wanted to go but he had no choice. He left no wiser than when he went in.

It was almost early evening as he sat back in his chair pushing the last of the blackberry jam Danish pastry into his mouth. He chewed it furiously for several seconds, tried to wash it down with a swig of his macchiato 'to go' and mumbled between swallowing: "Well? What do you think? Is it him?"

Degsy leant forward in his chair, looking intently at the image of the bearded man with the hat. Several seconds passed. "As far as I'm concerned, Boss," he said eventually. "That's him. I'm pretty certain that's the guy I saw at Dickie Trimble's do. That's Nickson." He looked at Thurstan. He'd expected him to be happier.

Thurstan looked back at him. "I know. You'd think I could at least crack a smile, but I've had time to think about it. Alright, it confirms our suspicions which, let's face it, are based on some blurry images, odd money transactions and the fact he's failed to contact us following our visit to his parents. But it doesn't take us significantly further forward in terms of actual hard evidence." Degsy looked as if he was about to say something but Thurstan ignored him. "Yes, we *can* now put him close to the scene of a murder, within minutes of the crime taking place, but we've got no DNA, no fingerprints, no weapon, no eyewitnesses. In fact we've got nothing whatsoever. Not even the bloody registration number of that car! Although, to be honest, I suspect it wouldn't help us either; probably false plates. In addition, we're not being allowed to investigate that particular crime and in relation to the murder we *are* being allowed to investigate, well ...we haven't even got that much." He couldn't help letting a half laugh escape. "Tell me I'm wrong."

"It's a bugger, I know, Boss," Degsy offered lamely.

"A slight understatement I think Derek. Anyway, onwards and upwards ... hopefully." He pointed at the large buff folder Degsy had placed earlier on the chair beside him. "Is that my hotels list?"

"Yes, Boss, everything you asked for, and it's bang up to date as of today including anything flagging up an anomaly with voters checks, liaison with Royal Mail or credit and Intel checks. Also, all addresses verified as rental. As you said, people move in and out of these places all the time so to a casual enquiry it wouldn't be unusual for names not to show up." Pausing, he ran his hand over his eyes then apologetically said: "And this is just the lists from the last two weeks." Standing up, he placed the stack of A4 sheets onto Thurstan's desk.

The DCI dragged the folder across the table. "Where's the rest?"

"Well, I thought it would be best to start from now and work backwards through the month, Boss. Gandalph has the remaining anomaly files, as well as the full guest lists. I think he's made an armchair out of them." Degsy sat down again. "He's not in the list, Boss, not under his own name anyway." He looked weary. "Do you want to go through it now?"

Thurstan shot his DS a glance and decided to take pity on him; he'd had enough himself. "No, I think we'll call it a day. Go home to the wife and kids, Derek. We'll look at this tomorrow."

Degsy smiled a tired smile of thanks. "Have a nice night, Boss," he said and left to sign out.

The late shift had come on duty and were quietly busying themselves with various tasks having been briefed by their supervisor. The day crew had already gone home, or wherever it was they went when not working, and Thurstan wandered through the office to 'hit the book'.

"Off home, Boss?" Lizzie said as she walked past carrying a stack of bulky folders.

Thurstan looked up, temporarily startled. "What? Oh... yeah... I'm.. er... I'm done, Liz. Enough is enough."

"Well, drive carefully and I hope you have a nice night," she replied, flashing him the smile he'd come to admire. Then she turned thoughtfully and walked off across the office.

"I'll try," he called after her. She'd sounded as if she'd meant it, he thought. He stood for a moment, watching her traverse the floor, then turned and ambled off towards the lifts and home.

Within a minute he strode briskly back towards his desk.

"I thought you were going, Boss?" Iqbal enquired as Thurstan shot past him.

"So did I," he called back over his shoulder, entering his office.

Five minutes later, carrying a large buff folder under his arm, he stepped out into a fine drizzle and strode across the HQ car park towards his car.

On his driveway, he took out his mobile and used an app to turn on the house interior lights and SoundTouch music system. Grabbing the folder and a carrier bag of shopping from the rear seat, he engaged in a short trivial conversation with a neighbour while he found his front door key. The car's indicators flashed. Entering the hallway, the sounds of classical music washed over him. He wasn't an ardent fan, but he knew what he liked. The CD 'Classics from Adverts' fulfilled all his needs in this area.

He dumped the folder and shopping on the table and headed for the fridge, took out a bottle from his selection of Belgian beers and poured its golden brown contents into the large, bulbous, stemmed glass he'd bought on a trip to Bruges. Two long mouthfuls later, he took his coat and jacket off, hung them on the hooks in the hall, opened another beer and topped up his glass. Stripping off his tie and shirt he headed for the shower.

Sat in a T-shirt and shorts, he downed his knife and fork on the empty plate and wiped his mouth with a paper towel. He was pleased to admit his skills were improving. Whilst ready meals were not quite a thing of the past, he found cooking from 'fresh' interesting, entertaining and therapeutic, particularly with a couple of beers. The benefits of watching TV cookery programmes were starting to become evident.

He placed the plate in the sink, opened the cupboard next to the fridge, took out the bottle of Bushmills Black Bush and the Braemar crystal tumbler, added two ice cubes from the ice dispenser and poured himself a large tot. Sitting down at the table, he dragged the buff folder towards him and took a swig of the whiskey. Prefab Sprout sang quietly in the background as he began to sift through the information before him. No rush. As always, he had all night.

CHAPTER 47

1st April 2014

"Morning, Boss, you wanted to see me?" Degsy was looking refreshed, more than could be said for his DCI.

"Yes, Derek." He rubbed his eyes and yawned. "This folder. I need to bring you up to speed. Close the door, will you?"

Degsy pushed the door to. "I take it you didn't get much sleep last night?"

Thurstan looked back at him. "Is it that obvious?"

Degsy shook his head, "No. Well, just a bit." He flashed a faint smile.

"Right. Well, it can't be helped. I was up most of the night wading through this lot." He stabbed the folder with his forefinger then opened it and pulled out a sheet of A4 containing a list of names. He passed it across the desk to his Sergeant. "Take a look at this."

Degsy sat down in silence, read the sheet then looked up and said: "I don't want to look stupid, Boss, but..." He shrugged his shoulders.

"Exactly!" Thurstan was coming to life. "But!" He shoved another sheet across the desk. "Don't look at that yet." He sat back in his chair.

"Last night, I idly remembered a game I used to play with the SK at Speke when it was one of those really, really quiet nights. I'd be in my office doing some paperwork and he'd be on the front desk, minding the station. We used to phone each other up with odd names that had a double meaning or made a sentence. It would start off with simple stuff like 'if your surname was Green, would you call your daughter Theresa?' Or 'if your surname was Off-Shotgun, would you call your son Shaun?' progressing to vaguer things such as 'if your surname was Noone, would you call your son Ian Martin?" One look at Degsy told him that one hadn't registered. "I. M. Noone. I AM NO ONE. With me now? Anyway, it was that sort of nonsense. We kept a score. It was puerile but it kept us awake." He leaned forward, shaking his right forefinger with meaning at Degsy. "And that's what triggered it. I. M. Noone. It's on the top of the first list. You got it?" Degsy nodded. "Well, I remembered I'd seen one or two other odd little names so I went through the whole bloody thing again." He stabbed the sheet of paper on his desk with his finger. "Take a look at that, Derek."

Degsy picked it up. On one side of the sheet were the names in full; overleaf the shortened versions. He slowly scanned the reverse.

I M Noone

William Tredwell

I N Hughes

Samuel E Goole

J S Tyce

Donald T Forlow

P Lees

M L Eveler

Beneath was written, 'I am no one. (I) will tread well. I and yous (have) same goal. Justice. Don't follow please. (I) am Level(l)er.'

Degsy looked up at Thurstan. "Is he taking the piss, Boss?"

Thurstan looked back at him deliberately and shook his head. "Despite the significance of today's date, Derek, I don't believe this is an April's Fool. No, I don't think he's taking the piss. I think he's being very serious."

Degsy shot Thurstan a look of curiosity. "Well, what does he mean 'I am no one'? He's told us who or what he *is*? And what on earth is a Leveller anyway?"

The DCI released a tired smile. "Well, *I think* he's telling us he's one of many, in the bigger picture, he's no one, and I have to admit I had to look up Leveller on the internet."

He paused and picked up a sheet of paper from his blotting pad. "Dictionary definition, Derek?" then read it aloud. "It's 'One that levels *or* one of a group of radicals arising during the English Civil War and advocating equality before the law and religious toleration *or* one favouring the removal of political, social, or economic inequalities *or* something that tends to reduce or eliminate differences among individuals'." He put the sheet of paper back down. "Look at the fifth name on the list – Justin Tyce. I discovered last night, Derek, that another form of Justin, is actually the name 'Justice', and that 'Tyce', according to the internet, can mean 'Fiery'. It seemed a bit dramatic so, I looked up synonyms and found 'Torrid' is one of them and the dictionary tells me one of *its* meanings is 'hurried or rapid'. *Rapid Justice.* Now, Derek, don't tell me *that* doesn't fit with what's happening here." Degsy couldn't.

Thurstan leant back in his chair. "And take a look at the last hotel he used, in particular the date."

Degsy picked up the first list he'd been given. After several seconds he exclaimed: "He left it yesterday morning!" He rose and started towards the door. "I'll get Gandalph and a couple of the others to start phoning around, see if we can find out where he is now, Boss."

"I wouldn't bother, Derek," Thurstan reigned him back in, then stood up and calmly walked over to the coat stand, removed his jacket and started putting it on as he spoke. "I contacted the Border Agency earlier. He left Liverpool yesterday afternoon for Berlin."

"Shit!" The DS looked disheartened.

Thurstan looked at him benevolently. "I know. It would destroy lesser men, Derek. But, we are not lesser men. We are the Plod! And we shall keep plodding on, like those Mummies in the horror films. You know, where the victims are running through the woods hell for leather yet the Mummy, dragging its foot, is always right behind them, gaining ground." He smiled. "Until."

He grabbed his phone from the desk and patted Degsy on the arm. "In the meantime we have a hotel to visit. I'm pretty sure they will still have some CCTV we can look at. And who knows, it might even be worthwhile."

CHAPTER 48

Degsy paid for the teas, handed Thurstan his, and bade the vendor farewell. "And tell your kid I'll see him at the match on Saturday, Brian."

"Right yer ar, Degs," Brian replied with a smile.

Thurstan pointed to the seating area encircling the nearest tree. They wandered slowly over to it, leaving the red coloured hot dog and burger stand behind them.

Sipping their tea in silence it was a while before Thurstan spoke. "Ok, not what we might have hoped for, but interesting nonetheless. Helps build up the picture." He threw Degsy a weak smile, intended as encouragement.

Degsy missed it and sat staring into the flimsy plastic cup. Eventually he declared: "It's an absolute waste of time, Boss, having cameras in your reception area if you're going to have them set at such a crazy angle. I mean, it *is* useful if we only arrested people after inspecting the tops of their heads, know what I mean?"

Thurstan chuckled and took another sip of tea. "I know. But look on the bright side, Derek. It's not as if we have less than we had before. In fact, we *are* a little bit richer for it. The cleaner's comment about how clean the room was when he left *and* how the bed sheets were untouched. Did you catch it?" He glanced at Degsy. 'Like he hadn't slept in it', she said. At least we know there's not much point in getting overexcited about finding a room he's just vacated. DNA and fingerprints? I think we've more chance of winning the lottery."

Degsy looked up from his tea. "Yeah, I caught that. You think he slept somewhere else or just slept on the top cover?"

Thurstan sipped his tea again. "I think he's using a sleeping bag," he said quietly. "It makes sense to me. Don't get me wrong, Derek. I'm not saying we don't forensically examine a room he's left. If we can get to it before the cleaners have moved in then it would be silly not to, really. But I'm just saying, let's not wet ourselves with excitement. We've got no DNA from the scenes. What we need it for, why it would be nice to have it, is because, at some stage in the future, he's going to fuck up. They always do. It's just a case of how long. Hopefully we won't be retired by then." He laughed.

Degsy smiled back at him. "I might not, but …" he said with a shrug then, as he felt his phone buzzing in his pocket. "'Scuse me, Boss."

He stood up and threw his cup in the nearby bin as he spoke. "DS Drayton... Yeah?... We'll be back shortly then. Ask Chalkie to hang on. Nah, we don't need a lift. We're just at Holy Corner." He hung up. "Chalkie's waiting for us to get back, Boss, so he can give you an update on the Masterson job before he goes home. Says it's important."

Thurstan poured the remainder of his tea over the base of the tree. Degsy took the cup from him and threw it in the bin. Less than 10 minutes later they walked into MIT and went their separate ways.

Thurstan walked over to Chalkie's office where he found him standing with his coat on, holding a sumptuous bouquet of flowers.

"Chalkie! You shouldn't have. They're wonderful!" Thurstan said waving his splayed fingers in front of his eyes.

"Fuck off, Thurstan!" Chalkie replied, grinning. "They're for the wife. It's our anniversary."

"So which one is this then? Stone, plastic, granite or polystyrene?" Thurstan retorted.

Chalkie looked back at him in mock disgust. "You haven't got a clue, have you?"

"No," Thurstan replied, "And, taking into account your attempt at deflection, neither have you." He smiled a winner's smile. "So, Masterson?"

Chalkie sat on the edge of his desk. "We've charged them both and they'll be appearing in custody tomorrow morning. They've maintained the 'no comment' stance but what with the fibres, DNA, fingerprints and the motorway CCTV, I think we're sound and so do the CPS."

"Good news, Chalkie, and thanks for hanging on to tell me yourself. I appreciate it. And at least we have some evidence to clearly connect Tony MacMahon to the job."

Chalkie smiled ruefully. "Yeah, his prints found on some of the recovered money have done that alright." He stood up. "I suspect it was probably 'half now and the rest later'. What price 'love', hey?"

"Forty thousand, apparently," Thurstan replied frankly. "Now, you'd better get a move on. Going anywhere nice tonight?"

"Well, I'm meeting her at the Radisson," Chalkie said as he readjusted his flowers. "She thinks we're just having a drink, but my sister, who's going to keep the kids occupied, helped me pack some stuff for her which I stuck in the room earlier. So it's a River View suite then a special meal at the Panoramic restaurant next door and tomorrow, well, I thought the old Ferry across the Mersey and some retail therapy for her." He grinned a big happy grin which clearly said he was very pleased with himself.

Thurstan patted him on the arm. "Chalkie, you are, indeed, a very clever and cunning man."

They walked into the main office where Thurstan added, with a look of gravity: "Seriously though. Don't forget to buy some condoms on the way out. A DI's pay will only support four kids." He grinned.

Chalkie turned, smiled condescendingly, and tapped his top pocket.

Thurstan laughed and patted him on the back. "Enjoy your anniversary," he said then peeled off and strode over towards the Sergeants' side of the office.

Lizzie glanced up from her desk and smiled as he approached. Thurstan couldn't help but smile back. He wasn't sure what the hell was happening, but it felt as if something was. The little man in his head told him to forget it.

"Derek, I need a quick update on anything the hotels team have come up with and I've just remembered we were going to make some enquiries in Hungary, do you remember?" he said.

Degsy looked up from his desk and held up his forefinger as he spoke into the phone: "Ok, love, I'll sort it out when I get home. Got to go now, the Boss wants me. Yeah, and I love you too." He started to laugh. "No, I'm not doing that! All I can say is ditto." He put the phone down. "Sorry, Boss. Yeah, can you give me five minutes and I'll see you in your office?"

"Not a problem. I need to go somewhere first. Five minutes then." The DCI turned and wandered off towards the corridor. Lizzie, who was now on the phone, looked up and watched him leave.

Ten minutes later, he and Degsy were ensconced in his office. "Sorry about that, Boss, I needed to speak to Soapy and he'd gone walkabout." The DS sat down, paused for a few seconds, then said: "Right, as we know, he came in on the seventeenth of February so I had Soapy start from that date working towards your list and Gandalph kept working back the other way. They found some names that are highly probable to be him simply because they fit the profile of being odd. There's a Christian Phillip Bacon, Chris P Bacon." He caught the grimace on Thurstan's face. "I know, they're all like that," he offered apologetically before continuing: "There's a Richard Stroker, Jack Goff and Robin Graves. But there's gaps where he must have been using conventional names. Now, Gandalph pointed out that none of these names, so far, actually consist of his own forenames so we discounted, for the time being, any names that did. That narrowed things down a bit but there's still days missing in his trail of hotels. We identified several more rooms he'd used but, as you mentioned, especially after this length of time, forensics is pointless. We did, however, get a confirmation of a sleeping bag. Soapy didn't realise the significance until I happened to mention it. He said one of the chambermaids saw it. She and several others also commented on how clean he left his rooms. Some remembered him by his description, having spoken to him when he declined having the room serviced and one of them commented she thought he had OCD."

Thurstan shot him a quizzical glance.

"She saw him doing some repetitive stuff. Closing his door several times, returning to touch the door handle. She said she recognised the behaviour because her brother's got it, does the same sort of thing."

"Hmm..." Thurstan raised his eyebrows. "OCD. Intriguing. Not quite sure where it gets us but interesting all the same. What about the Hungary enquiry?"

Degsy was looking at his notes. "Yeah. That was the transport links thing. The 'man in the wall'. It's two stops away on the underground from ..." he hesitated briefly. "Looks like you pronounce it Delly Pallyowdvar. Anyway it's the Budapest train station for getting to the west of Hungary. There's another two big stations but they're on the opposite side of the river. One of them basically serves the east and south of the country and the other one is the main international and intercity terminal."

The DCI looked thoughtful. "I don't think he would have made that withdrawal if he lived in the City or even nearby. So, probability is that he's living in the west of the country." He fell silent a moment. "Or he wants us to believe he lives in the west of the country. It's something, yet it's nothing." It was his turn now to look apologetic. "Ok, let everyone know I'm very grateful and they've done a great job, but let's just dot the i's and cross the t's, if we can."

"Will do, Boss." Degsy, sensed the briefing was at an end. He rose from his seat then added: "Do you think he'll be back?"

Thurstan rubbed his chin. "Do you know what? I've got absolutely nothing more than a gut feeling but, yes. I think he *will* come back. I don't think it's finished yet." He yawned then stood up. "Right, I'm going to take some 'time due', Derek, and head home. I noticed the other day you've got some time owing to you so if you want to do the same, seeing as you obviously have something needs sorting ... I've no objections. Just make sure all your lot are accounted for and let Lizzie know what you're doing."

Degsy nodded. "If you don't mind, it would be handy, Boss," he said, then made for the door.

Thurstan called after him, "Oh, and Derek!" Degsy halted and looked back. "You're doing a great job too. Thanks very much. I mean it."

CHAPTER 49
14th April 2014

"Just drop me off at Old Hall Street. You won't have to dick about to get me to the hotel. I need to clear my head and anyway it's better for us both this way."

It was a week since Nicks had returned from Hungary where he'd administered retribution on behalf of young Katalin Lukács and her family. Her resemblance to Anca was seldom far from his mind. He took a mouthful of water then pushed the bottle down the side of his day sack, nestling it against his fleece.

Making safe the Yarygin pistol he slid it into the right hand leg pocket of his distinctive, unmistakably Russian, combat pants.

Their current target, a leading Newcastle gangster, had newly emerging links to Russian 'Mafia' people in London. Like the weapon and ammunition, the pants were an easy clue. The Police had a tendency to like easy clues. It saved them from having to think out of the box.

Simon looked at him briefly.

"You sure? I must admit I'm absolutely knackered and every minute counts when there's another early start."

Nicks looked back at him. He could see how tired he was. They'd spent the whole day driving around the North-East of England to no avail, waiting for the surveillance to highlight an opportunity for him to use his skills.

"Yeah, I'm sure," he said, slipping the suppressor into his left leg pocket.

"Just here, Si, on the corner will be great. Go and get your head down and I'll see you later on. Same place as you picked me up."

Simon pulled over and Nicks got out. As he walked away Simon called after him.

"Don't forget, seven o'clock."

Nicks turned and waved. "Yeah, yeah. I know. Stop worrying."

CHAPTER 50

Four monitors bathed the otherwise unlit room in a soft glow. The ticking of the wall clock supplied a soundtrack for the night. Two switched rhythmically between internal views, another alternated views of the rear. The last maintained a steady oversight of the glass entrance doors and the street beyond.

The business sector on the northern edge of the city centre had no attraction for the average party animal, despite its proximity to several nightclubs. There was no fast food, no flashing lights and no night taxi rank. This put it in a no go zone for all but the few in a hotel room or apartment there. After midnight, if there was tumbleweed in Liverpool, this is where you'd find it.

It had been months since anything interesting had appeared on three of the monitors. The last time was when two hooded figures broke in and stayed long enough to be captured by the Police. The footage of one of them trying to outrun the Police dog was particularly amusing and ultimately very satisfying for those privileged enough to see it.

The front entrance was different. Often it'd revealed comedy drunks, male and female urinators, couples having sex and the occasional 'domestic' dispute. Tonight, since not long after midnight, it'd stolidly recorded the building facades opposite, together with the dark entrance to the narrow cobbled roadway cutting between them.

Until, that is, just after 3am. On the opposite pavement, a woman coming from the direction of the city centre walked unsteadily past.

She stopped then returned to stare into the gloom of the alley. After checking to her right and left, she disappeared into its depths. Twenty seconds later, a figure dressed in dark clothing, hoodie covering his face, walked briskly into view. Without hesitation, he followed her into the gloom.

A full two minutes elapsed before the man in the odd pants with a small light coloured rucksack on his back walked past the entrance and continued out of view into the city. Fifteen seconds later, he came back and walked slowly along the cobbles. When he reached the periphery of light, he stood still.

CHAPTER 51

He waited on the edge of darkness as if he was on the threshold of space. Had he really heard something or just imagined it? He was tired and yearning to get to bed, another long day to come. Part of him wanted to turn and walk off. Another wanted just a few more minutes to be sure. He listened intently. There it was again. A low, almost distant, squeal. Silence. Now a muffled sobbing.

Quietly and slowly, he took several paces into the shadows until he reached some railings he'd not seen from the street. Satisfied he couldn't be seen, he removed the Yarygin from his leg pocket, regretting having made it safe in the car.

Turning his back to the darkness, hoping his body would help suppress any sound, he carefully racked a round into the chamber under control; a misfeed *could* prevent him getting a first shot off but his drills would correct that, if he had time. It was a risk he preferred to take for the advantage of surprise. Facing back into the gloom, he slowly screwed the 'silencer' onto the weapon and took a deep breath before casually but carefully walking along the middle of the setts that formed the narrow roadway, adjusting his eyes to the dark, weapon held firmly to his side.

There it was again. Sobbing. Faint but unmistakable.

It came from an area to his left, ahead of him. He quickened his pace. Suddenly, his foot made contact with something, sending it scuttling briefly across the cobbles. He winced with annoyance. The sound hadn't been loud, but it *was* a sound. Stood frozen for several seconds, he took another couple of steps and found his foot was now on the object. He crouched down. A woman's high heeled shoe.

Following the line of spiked railings to his left, he was about halfway along the street when he heard a short deep moan followed by a noise the nature of which he couldn't distinguish. Movement? A whisper? He didn't know, but both came from behind and below. He stepped back.

A set of steps led down to an enclosed basement. Warily he descended them, the weapon ready at his hip, slightly extended in front of him, his left hand holding the guard rail. The lack of unevenness on the steps told him they were iron, not stone. There would be a space beneath them he'd need to take into consideration; another place for someone to hide.

Despite having obtained some night vision, the further he went the less he saw. The phrase 'blacker than a very black thing' flitted through his mind as he reached what felt like the floor of the basement. He probed in front with his right foot. Satisfied he was on solid ground, he fumbled around with his left hand for the small lighter with its little torch he knew he had somewhere and instinctively turned to follow the stair's guard rail back on itself.

Sobbing erupted from the void ahead of him. At the same time, he was struck heavily by someone bursting out from the darkness beneath the stairs. The initial contact on his left side was almost simultaneous with the full blow of a body which took him off his feet and slammed him into the pitch-black recessed doorway to his right. As he lay

199

slumped against the door, his head swimming from the impact of the doorframe, he could dimly discern a figure running up the steps. Without thinking, he raised the Yarygin and pulled the trigger. He'd no idea where the round had gone, it was completely instinctive. Had he thought about it, he knew he wouldn't have done it. It complicated things. Now he *had* to finish it.

Nicks reached the top of the stairs with a high pitched buzzing in his ears. A sharp pain in his side accompanied a sudden feeling of nausea. He steadied himself momentarily with his left hand on the railing; his legs didn't feel right, he felt weak.

He knew he couldn't pursue his attacker, silhouetted ahead of him against the fatigued light from an unseen streetlamp. He'd thought they'd be running much faster but dismissed it from his mind as he raised the weapon in a weaver stance and fired in quick succession. Klak!Klak!Klak!

The first round hit the figure centrally in the lower back tearing the muscles, deforming as it did so, shattering its way through the sacral plexus. The second hit the upper back, slightly to the left of the spine, passing through the muscle, narrowly missing the 7th and 8th thoracic vertebrae before ripping through the thoracic aorta and into the heart. The third round passed easily through the figure's jacket into clean flight and clipped the sign at the end of the alley, sailing wildly off into the darkness, well beyond the reach of the nearby street light. The figure stumbled forward and slapped itself unceremoniously onto the cobbled roadway.

Nicks walked forward, carefully stripping his left glove from his hand with his teeth, so his latex one remained in place. He shoved the outer into his pocket then stuffed his hand up inside his jacket so he could wipe the area where he'd been struck. He licked the back of his fingers. Blood.

Cautiously, he lightly kicked the prone form. No reaction. He knelt down beside it. The buzzing in his ears had disappeared. A faint gurgling sound was all he heard.

Abruptly remembering why he was there, he stood up, checked both ends of the street for movement and returned to the stairway. Slowly descending the steps, he tried again to adjust his eyes to the darkness. He could hear muffled whimpering. Turning the corner on leaving the last step, he cautiously edged his way forward, as silently as he could.

After a few steps, he felt something underneath his foot and dropped to one knee. It was the lighter he'd lost when struck. Alert for any movement, side throbbing, weapon readied in front of him, he found the button at its base and pressed. Its weak white light was enough for him to see the figure of a woman lying on her right side, almost foetus like, her back to a wall, her jumper pulled up and over her head exposing her bra and the breasts that hung from it. Her dark trousers were pulled down to just below her knees, her white briefs just above them. He could see her arms were held behind her back and through whatever was stuffed in her mouth he could hear her frightened whimpers gather into deep sobbing.

CHAPTER 52

"Ok, what have we got?"

Thurstan hung up his coat and accepted a steaming mug of coffee. Standing on a cold Liverpool street in the early hours of the morning was beginning to lose its attraction. Though he'd returned home to shower and change, he looked tired.

"We've viewed the CCTV," Lizzie replied. "I've got a copy here, and we've taken the victim's and witnesses' statements.

Thurstan squeezed himself between his seat and his desk and put the mug down on a coaster. His PC had already been turned on, so he entered his password and slid the disc into the machine. "Where's Derek?" he enquired.

"He's got his promotion board this morning, Boss, but he's briefed me. I've seen the footage and read the statements." Lizzie gave him her 'don't panic, I'm on top of it' smile.

He rubbed his face and eyes. "Damn! I'd forgotten about that."

Pretty sure he was being short changed by his shower gel, which promised he'd feel 'refreshed and invigorated', he swivelled his monitor so Lizzie could view it with him. The screen flashed into life as the compilation of images from three different cameras showed the victim, her assailant, and the murder suspect's approach to and into the alley.

"As you can see, Boss, it's not great footage. Too distant for the most part, other than the building opposite and even that's not what we'd hope for. It's from their reception area, the angle and glass doors make it difficult to see clearly. You can make out the figures and some detail, like that distinctive pattern on his pants, but not the stuff that matters like the face."

They sat in silence as they watched, Thurstan sipping his coffee.

Eventually Lizzie said: "There's a fair gap here where nothing happens. It's around ten minutes before you see them coming out again."

Thurstan nodded, picked up the statements and began to speed read them, bypassing the usual introductory personal information. Between sips of coffee, he occasionally glanced at the monitor. Lizzie got up. "Just getting myself a drink," she explained and left.

As she walked back into the office with her cup of tea she glanced at her watch and said: "It'll be coming up soon, Boss."

Thurstan put the statements down, took another sip of coffee, and rested his elbows on the desk. He watched the victim and her 'rescuer' emerge from the depths of the alley. They walked to the steps of a building slightly further up the main street where he sat her down before calling and waving to someone, unseen, back towards where they had just come from. Seconds later, a couple, a man and woman, entered into shot. After a short conversation, the female sat next to the victim, putting her arm around her. The male took out his phone to make the call for assistance which the Police Control Room had recorded. The 'rescuer' appeared to say something to the male then walked back into the alley where he disappeared from view. From the statement he'd just read, Thurstan knew the 'rescuer' told the male he was going to find the victim's handbag, which she was asking for, and he'd be back soon. On the CCTV footage looking into the alley, several small flashes of light could be periodically seen in the two minutes it took for the first Police patrol to arrive.

Thurstan didn't need to see anymore. He knew, from the first Officers to search the alley, what they had and hadn't found. They *had* found a man lying dead, a bloodstained knife, a woman's handbag and four empty cartridge cases. They'd not found the 'mystery rescuer and chief murder suspect'. It mattered not. Thurstan was fairly certain he knew who he was dealing with.

CHAPTER 53

Seeing the first flashes of blue splashing across the walls at the far end of the street, Nicks knew he had to abandon his search for the knife. Despite the handkerchief beneath his jacket, he could feel the warm wetness of the blood oozing out of him. Leaving the alleyway, he turned right and stopped briefly to get his bearings, shielded by the building line. He could hear the siren closing rapidly; more, almost iridescent, blue bouncing over the walls and windows of the buildings further down on the main road.

The path through the little un-gated 'park' opposite beckoned. He desperately tried to remember where it exited, if at all. Pall Mall! It had an exit there! He crossed the narrow street and was quickly absorbed by the darkness, masked by the old Exchange railway station. As he walked, he took out his phone.

"What's up?" Simon answered.

An unscheduled call from Nicks was not common, especially at this hour.

"Si, I need a bit of assistance. I've been stabbed," he said casually.

"You've been stabbed! How the fuck've you managed that?" Simon replied incredulously.

Nicks sighed. "Too long a story, mate, but I need to get to a doctor."

"How bad is it?" Simon wandered around his bedroom trying to remember where he'd thrown his pants.

"I don't know, but it's hurting and I'm losing blood."

"Well, take a look, for fuck's sake! How much is it bleeding?"

He sighed again, impatiently this time. "I don't know. Enough. I don't want to look and I'm not in a position to start stripping my kit off."

"Ok, fine. I take it you're not at the hotel, so where are you?" Simon danced on one leg as he unsuccessfully attempted to insert the other into his trousers before collapsing sideways through the curtained opening of his walk-in wardrobe, bringing the curtain and rail down with him.

"I'll be on Pall Mall at the entrance to the little park behind Exchange Station." He stopped walking. "What the fuck was that? You ok? Simon?"

He leapt back to his feet, phone still in hand. "Yeah! Everything's fine. No problems. You stay there, and I'll have somebody with you within five minutes."

The phone went dead. Nicks looked forlornly at the screen then pocketed it. He was almost at the exit point, a long narrow path bordered by a wall and shrubs to his right, a low wall and trees to his left. He crouched down amongst the shrubs and removed his day sack; pulling out the fleece which he stuffed up the inside of his jacket against the wound. He wasn't sure how effective it would be, but it made him feel better. Something was throbbing.

It was the phone in his pocket. "Yeah," he said laconically.

"Black hackney cab. Two minutes. Plate number 723. Driver's called Phil. He'll sort you out. I'll speak to you later." It was Simon. The phone went dead.

On the soil under the shrub, hidden from the road, he took out the small bottle of water from the day sack and gulped down several mouthfuls before replacing it in the bag. He didn't feel too bad under the circumstances, 'all things considered', as his Dad would say. He stood up and hugged the bag to his chest, grimacing slightly. He was tired again. The adrenalin gone.

The phone buzzed in his pocket. Before he could say anything, a voice said: "Hi, it's Phil. I'm on Pall Mall now. Will you be able to make it to the cab or do you need some help?"

He smiled. Relief flooded through him. "I can make it to the cab ok."

Seconds later the hackney pulled up, exactly opposite the exit to the park, and Nicks left the shadows, clambering into the rear.

Phil got out and jumped in the back, wrapping him in a foil 'space' blanket then a tartan rug. He pulled down the 'jump' seat and rested Nicks' feet on it.

"You sure you're ok for now? It won't be a long journey," he said, then got back into the driving seat.

As they drove away, he initiated a long conversation which just about covered everything. Football (it was evident from the pendant dangling from the dashboard he was an Everton supporter); politics (socialist, definitely); religion (agnostic bordering on 'God's a spaceman'); holidays (Europe's fine, but Wales has a lot to offer) and cookery (you can't beat a good Sunday roast). It was an interesting 15 minutes or so. Nicks knew what he was doing and joined in as enthusiastically as he could, in the circumstances … all things considered.

Phil stopped the cab midway along a deserted and silent Marine Crescent in Waterloo. The Crescent was remarkable for two things. It was once the home of Captain Edward John Smith, the first and last Captain of the R.M.S. Titanic, and it wasn't actually crescent shaped at all. Constructed between 1826 and 1830, the Grade II listed buildings sat serenely gazing out across the adjacent marine lake and its sand hills; the River Mersey and Welsh mountains beyond. In winter, a walk past its snow covered Victorian lamp posts evoked memories of Narnia.

Phil quickly jumped in the back of the cab. Lifting up the free portion of the rear seat he took out what Nicks recognised as a ballistic bag. "Do you want to unload it or shall I do it for you?" he asked, pulling on a pair of forensic gloves.

Nicks slowly slid the weapon from his leg pocket, carefully offering it to Phil, then the same with the suppressor. "You ok doing it? I feel a bit too shaky at the moment. It's loaded with one up the spout."

"Yeah, no problem," Phil grinned.

He pointed the pistol into the ballistic bag, unloaded and cleared it then placed everything inside, zipped it up and returned it to its hiding place. Taking the day sack, he jumped out and held the rear door open.

"Ok, you still alright? Manage by yourself?"

He nodded. "Yeah, I should be able to." Holding the improvised fleece 'bandage' with his left arm, he levered himself up by the door frame with his free hand and eased himself onto the footpath. For some reason he ached all over. Phil handed him his rucksack and said: "Straight up the path. They're expecting you."

Nicks' eyes followed the line of the path from the wrought iron gate to the Victorian stained glass panelled front door, two wide floor to ceiling bay windows guarding the entrance. A warm glow was visible through the curtains on the left hand side. At that moment the stained glass panels flickered into life and the front door opened, the gentle hall lighting escaping into the garden. A small matronly figure came out to greet him. Putting her arm around him, she waved at Phil and guided Nicks into the house.

"I believe you've been in the wars, my dear. Come this way and my husband Maurice will sort everything out for you. And after, if you're able, I'll give you a nice cup of hot sweet tea." Then she called: "Maury, the young man's here." Young man. A faint smile flickered over his lips. She smiled sweetly at him. For the first time that night he felt completely safe.

Doctor Maury was a short stocky man with faded sandy coloured hair and matching moustache. He looked Nicks up and down.

"You know you're very lucky. If it hadn't been for your padded jacket and that bit of excess weight you're carrying around your waist, it could have been much worse."

"How much worse?"

"Oh, considerably worse," Doc Maury smiled. "If it *had* perforated your large intestine, it would have opened up a whole can of worms. Lots of problems involved there, but the blade didn't penetrate further than your internal oblique muscle, so I'm satisfied you'll be fine. Judging by the wound and the amount of blood it produced, I'd say you were stabbed with a double edged blade, quite sharp, something like a 'commando' dagger or a 'switchblade' I think they call them. Anyway, you'll need to come back in ten days and I should be able to take the stitches out then. In the meantime, don't exert yourself too much." He smiled again. "Now, I just have to give you a tetanus injection and we're finished here, but you'll be staying the night in the guest room." As Nicks tried to protest, Doc Maury raised his left hand, palm towards his patient, then placed his forefinger against his lips briefly. "Don't waste your breath. You *will* be staying in the guest room. My wife will have made a considerable effort to make you comfortable and we mustn't disappoint her. There, that's done. Good for another ten years."

He looked for his bloodied T shirt. It had gone, replaced by a fresh one. He hadn't even noticed her.

The Doc patted his arm. "Right! Time for some hot sweet tea and a chocolate digestive, I think."

CHAPTER 54

"Apparently my love handles saved my life." Nicks was speaking to Simon on his mobile as he walked to the railway station later that day. "Well, that and my big 'fuck off' padded jacket, of course."

"Wonderful, Nicks. Naturally I'm thrilled for you, but your antics have thrown everything out of sync somewhat." Simon sounded tetchy.

Nicks ignored the seeming lack of sympathy. "It's not as if I planned it, Si."

"I know, but they're not exactly overjoyed with the unscheduled body count. Anyway, you're off the plot for the next ten days at least, so the Newcastle job's been reallocated to another Leveller. One less thing for us to think about, but don't leave the country because there are things in the pipeline. May happen, may not."

"Does Wales count?" Nicks smirked to himself. He felt a strange urge to wind Simon up, which he could only put down to the 'joy of life'.

"Wales? Count as what?" Simon was bemused, then the penny dropped. "Fucking hell, Nicks! You know Wales is fine, just don't leave the mainland. I'm under pressure here, mate."

"Sorry, Si," He reined himself back in. "I think I'm just happy to be alive."

"Yeah, well, so was I until this morning. First you frighten the shit out of me and then the bollockings started via Don from some fuckers

I can only describe as the Y Department." Nicks heard his exhalation of breath. "*Why* didn't you drop him off at the Hotel? *Why* did he still have the weapon? *Why* haven't you got more control over him? *Why* didn't you tell someone earlier he couldn't do the Newcastle job? Jeez, I'm not a fucking psychic. And if you dare tell me to fucking chillax I'll find you, so help me God."

"Furthest thought from my head," Nicks interrupted, lying. "Look, Si, if you need me I'm going down to Llangrannog, the Pentre Arms for a few days. Why don't you come down there when you get the time? We could do a little fishing."

Simon tried, but couldn't stifle a chuckle. "You don't know how to fish! Apart from tinned mackerel in sauce, you hate fish!"

Nicks laughed. "Well, they've got those little fishing nets on sticks. We could look the part. I'll buy you a bucket and spade. What do you say?"

"Fuck you, Nicks, you're incredible mate!" The tension in Simon's voice had lifted. "Ok, give me a couple of days and I'll see you down there. And don't forget you're buying the first five rounds! You deserve to after what you've put me through."

"It's a deal. And if you're really lucky I might let you see my fluff collection. See you then." He pocketed the phone and entered the Station shop to buy a ticket.

He'd book the Pentre Arms on the journey into the city, buy the usual materials from the minimarket near his hotel and spend the evening on the ritual cleaning of his room before a good night's sleep.

CHAPTER 55
pm 14th April 2014

He took a sip of coffee and sat back in his chair. "Do we have any biscuits?" he asked. Before Lizzie could respond, he called out: "Taffy! Taffy! Are there any biscuits left in the tin?"

"I think we've got custard creams, Boss. I'll get you some," the Welshman replied looking up from his desk. Thurstan looked back at Lizzie, "Sorry, Liz, where were we? Yes! What else have we got?"

She looked down at her notes, a little smile playing across her lips. "We have, as yet, an unidentified male, approximately 30 years of age. No marks or scars. No identity documents, no cards, thirty pounds in cash, set of keys to a Ford something we haven't yet found and a set of house keys for somewhere or other. Fingerprints have been taken and are being checked, but at the moment it would seem he's never come to the attention of the Police before, at least not in this country. He had a number of bullet wounds; an entrance and exit wound to his right calf, indicating that particular shot came low from his right side, one to the lower back and the last to his upper left back which, I'm informed, most probably penetrated the heart before exiting. All to be confirmed by the post mortem, which will be carried out this afternoon.

"We've four spent cases, so the hole in the top left hand shoulder of his jacket was probably caused by the fourth bullet; we're still searching for that. Initial indications from the guys at Firearms Training are they're nine millimetre, possibly Russian or Bulgarian because they appear to have Cyrillic letters on the base. Fingerprints have taken a look, but it's negative there I'm afraid. They're clean. His DNA samples are being processed so there may be something to come back from them, but it could take a while and the knife found *was* the dead man's, fingerprints confirm, *and* we're getting a DNA profile done from the blood that's on it. Again, it could take a while." She paused, adding, "Oh, and the suspect's pants. I showed the Firearms guys the camera footage and one of them said they thought the pants he was wearing were probably Russian birch pattern camouflage. It seems some of them are into that sort of thing. He was pretty certain. Said you couldn't mistake it, it's so distinctive." She laid her notes flat on her knees and looked at Thurstan expectantly.

He rubbed his chin, thoughtfully.

"Any luck with finding CCTV from further afield?"

"Still being sorted, but I'll chase it up," she replied quietly.

"Four custard creams enough, Boss? I can get you more if you want." Taffy laid the saucer cradling the biscuits on the desk. "Actually, Sarge, I can update you on one of those matters. Chewbacca located something from one of the traffic cameras at Leeds Street, junction with Old Hall. Dark coloured Vauxhall Astra, old model, W plate, owner registered in Exeter, shows our suspect getting out and walking down Old Hall."

Thurstan leaned forward as he dunked a custard cream into his coffee. "And have we sent someone round to the owner's yet?"

"Sorted, Boss," Taffy replied, watching Thurstan holding his wet biscuit. "Chewy had the local uniforms pop round and it seems the car's not been off the drive for days. Owner's had the engine in bits in his garage." He hesitated. "I'd eat that pretty quick if I was you, Boss. They've been in the tin for a while."

Thurstan looked gloomily into his cup as he realised the tensile strength of a dunked biscuit had a direct relationship to its freshness. Lizzie leant forward and handed him some clean tissues from her bag.

"Do you want another drink, Boss? Taffy enquired. "I can get you one, no problem."

Thurstan busily mopped up the liquid which had cascaded onto the desk as one half of the custard cream had somersaulted into the cup. "No, it'll be fine, makes the last mouthful more interesting." He looked up. "Thanks for that information Taffy *and* the biscuits."

When he'd gone, Lizzie stood up and took the wet tissues from Thurstan's hand, used a clean one to round up the last few smears, and dropped them in the waste paper basket. She sat down again. "I've got some of the staff out looking for any CCTV from the city, now we know the route our female victim took when her boyfriend dumped her out of the car after their domestic. Hopefully we'll know soon, roughly, where she attracted the attention of our dead guy."

"Great stuff," Thurstan replied. "So, to recap, we have a dead sex attacker who's been killed with, possibly, Russian bullets from, possibly, a Russian gun by a man wearing, possibly, Russian pants. The gun fired, in the words of our victim witness, sounded like ...what did she say they were called?"

"Clackers," Liz responded.

"Clackers! That's right. So, sounded like Clackers, which makes me think silencer. Now, judging by our shooter's distinctive patterned

215

trousers he either doesn't mind being noticed or he actually wants to be. This is a man who apparently just happened to be walking past whilst armed to the teeth, having been dropped off at the end of the street from a car on false plates."

He sat back in his chair and ran his hand pensively across his mouth several times. "I'm pretty certain from the CCTV he was just strolling past on the way to somewhere else and at that time of night my gut feeling says the place was bed. So, he gets involved in an unplanned incident. But why the Russian thing? What was he doing *or* going to do that *he or they* wanted to blame on the Russians? Do we have a Russian problem?"

"Not that I know of, Boss, but I'll speak to someone in SB, see if they can tell us."

"Thanks. I know the Met have issues there. I'll speak to Chalkie when he comes in and you speak to SB. In the meantime, have a few of the staff check the hotels for any obvious Russian or Eastern European names. In fact, have Gandalph do it. He's built up a few contacts in that department."

He looked at Lizzie. *God, you're beautiful,* he suddenly thought and equally suddenly banished it from his head. He looked at her again. There was an awkward silence. "Right," he said, "Well, erm ... I've got nothing else I can think of. We good?"

She smiled at him and nodded. "We're good."

CHAPTER 56

Placing his basket on the counter, he stood patiently whilst the cashier began to check his items. A name tag declared him to be Marcus and his opening gambit was:

"Had a nice day today?"

"Yeah, not bad," Nicks tossed back as part of his warming up exercises.

"The weather's been good, hasn't it?" Marcus said as he scanned a bottle of bleach.

"Yes, it has." Nicks was on a roll.

Marcus re-scanned the bleach. "They say it's going to stay dry for the next few days at least."

Nicks began packing his carrier bag. "Really?" He was beginning to tire already.

"Yeah." Marcus passed him the bathroom cleaner and sponges. "Do anything interesting at the weekend?"

He'd been doing his best but felt this an intrusion too far.

"Did I do anything interesting? Let's see… Oh yes, I read my mail order copy of 'Naked and taking it up the arse' and spent the entire weekend masturbating." It had been Nicks' ambition to use this answer for a long time.

Clicking back to reality, he found himself saying: "Well, yeah, actually I went to…"

"That's £7.32p," Marcus interrupted, holding his hand out having exhausted all the interest he was paid to dispense per customer.

Nicks received his change in silence. He didn't bother to bid Marcus farewell. He could see he was otherwise engaged with his next victim.

CHAPTER 57

"I'll have the chicken curry, please. Rice, no chips," Thurstan told the young woman serving behind the counter at the HQ canteen.

"Alright, Boss. I'm back," Degsy sidled up to the DCI, dragging his tray along the counter. "Lasagne, please, and some broccoli as well."

"Ahh, Derek!" Thurstan looked up after pushing several buttons for the delivery of his Café Latte. "How did the interview go?"

Degsy shrugged his shoulders and exhaled sharply. "Who knows?"

"That's what I like, Derek. Positive attitude. Look, I'm just going to pay for this then I'm going to grab that table over by the window before someone else does. I'll see you over there."

Degsy waited for a new tray of lasagne to be brought from the kitchen. Thurstan wandered over to the table, glancing up at the lunchtime news: A Cabinet Minister's resignation in order to spend more time with his family, a senior Judge's unexpected early retirement and weather prospects which promised a warm and sunny start to the coming weekend.

Placing his plate and cup on the table he slid the tray onto the window ledge.

"So, come on. What happened?" he asked as Degsy joined him.

"Not much, Boss. I just don't feel confident. I mean I was ok in the interview. Felt good. I even thought I was doing well, but since coming out I just don't know." He took a swig of his bottled mineral water. "I mean, Chalkie spent a lot of time with me on the interview technique stuff and gave me some cracking examples of how to answer questions he felt certain were going to come up, and he was right. They did."

"So what's the problem, Derek?" Thurstan said between mouthfuls of curry.

Degsy stabbed at his broccoli and waved it absent-mindedly in front of his bemused face. "Well, basically, I left Derek Drayton outside and they interviewed Chalkie White. I only became Derek Drayton again when I closed the door behind me on the way out."

Thurstan looked at him seriously. "And your issue with this is...?"

Degsy swallowed his food before answering. "Well, if I get promoted it won't really be me they promoted. It'll be Chalkie. I feel a bit of a fraud."

Thurstan took another mouthful of curry and rice, chewed it thoughtfully, then put his fork down and took a sip of coffee. "It'll always be you they promoted, Derek. Just a wiser and better prepared 'you' than the 'you' that would have gone in having not taken appropriate advice. I did the same thing. Went in as 'me', not properly prepared the first time. Learnt from it, took the advice I was offered, went in next time and passed."

Degsy swallowed the lasagne he'd shovelled into his mouth and took another swig of water. "So, who did you go in as?"

Thurstan laughed and sipped his coffee. "Jerry Holden. You probably wouldn't know him. Retired now. Great bloke." He took another mouthful of curry. "It'll be fine. They'd be stupid not to promote you, and anyway, Chalkie knows his stuff, so stop worrying.

What's done is done." He scraped up a last mouthful and slid his plate to the side. "To change the subject, I have to take a couple of days off. Got gripped by the Superintendent earlier, said he'd authorised my carrying over some annual leave, but I had to start taking it *now*. So I'll be taking Thursday and Friday off. It'll give me a long weekend. I've got stuff to do at home on Thursday, after which I thought I'd have a couple of days away."

Degsy finished off his broccoli with another slice of lasagne and pushed his plate away. "Going anywhere nice, Boss?"

"Oh, just a little place I've been to once or twice over the years. It's nice and I can get a decent walk in as well. I'll have the job's phone with me." He looked at the plates. "You done?"

Degsy nodded. They put their dinner things and trays on the trolley in the corner and wandered out of the canteen over to the HQ building.

"I need to bring you up to speed about this morning, Derek," Thurstan said as they strolled along the walkway leading to the rear entrance into reception. "But first I'd like you to contact the Border Agency and check on our 'friend'. Use whatever contacts you have there."

"So you really think our alley killer could be him, Boss?"

"I think it's an extremely strong possibility, Derek. As we discussed this morning at the scene, there *are* significant similarities."

"But three or four shots? Not his usual M.O." They'd come to a mutual halt near to the doors. Degsy acknowledged two passing uniforms.

Thurstan lowered his voice. "Given a fleeing target, the distance and the lighting conditions, it was still a pretty decent bit of shooting *and*, given we now know from our witness that the killer was most probably knifed in the scuffle at the foot of the steps, well, it makes it even more commendable."

"Or maybe his OCD kicked in, Boss." He let out a little laugh.

"Maybe." Thurstan smiled back. "Anyway, sort that out for me."

"I'll get on to it straight away," Degsy nodded and held the door open.

They reached the lift and Thurstan patted Degsy's back.

"Look, you go on up. I just want to get something from the newsagent down the road. I won't be long. I'll bring you up to date when I get back."

Three quarters of an hour later, Degsy found Thurstan sitting in his office reading a well-known satirical news and current affairs magazine.

"Sorry I took so long, Boss, I was waiting for the Border guys to call back and I had to catch up on a few things."

Thurstan looked up. "Oh, no problem. What did they say?"

Degsy sat down. "He's not come back into the country, at least not through his normal route. He could have flown into Dublin and then got an internal flight from Belfast or a ferry, I suppose."

"Or he's using false documentation," The DCI said as he undid the top of a small mineral water and took a mouthful. "One way or another, I'm pretty certain he's here."

He paused, took another mouthful of water then, setting the bottle on his desk: "Anyway, did you see the news today? Cabinet minister? Prominent judge retiring?"

"Yeah, I've just seen it on the late lunchtime news. Why? Do you think they're connected to our councillor?"

"More so now I've read this, Derek." The DCI waved the magazine in the air, folded back some pages, leant over his desk and passed it to Degsy. "Left hand column. You need to read between the lines."

Degsy sat back reading the article.

"Interesting, Boss. I like this description: 'a bastion of public service and child welfare whose sudden, unexpected but understandable demise from an uncommon but 'natural' cause'. I suppose you could describe the bullet in his head like that. Natural justice, at least, maybe?" He placed the article back on Thurstan's desk.

"Exactly, Derek, and it seems to me Special Branch and the Security Service aren't going to find this one as simple as they thought. This is, probably, not the last we'll hear about this." He leant forward, recovered the magazine and slid it in his top drawer. "I think we may get another visit from them. Bully boy tactics, hot air and bluster, you know the score. They'll probably suspect we're a source for the article. Now, I know we're on solid ground as far as the councillor's concerned, but I don't want them inadvertently finding anything out about Nickson and then interfering with the MacMahon job. It could leech into what we have on Tommy Cole. Despite our general opinion of *him* I think he's astute enough to sell himself to them as a drugs source and I don't want any deals being done, not when we've got him by the balls."

"I think we're ok there, Boss. There's nothing on the Niche system to connect Nickson and I hid the intel checks amongst a list of others, all relevant to the investigation: suspects, hotel guests, that sort of thing. It should be ok."

Thurstan rubbed his chin. "What about the Border Agency?"

"Same again, Boss. They could've automatically notified us of his departures and arrivals, but it would have meant putting a marker on their system so I declined. He's just one of many now. Apparently they're doing crap loads of these checks every day. Someone would have to be looking specifically for *him* before the line of inquiry became apparent."

"Good." Thurstan sat back and relaxed. "Speaking of Tommy Cole, are you available all next week?"

"Yep, I'm on 'Days', Boss." He was intrigued.

"Right, sit here and read this whilst I go and have a chat with Chalkie." He handed Degsy a large file from the bottom of his tray. "Don't take it out of the room. Up to this point there's only me, Chalkie and Arthur know what's in it, but I think it's time we spoke to Mr. Cole about what he was doing on Oglet Lane two years ago."

CHAPTER 58

The small coastal village of Llangrannog lay in the valley of the little River Hawen, on the Ceredigion Coastal Path. On a sunny day, as one drove down past the houses to the beach, it could be mistaken for a Cornish village. However, this was Wales and the beauty of Cardigan Bay. Nicks had discovered it quite by chance as he drove aimlessly around the area, finding accommodation as he travelled; trying to put some normality back into his life in the days before he and Anca had met.

He'd stopped at the Pentre Arms and sat, watching the families on the beach, sipping a pint; waiting for confirmation a room was available. Its simple magic had infected him. Since then he'd been back several times over the years, but never often enough to be recognised by the staff. Once, a wild sea battered the shuttered windows so hard he thought they would implode. The locals hadn't batted an eyelid.

In the afternoon of his second day Simon joined him, stipulating he could only spare two nights then had to get back; there were 'things' to be sorted out.

The weather was good. The first evening was spent drinking whilst watching the sunset over the little cove which Nicks always thought had an element of 'pirate' about it. Had it not been just him and Simon, it may have been romantic.

The day after, he dragged Simon's reluctant mind and body up out of the cove and along the coastal path where they experienced some magnificent views amidst Simon's periodic whining enquiries of "Is this going to take much longer?...Is it far now?" and "are you absolutely certain there's a pub at the end of this bloody thing?" Nicks answered: "Not long...not far" and "yes." Only once did he have to say: "Yes, I've bloody told you twice!"

After 9 miles they reached New Quay with its picturesque harbour and expansive sandy beach. Stepping through the stile from the path onto tarmac, Simon suddenly gained new vigour striding off along Rock Street like a man on a mission. It was a beer mission. He could see the harbour wall and figured the pub couldn't be far now. Nicks couldn't help but smile.

After a couple of pints and a meal, they'd explored further, visiting several pubs before ending up at the Penrhiwllan Inn where they sat outside in the sunshine watching the world go by before catching a taxi back to the Pentre Arms. The next day Simon left Nicks to his own devices, having grudgingly admitted he'd enjoyed himself.

The following morning after a breakfast of two poached eggs with mushrooms on toast, Nicks showered, packed his stuff and vacated the room. Then he strolled across to the village car park, threw his rucksack in the boot of the hired Nissan SUV and returned to the Pentre where he sat in the dining room, with a newspaper and a coffee, until he felt it was time to pay.

As he entered the bar a sudden feeling gripped the pit of his stomach. He turned abruptly, scuttling back into the dining room where, from behind a newspaper in a corner seat, he was shielded from view but could still see anyone going to their room.

"No, it's quite alright. I can manage," the man said as he left the bar.

Nicks peered over the paper and watched him disappear up the stairs before quickly re-entering the bar.

"Good morning, Sir. Are you paying your bill now?" she said with a smile. He nodded. "Just a moment. Ahh, here it is. Is it cash or card, Sir?"

"Cash," Nicks replied, glancing at the receipt she gave him. "I hope you don't mind, but that gentleman who just went upstairs looked familiar. I think I used to work with him many years ago, but can't for the life of me remember his name."

"Oh, yes, he had an unusual name," she looked at the reservations screen on the computer. "Yes, it's Thurstan Baddeley," she said, then added, thoughtfully: "It's got a nice sound to it, hasn't it?"

"Yes! That's it! I thought it was him." Nicks was doing his best not to seem hurried.

"Well, you'll be able to have a chat because he said he was just going to unpack and then come down for a drink." She smiled again.

"Unfortunately, I have a train to catch." He handed her a £5 note. "I wonder if I can give you this and ask you to pull him a pint of Guinness when he comes down but make sure it's the normal stuff, not the chilled. He doesn't like the chilled stuff." He felt a desperate urge to leave, and quickly, but managed to maintain his air of calm as he

227

smiled at her and said: "Give him my regards and please keep the change." As he turned and walked away he heard her say:

"I will and thank you very much. Come again soon."

Leaving the bar he made his way back to the Nissan, only quickening his step when he knew he was out of sight of the Pentre. Settled in the driving seat, he drove onto the narrow B4321 gunning up the hill towards the main road where instead of turning left and taking the more direct route back to Liverpool, he would turn right and head across country to Hereford; joining the A49 for home.

Thurstan unpacked his weekend bag and, after peering out of the small recessed window that overlooked the cove, he locked his room and descended to the bar wearing the same grey chinos, blue polo shirt and brown casual shoes he'd travelled down in. He looked around for somewhere nice to sit. Having chosen his spot, he turned to the girl behind the bar to order his drink, but hesitated on seeing her pulling a pint of un-chilled Guinness which he assumed was for another, temporarily absent, customer.

"How's the Guinness today?" he casually enquired, immediately regretting it in the realisation she wasn't likely to say: 'It's shit, I wouldn't touch it with a bargepole."

"Well, you tell me," she smiled, placing the dark creamy topped pint in front of him. "That's from your friend who left about five minutes ago. He said you used to work together, and to give you his regards, but he couldn't stop because he'd a train to catch."

Thurstan was pleasantly stunned. It was always nice to get a free pint. He lifted the glass to his lips and took a satisfying mouthful of foam and liquid. The Guinness was indeed good. He wiped his mouth. "Did this chap say what his name was, at all?"

"Ooh! No, he didn't. I forgot to ask him, but I'll check his room details for you." She pushed a few keys on the computer then said:"His name was John Steed."

Thurstan looked confused. "Well, it rings a bell. Certainly sounds familiar, but I can't place him at the moment. Did he say where we worked together?"

She shook her head. "No, just to give you his regards."

"I dare say it'll come back to me. Probably at three in the morning. Don't worry, I won't phone you."

She looked blankly back at him. Sometimes, he thought, humour was wasted on the young. He took his pint and sat down at a small table by the picture window and looked out onto the beach pondering the mysterious Mr Steed. Eventually he gave up and settled down to enjoy his drink as he read the lunchtime menu.

After lunch, he had a walk around the village and meandered through one of the shops. It sold all the things interesting to small children on holiday and he reacquainted himself with fishing nets, plastic buckets in the shape of castles, cowboy pistols and the like. Afterwards, he bought himself an ice cream and wandered up the hill overlooking the bay.

At the top he sat on a bench for some quiet reflection and it wasn't long before his thoughts turned to Lizzie. Just thinking about her made him feel good. Was he misreading the 'signs'? Maybe when she smiled 'that smile', it wasn't just for him. Maybe it was just the way she smiled at everyone. He'd no idea. He needed to pay more attention.

"Sorry, did you say something?"

He spun round on the bench. A couple of walkers were looking at him.

Thurstan blushed with embarrassment. "Oh! Um. Sorry. I didn't realise I was err..."

The woman smiled. "Oh that's alright. I do the same myself, quite often."

He threw them a smile, grabbed his jacket and walked back down the path to the village.

Later that evening, after a shower, he had dinner in the restaurant then entered the bar, carefully scanning its occupants for the 'walking couple'. Their absence a relief, he was able to enjoy a pleasant evening in conversation with several locals.

The following day he walked south along the coastal path to Aberporth, after which, filled with a sense of achievement, he lay on his bed and idly flicked through the TV stations waiting for his attention to be caught.

"Is that you, Steed?" the attractive woman, bound to a chair by heavy rope, called out.

A dapper man in a suit, wearing a bowler hat at a jaunty angle, leaned against a doorway smiling flirtatiously, waving his umbrella at her.

"Ah, Mrs Peel. I see you're a bit tied up at the moment. Shall I come back later?"

The end titles rolled and the music played as Thurstan, now sitting bolt upright, stared at the screen.

"And you can join John Steed and Mrs Peel tomorrow at the same time as we air another classic episode of The Avengers."

"Ahhhh! That's it! That's why the bloody name's familiar," he declared aloud to himself as he scrabbled about the bed for his phone. Quickly he connected to the internet and typed in 'John Steed' then clicked into several sites before he began to feverishly scribble down something on the writing paper provided in his room's welcome pack.

Slipping his shoes on, he left the room and went to the bar. She was there. He asked for a Guinness. She was about to ask whether he wanted chilled or un-chilled when she recognised him. As she pulled the pint he asked her if she could look up his 'friends'' address on the computer and confirm whether he had the right one. He waved the piece of paper at her.

She smiled sympathetically. "I'm not allowed to give you people's addresses and things. I shouldn't really have given you his name. It's something called Data Protection, you see."

"I know all about Data Protection. I'm a policeman. You don't have to give me anything because I'm giving you the address and all you have to do is nod or shake your head," Thurstan said pleasantly.

"Oh, a policeman. You don't look like a policeman," she replied.

"Thank you, I do my best," Thurstan retorted, handing her the piece of paper.

She took it from him.

"I don't need to look it up anyway. I can remember it. One of those Mews places."

She looked at the address Thurstan had written down.

"There's your Guinness" she said as she placed it carefully in front of him and passed him back the note. Then she nodded.

"Thank you very much and please, please keep the change," Thurstan said as he handed her a £5 note.

Stepping over to an empty table, he sat down, took a large mouthful of beer, leant back and said quietly: "You cheeky bastard."

CHAPTER 59
21st April 2014

"Good morning, Boss. How was your weekend?" Degsy cheerily greeted him as the DCI took off his coat and hung it on the coat stand.

"My weekend, Derek, was both extremely refreshing and gut wrenchingly frustrating."

He threw his mobile in his top drawer and plonked himself in his chair.

"Well, you'll probably *need* this then."

Degsy offered Thurstan the mug of coffee he'd started making on seeing the Boss striding purposefully across the HQ car park. There was something about his demeanour, even at that distance, that had made him think all was not well.

Thurstan took the mug, placing it on his blotting pad.

"What happened, Boss?" Degsy asked more out of politeness than curiosity.

The DCI took a mouthful of coffee and said: "He was there, Derek. He was *fucking* there." Degsy looked at him blankly.

"Nickson, Derek. Nickson! He was actually staying at the same hotel. Left just as I was booking in."

"Did you see him?" He sat down on the edge of the nearest chair.

"No," Thurstan replied curtly. "But I'll tell you how I know."

For several minutes he recounted the incident at Llangrannog as his Sergeant sat engrossed.

"Even the description they were able to give me matches what we have of him at the moment and he's still got the beard. Plus, he was down there with another bloke; shorter in height, fair hair, in his forties, wearing glasses, slightly overweight or stocky, depending on who I spoke to. I don't know? Connected to the jobs? It could be the driver, given he's used a false name and address as well, and paid cash too. I doubt very much he's just a mate. But what were they doing there? Apparently they went walking along the north coastal path. They made it to New Quay because someone at the Pentre saw them come back in a taxi and I checked with the firm. They were picked up outside a pub there so, if they were doing a recce for a job, it has to concern someone living or working somewhere along *that* section of the path. We need to look into the possibility, Derek."

Degsy had taken a sheet of blank paper from the desk, folded it notebook size and was furiously writing on it as Thurstan spoke.

"I mean, the name and address he gave." Thurstan wasn't entirely sure whether he was still trying to convince himself or just Degsy at this point. "It's pure *him* as far as I'm concerned."

"At least we know he's an Avengers fan," Degsy quipped without looking up from his piece of paper. "And from what they told you of his drinking habits, like yourself, a fan of un-chilled Guinness."

He'd stopped writing and was looking at Thurstan, who took another sip of coffee then said: "Well, I don't mind telling you, Derek, that little comment of his almost drove me paranoid on Sunday night when the significance properly hit me. But, having given it quite some thought, I've decided it's a titbit about me probably anyone I've ever

234

had a drink with knows about ever since they brought the chilled stuff out. That they've been gathering such information is interesting. A little warning shot, I think, just to let me know. Just to let *us* know."

"Do you think we should be worried?"

Degsy was suddenly thinking of the wife and kids and Thurstan saw it.

"No, Derek, not at all," he tried to reassure him. "It's just a message. A bit of mental jousting designed to disturb our focus and it certainly did that to me last night." He sipped his coffee again, deep in thought. "No, that information most probably came from further afield than this office. I've never been for a drink with any of the staff, as yet, and even *you* didn't know that about me, did you?"

"Well, I did actually," Degsy confessed.

Thurstan frowned. "Who told you?"

"Well, Ralph, the porter at Lower Lane. I believe you used to work together once, when he was on the job. I was chatting to him a few weeks ago," Degsy smiled.

"Well, there you go! Idle chatter picked up in passing. One of the foundations of intelligence gathering," Thurstan said expansively, then added: "How is Ralphy, by the way?"

"He's fine, Boss. He said if you're ever out that way to give him a call and he'll take a can of Guinness out of his fridge and put it on a radiator for ten minutes."

"Good!" laughed the DCI then slapped his palms gently on the desk and stood up. "Right, let's make some of those enquiries. Get Gandalph to help you and, if need be, Taffy. He might have some contacts out that way and, if not, just the fact he can speak the local lingo might help." He eyed the clock on the wall. "I've got a meeting I have to attend *so* I need to get a move on."

CHAPTER 60
7th May 2014

"Is that it then, love?" the middle aged woman behind the cash till enquired.

"Yeah, just the chicken wrap and a decaf to go."

"The healthy option," she said and they smiled at each other.

Sliding his empty tray in with the others, he started his walk back to the canteen entrance when he heard: "Degsy!"

Someone was waving at him from a table in the far corner. The figure got up and came towards him.

"Terry!" Degsy said as they shook hands. "Sorry, mate, I didn't see you when I came in."

"Not a problem, Degs," Terry replied. "How's things? Still enjoying MIT?"

Degsy nodded. "Yeah, still enjoying it. What about you?" he asked, looking Terry's suit up and down as he stood in front of him. "Uniform a thing of the past?"

"I'd like to think so, mate," Terry grinned. "SB now, you know! Out at the Airport."

"So what brings you to Fantasy Island?" Degsy asked, using the Forcewide nickname for Headquarters.

"Oh, my oppo just had to pop in to drop something off and have his appraisal with the Chief Super. Not much point in hanging around the office. I'm the new boy. No one'll tell me fuck all, so I thought I'd just grab a coffee. It's handy I saw you, actually. I gave you a bell the other day, but you were out."

"Why, what's up?" Degsy asked as he gave a quick wave to another former colleague at a table some distance away.

"*Guess* who I saw last week?" He didn't wait for an answer. "Nicks!" He saw the lack of recognition. "Chris Nickson! You were asking me about him a while back."

"Oh! Chris Nickson. Yeah." Outwardly he appeared calm but inside Degsy felt a strange combination of interest, excitement and concern. "How's he doing?"

"Good, so he tells me. Saw him at the airport. I told him you'd been asking after him and he sends his regards. Still living in Berlin, lucky sod."

"Really!" was all Degsy could manage at this point.

"Yeah. He's looking well. Still sporting the beard. Gives him a distinct middle eastern look, I think. I was just glad he wasn't wearing a fuckin' rucksack!" Terry laughed.

"Did he say what he was doing there?" Degsy asked casually. "Picking someone up, I presume?"

Terry nodded, breaking off to speak to another suit who'd approached them. "I'm sitting over there, Dave. Give us two minutes and I'll be with you." The suit smiled and wandered off. "Sorry, Degs. Well, he *was* the first time I saw him. Now, last time, he said he was there buying a ticket for his German mate. I suppose that's who he was waiting for the first time."

Degsy was intrigued. "So you saw him twice?"

238

"Yeah. Same week, funnily enough. First time I saw him he was coming in." Terry flashed a mischievous grin before continuing. "So I sidled up to him, gripped his arm and said, dead official like, 'Would you mind coming this way, Sir?' He nearly shat himself! Funny as fuck!"

Degsy managed to force what he hoped would at least pass for a chuckle, then enquired, "So his er... his mate's name? Did he mention it? It's just I met a German mate of his once, years ago. Nice bloke. Name's on the tip of my tongue, just can't get it."

"What are you like with names, mate!" Terry laughed, looked thoughtful then triumphantly exclaimed: "Dieter Ackermann! That's who his mate was. I'll tell you why I remember. I knew a bloke with the same name, years ago. Well, not exactly the same name because that would've been spooky. No, *his* name was Rudi, owned a bar. Great fellah."

Terry's mind worked a bit like a neon scrolling information sign in a Travel Agent's window. Sometimes the next piece of information was connected to the previous, often it was the beginning of a whole new thing.

Knowing this, Degsy clarified. "So, it was *Dieter* Ackermann who was Nicks's mate, not the bar owner?"

"Yeah, spot on!" Terry replied.

"No, doesn't ring any bells," Degsy said, shaking his head in fake bewilderment.

"And I'll tell you how I know," Terry continued. "I saw the surname on the ticket he was holding and said to him 'That wouldn't be for a bloke called Rudi Ackermann, would it? 'cause he's a good bloke and handy to know', and he said, 'No, his name's Dieter' and then, of course," he paused and gave a shrug of his shoulders. "I had to explain the whole Rudi thing blah, blah, blah!"

His oppo approached waving his mobile, "We're needed down the Ferry Terminal."

Terry nodded, looking apologetically at Degsy. "Sorry, Degs, *got* to go. Anyway, great to see you again, mate. Give us a bell at the Airport and we'll go for a pint sometime."

"Yeah, no problem," Degsy replied. After a moment he called after him. "Terry, just out of interest. What was the airline?"

"Easyjet, matey. If you're thinking of trying to catch him and his mate at the airport for a pint, you'll have to be quick. The flight's sometime tonight. Six o'clock, I think." With that, Terry waved and disappeared into the depths of the stairwell.

CHAPTER 61

When Degsy reached the doorway of the DCI's office Lizzie was just leaving. She turned back to face Thurstan, "So, Sunday then?"

"Yes, definitely," he replied, standing up behind his desk before confirming. "A normal Sunday lunch with the family. Just a small, informal, sort of thing." He paused. "How many exactly?"

Lizzie laughed, catching his concern. "Well, there'll be me, my Mum and Dad, my Nana and Gramps, my three sisters and three of my brothers. My brother Melvin is still in Afghanistan." Then she added, "Oh, and Auntie Lydia." She flashed him a sparkling smile, noticing he seemed to have lost some colour from his cheeks.

"Oh, good. Nothing to worry about then?"

"No, nothing to worry about," she laughed. "Just a normal Sunday lunch." She turned, smiled at Degsy and strolled across the main office to her desk.

Having waited patiently for the interaction to come to a natural end, somehow he couldn't help but join Thurstan in watching her progress.

"You obviously want to see me, Derek." Thurstan said, breaking the spell.

"Er... yes, Boss! I've just been speaking to a mate in the canteen. He works at the Airport. SB..."

Thurstan let him finish then said: "So, you think it's Nickson leaving on this flight?"

"Yes, Boss. It's got to be, surely! Officially he's not in the country, so this is how he did it. Your being there at the same hotel probably spooked him and he's taking the first opportunity he could to do one."

Thurstan looked thoughtful. "I'm not so sure, *but...*" He rubbed his chin. "I think you're right. It could be him and it's *too* good an opportunity to waste. If we can lock him up on the passport offence we can, at the very least, get his bloody DNA and keep him in custody." He looked at his watch. "You said the flight's around six?"

Degsy nodded. "I could phone the Airport and check?"

Thurstan shook his head. "No. It'll take too long. The traffic's going to be bad this time of day. We need to get up there now, Derek. Right now!"

"I'll get the job's car, Boss. It's got blues and twos and I'll see you in the top car park by reception."

Thurstan pulled on his jacket and grabbed his mobile from the drawer. "Somebody get me a radio with a fresh battery, please," he called from the doorway of his office before returning to his desk and phoning the Control Room. Requesting a doubly manned patrol to meet him in front of Liverpool Airport terminal he then strode out of his office, snatching the Airwaves radio Arthur presented to him.

"Book me out, Arthur, will you? Speke Airport," he told him and walked briskly to the office exit just as the SB Superintendent entered, impeding his progress.

"Baddeley, I want a word with *you*, in your office!"

Without pause, Thurstan looked at him disdainfully and brushed past. "*Not now!*" The SB man was left flapping in the wind.

Once in the passenger seat, Thurstan wound down his window and deposited the small but powerful, blue, magnetic strobe light on the roof. Driving down the ramp and out onto the main road, Degsy switched on the yelp siren and with alternating flashing headlights began to weave his way through the traffic.

"Have you used these sirens before, Boss, or just the two tones?" Degsy shouted over the noise as he accelerated away from an intersection.

"It was just two tones in my day, Derek. I must admit this looks confusing," Thurstan confessed loudly, perusing the emergency equipment control box.

"No problem, Boss. Ignore everything else and just press wail when we're on a straight run, the sound carries better, and yelp when we're approaching and going through a junction, it's an attention grabber."

At each set of red traffic lights they encountered, Degsy manoeuvred to the front, checking right, left and ahead before accelerating through the junction when safe to do so. At green lights, he was looking for pedestrians, cyclists and random thinkers.

It'd been a long time since Thurstan had experienced the thrill of a 'blue light run' and it was only after some challenging and inventive manoeuvres on Degsy's part that he felt able to relax as they eventually turned into Speke Hall Avenue, the dual carriageway leading to the industrial estates and JLA. As they shot down the near empty road he turned off the sirens.

Less than two minutes later they pulled up behind the marked Police car parked on the 'Emergency' hatchings in front of the first entrance to the Terminal. Thurstan took the blue light from the roof and stowed it in the footwell; two uniformed Officers got out of their vehicle and donned their hats. Thurstan slammed the door behind him, slapped the smaller of the Officers on the shoulder and told him: "You mind the vehicles, son." The other Officer was muscular. "You come with me, big fella," he added, racing towards the entrance.

Nicks popped an earphone into one ear, leaving the other dangling. He pressed play on his iPod and settled back in his seat, glancing briefly out of the emergency door window. Beyond the wing he could see his fellow passengers walking from the Terminal towards the aircraft. He wondered how many more there would be. Buckling his seat belt, he perused the emergency instructions read 'a thousand times' before and inspected the emergency door confirming it agreed with what he'd seen on the card. Satisfied, he closed his eyes and leant his head against the cabin wall.

Walking briskly through the concourse, Thurstan located the airline desk and flashed his badge. "Detective Chief Inspector Baddeley. I'm after a person wanted for questioning in connection with a murder and I believe they're booked onto your flight to Berlin today. His name's Ackermann. Dieter Ackermann."

The woman behind the desk stabbed a few keys on her computer.

"Yes, he's on the flight. But you'll need to hurry. They're boarding now, Sir, Gate five. I'll get security to take you through." She called and waved to a security guard who was standing by the check-in desks opposite. He ambled over towards them.

As Thurstan impatiently watched his progress, he instructed the woman.

"Contact the gate and let them know we're on our way. And if need be, you'll have to delay the flight. Do you know what seat he's in?"

"Ten F, extra leg room. As you go in from the front it's the first row on your left over the wings." He lost patience and strode off to meet the security officer strolling towards them. She shouted after him: "He should be in the window seat."

Thurstan showed the guard his badge, took the man by the arm, spun him round and guided him towards the departures gates whilst explaining the situation. The former lethargic attitude changed in an instant and the security man set off at a fast pace, gabbling into his radio, causing Thurstan, Degsy and the uniformed Officer to jog after him in order to make up the ground.

At the departure gate they were joined by other security officers and Thurstan quickly briefed them. "I want all exits to the plane covered and no one, absolutely no one leaves that plane until I or DS Drayton here okays it first. Clear?" Nods all round.

They stood and watched the last of the passengers exit the main building and walk across the apron towards the plane. As they ascended the stairs, the security officers took up their positions. Thurstan, Degsy and their colleague joined the last passengers as they entered the aircraft. After a few quiet words with the cabin crew Thurstan looked over in the direction they indicated. Between passengers stowing their luggage, he caught fleeting glimpses of an arm and then the top of the head of the person sat in seat 10F.

Beckoning the others, he weaved his way towards his prey, feeling the rush of adrenalin he always felt when making an arrest. "Police," he said to the man sitting next to the window. "Dieter Ackermann?"

From underneath a baseball cap, the man looked up at him and replied: "Yes, I'm Dieter Ackermann."

CHAPTER 62

Whilst the aircraft moved slowly from its gate, Nicks watched two suits and a uniform escort Ackermann from the adjacent Berlin flight and stride across the tarmac towards the terminal building. He allowed himself a little smile, removed his earphone and turned off his iPod, directing his attention to the flight safety demonstration. He felt it was incumbent upon him to do so, seeing as they were always kind enough to provide it.

As they trudged up the stairs, Degsy explained to the hapless Dieter how the procedure would unfold and the possible consequences should things not be as the German was insisting. Thurstan stopped on one of the half-landings and watched an aircraft taxi out towards the runway.

"Where's that one going to?" he called to the accompanying Security Officer.

The security man turned and came back down the steps to be alongside the DCI. "What? That one there?" He pointed at the same aircraft the nodding Thurstan had enquired about.

"Palma de Mallorca," he said and, readying his pass, scuttled back up the stairs to join the others, now waiting at the security door. Thurstan followed him slowly. "*Don't* take him to the SB office, Derek," he called. "Use Security's."

Once ensconced away from prying eyes, Thurstan told Degsy to carry out the necessary checks via the MIT office.

"They want to know if they should unload his hold luggage," the Security man asked.

"Basically, you mean how long is he going to be? Tell them not to do it for now. I just need to check something out, then I'll confirm. Give me 10 minutes. Derek, I'm off to the airline desk."

Degsy looked up. "That'll be great, do that then," he said into the phone as he nodded back to Thurstan.

Ten minutes later, Thurstan returned. "Any news?" he asked.

"Yes, Boss," Degsy replied. "By a stroke of luck, Gandalph was speaking on the phone to an on duty German mate of his when I called him. They're both in the IPA. He's been able to shortcut the checks on Mister Ackermann here. Checks out okay, here *and* there. Not known."

Thurstan smiled: "Well, young Mister Ackermann, I'm sorry we delayed you and I do apologise for the inconvenience caused. This Security Officer will escort you back to your plane. Have a safe flight and I hope all goes well at home." He nodded to the Security man who escorted the relieved German from the office.

Degsy looked at the DCI who shook his head. "No, Derek, I doubt we'd gain anything further from him if we took him into custody. I think what he's been telling us is the truth. Besides, I've just had a look at the passenger list for the other flight that was leaving as we came back into the terminal. Nickson was on it. Using his own details and sitting in the same bloody seat."

"Should we get him pulled when it lands, do you think, Boss?"

"No. We're still in the same boat. No hard evidence and you need at least *something* if you're going to extradite someone." He shook his head sadly as he rubbed his chin. "No, best to let it be for the time being. Come on! Let's get back."

Walking through the terminal towards the exit Degsy said: "It's my fault, Boss. I should have thought this out better. I should have thought out of the box."

Thurstan shot him a glance and smiled. "It's not your fault Derek. It would have been foolish not to have gone for it. Anyway, it's not easy to 'think out of the box' when you don't know you're in one." He let out a little laugh. "We did exactly what he wanted us to do and I don't think he was taunting us, if that's what you're thinking. No. He wanted us to know he's left but he didn't want us to be there, not right there, when he did. I think we've just witnessed the difference between a concert pianist and Chas and Dave."

"I don't suppose we're the concert pianist, are we, Boss?" Degsy replied with a slight smile.

"Most probably not, Derek," Thurstan said, patting him on the back as they left the building. "Most probably not."

CHAPTER 63
a.m. 12th May 2014

"I'm sorry about the other day, but I had to dash. Urgent enquiry," he said, affecting an air of pleasantry a long way from how he actually felt. There was something about the SB Superintendent that always made his teeth itch.

"Anything I should know about? Something you're not telling me?" the SB man said as he sat, his hands held to his lips as if in prayer, fixing Thurstan with a long stare.

"No," he replied, adding "and anyway it's a *need to know basis*." It was SB's own mantra.

The Superintendent narrowed his eyes in annoyance.

"*I* think I *do* need to know."

Thurstan stared back at him.

"That may well be, but *I know* you don't."

An awkward silence, then: "Why didn't you provide us straight away with the camera footage you recovered of the vehicle and occupants you knew would be of interest to us in connection with the Councillor's murder?" He was more forceful in his tone this time.

"I did," Thurstan prevaricated.

"Oh no, you didn't, Chief Inspector!" the SB man retorted. His dropping of the word 'Detective' from Thurstan's title was deliberate. "Effectively *you kept* that piece of information from us for a week! We should have had it when you handed over all the original statements and evidence. You're well aware of that!"

Thurstan leant forward on his desk, his voice raised slightly. "Yes! However I couldn't give you something which, at that time, I didn't have, hadn't seen and couldn't assess!"

"And this simple task took a week! I should have expected nothing better," the SB man replied condescendingly.

"No, it didn't take a week!" Thurstan could feel his annoyance rising. "I delivered those discs to the SB office, properly labelled and exhibited, within two days."

"Oh, really!" His opponent's voice was raised. "Then why did you fail to highlight to my Exhibits Officer the importance of what they contained? Why didn't you bring them directly to me?"

Thurstan leant back in his chair. "You weren't there," he said casually. "Anyway, it was all on the report I left."

"So what did you do? Sneak in when he was on his lunch and casually leave it in a pile of other items on his desk? Oh, granted, there was a report! In a separate envelope which was, mysteriously enough, found on *someone else's* desk!"

Thurstan leant forward again. "Listen to me very carefully. I don't sneak! That's your department. I left *those* items. If your office management isn't up to it then you need to get your act together!"

Taffy sat at his desk. Gandalph passed him a coffee 'to go' and a bacon sandwich from the cardboard holder he'd carefully balanced all the way from the canteen. He placed his own coffee on the desk, pulled up a chair and unwrapped his coronation chicken sandwich.

"You didn't forget the brown sauce, did you?" Taffy enquired as he took a sip of his coffee and pulled his brunch from its paper bag.

Gandalph took a big mouthful of sandwich and shook his head.

"Oh, look at that!" Taffy said as he peeled the top layer of toast from his sandwich revealing the succulent bacon, smothered in tangy brown sauce. "Lush, that is," he said, replacing the toast and taking a big bite.

They sat in silence, chewing steadily, watching from a distance as Thurstan and the SB man's discussion became more and more animated. They couldn't hear what was being said but every now and then the voices rose loud enough for them to discern a "what!" or a "how dare you!"

Taffy, having finished the first half of his sandwich, started on the other. Gandalph wiped his hands on a serviette, thoughtfully provided by the canteen, before taking a swig of his coffee, his cheeks bulging with the remains of his coronation chicken.

"I've not seen him this angry before, have you?" Taffy observed.

Gandalph shook his head, held his hand up, pointing to his bursting cheeks. He took another swig of coffee and swallowed several times. "No," he eventually answered.

Suddenly the door to the DCI's office flew open and the SB Superintendent shouted: "Well, don't say I didn't warn you. I'm off to Personnel!" and stormed off through the main office towards the exit. Thurstan stood in the doorway. Taffy and Gandalph had the impression he was going to say something else, but he shot them a glance then simply shouted back: "You do that!"

Thurstan slammed his office door shut and returned to his desk.

Gandalph, finishing his coffee, switched on his computer and keyed in his password. As he waited for access to be granted he idly glanced at the news report on the office television. A Newcastle gangster had been machine gunned to death, in a quiet corner of a local industrial estate, by the pillion passenger of a motorbike. The DCI giving the interview to the news crew seemed to think, for some reason, there was a link to eastern European organised crime in the London area.

Thurstan knew what the SB Superintendent was inferring when he said he was 'off to Personnel'. A veiled threat, his personal file was going to be marked in such a manner it would 'limit' his future career in some way. He'd heard other people complaining this'd been done to them. The 'conspiracy theorists' had maintained 'you can never find out what's been done because they take it out of the file before they let you see it.'

He'd taken it with a pinch of salt, but knew the SB Super would hurt him if he could. The man had waited a long time. Of course, he could've followed him up there, but it would've undoubtedly resulted in a 'scene' and Thurstan was trying hard not to draw attention to himself and his enquiries, at least for the time being.

He sat down and scratched the Personnel Department and Special Branch from the career 'to do' list he hadn't written. At the same time, in the main office, Taffy scrolled down the information on his computer screen and chewed thoughtfully on the remains of his bacon toasty.

CHAPTER 64
p.m. 12th May 2014

Striding across the main office, he'd almost made it to the exit when Arthur hailed him.

"Thurstan! Phone." He held it up to reinforce the message.

Thurstan sighed, then called: "Tell whoever it is I'll phone them back in 30 minutes."

Arthur shook his head. "I think you should take this now. It's Bill Cheesewright and it's important."

Bill Cheesewright was the DCI running the St.Helens murders enquiry. Thurstan huffed and pointed back to his office. The phone rang as he entered. He looked back at Arthur who nodded feverishly in return.

"Bill! Thurstan. To what do I owe the pleasure?" he said affably.

"Hello, Thurstan," Bill replied. "I assume from your greeting you're not aware."

"Aware of what?" Thurstan said as he made himself comfortable in his swivel chair.

Bill laughed.

"I thought as much. It's the way they've sent out the notification, you know, the one regarding your alley victim's DNA profile? Now, would I be right in suggesting the one you received simply told you they'd profiled him and he's not known."

Thurstan's interest was aroused.

"Yes, you'd be absolutely right. Are you going to tell me otherwise, Bill?"

"I am indeed, mate. I received a similar notification." He paused and Thurstan could hear him saying: "Two sugars, please" before he continued. "But mine tells me who he is."

Thurstan leaned forward, elbows on his desk. "And who is he, Bill?"

"Thank you, just put it there," he heard Bill whisper before saying: "Well, it's not so much who he is, Thurstan, but *what* he is." A pause. "He's our serial killer, mate."

CHAPTER 65
12th May 2014

He sipped freshly made iced lemonade, beneath a large white parasol, as Anca stepped into the pool and waded up to her waist.

"It's not as cold as you'd think," she called to him before launching herself fully into the water. She wore the black and white one piece bathing suit she'd bought in Budapest, two years previously. She always looked particularly cute in it.

He lay back and watched her swim up and down. On the table beside him were the books he was currently reading: Jim Marr's *Crossfire* and Jim Garrison's *On the Trail of the Assassins*.

When he'd pulled them from his rucksack, Anca had looked at him tenderly. Running her palm gently down the side of his face she'd smiled, softly. "Again?"

He took another mouthful of lemonade and pressed the cool glass against his forehead, like he'd seen her do sometimes. She always made it look like a sensual wonderland. It was cold and wet, he concluded, wiping his face with the towel. He'd expected more.

They'd been lucky getting a place at such short notice. He'd been hanging around Liverpool waiting for the next job, idly surfing holiday locations when he saw the villa in the mountains with its own pool, magnificent views and solitude. It was perfect. As if it were fate, Simon called him saying everything was on hold and he was free to go home. It'd been too much to resist.

Having bumped into Terry at the airport, he thought he'd have to abandon the idea of leaving direct from Liverpool, making up the story of meeting a friend as a means of escape. But then he met Dieter Ackermann.

The idea had formed only when he'd overheard the young German in the pub, explaining to a relative on his mobile phone that he doubted he'd be home for the funeral because he didn't get paid for another week.

Telling Dieter he'd already bought a ticket for a flight to Berlin but couldn't now use it, he explained someone had done something similar for him when he was younger and he felt he had to carry on the 'vibe'. All that had to be done was the change of name and the ticket was his.

Dieter was only too pleased to accept and promised to do the same, one day, if he were able. He even complimented Nicks on his German and on the strength of this Nicks had booked him extra legroom. Returning to the airport to buy the ticket he deliberately sought another encounter with Terry. Nicks had to hang around for only fifteen minutes before he'd appeared, almost on time.

He was a nice guy, but tended to talk a bit too much, having all the hallmarks of a gossip genuinely enjoying the experience. Nicks wasn't sure SB was the safest place for him, concluding he probably hadn't been asked the right questions in his interview. The name Drayton had been vaguely familiar to him on their first meeting, but it was only when Terry mentioned his working at the MIT that the penny had dropped. Knowing Terry's primal urge meant he would tell whoever he liked of their encounters, Nicks was fairly certain he now had it covered.

"Come on in, sweetheart!" she called, waving excitedly. "We can have a race!" He smiled and waved back. Peeling off his T-shirt, he descended the steps from the terrace to the pool.

CHAPTER 66
14th May 2014

"Derek!" I'm glad you've managed to turn up... finally," Thurstan said as he took his arm, guiding him back towards the office entrance.

"Arthur, book us out somewhere nice, will you? I'll speak to you later," It was the 'code' he and Arthur used for those occasions when he wanted to avoid someone such as the Superintendent or another Senior Officer, or for when he needed to camouflage the nature of his enquiries. Arthur had a flair for this sort of thing.

"Boss, *you* told me I could come in late," Degsy protested as Thurstan propelled him along the corridor towards the lifts.

"Yes, yes," Thurstan told him impatiently. "But it was before I decided we have to do something that *must* be done. Come on! We can catch that lift if we're quick."

Bundling him out of the lift on the ground floor, Thurstan led Degsy across the reception area and out onto the car park.

"You want me to do what!? Steal a toothbrush?" Degsy asked incredulously as they cleared the entrance.

Thurstan strode meaningfully towards his car.

"For pity's sake, Derek, I'm not asking for the world," he replied as the indicators of his car flashed several times. He hesitated as he opened the driver's door. "Just get in and I'll tell you everything en route."

They were driving towards the Dock Road. "I've just received the DNA profile from the knife found in the alley," Thurstan said, "and I need to get some form of confirmation regarding Nickson, something that will let us know we're definitely on the right track. Well, today's the best day to get it. His Dad meets up with a few pals at the Masonic Hall every Wednesday leaving his Mum on her own. So, I thought we _"

"How do you know that, Boss?"

"Know what?" Thurstan checked over his shoulder then slipped into the nearside lane.

Degsy replied deliberately: "Know that his Dad's going to the Masons this afternoon."

"Well," Thurstan began then paused as he negotiated the roundabout before continuing. "You're not the only one with contacts or influence. A friend of mine is running the surveillance courses that've been going on recently so, because we couldn't do it officially, too many questions, I asked him if he could use Nickson's parents as their training targets. I gave him a cover story, of course. Thing is, they weren't able to cover it round the clock, *but* no sightings of Nickson *and* they managed to pick up this behavioural pattern of his parents. Today's the day and we can't afford to waste time."

Degsy was thoughtful for a moment. "Boss? I *can* actually see where you're going with the toothbrush thing, but … why do I have to be the one to nick it?"

Thurstan threw him a scathing glance. "Because, Derek, I'm a DCI. We don't do this sort of thing."

"But I do?"

Thurstan grinned. "Do you want to get on in this job or not?"

"That's unfair, Boss," Degsy complained, with a hint of a smile. "Anyway, what am I supposed to do? Ask if I can use the toilet again? She'll think I've got some kind of problem."

"Perfect! Good thinking!" Thurstan exclaimed. "I'll tell her you've got a prostate issue, but you're too embarrassed to talk about it."

"Great! Thanks very much!" Degsy replied. "And what if there's no toothbrushes? What if they've both got false teeth?"

"Then, Derek ... we're fucked," He paused thoughtfully. "However ..."

CHAPTER 67
Thursday 15th May 2014

"The problem is the Chief blows hot and cold. When he's on his cold cycle, meetings can be somewhat tense. That's why the senior management avoids them if they possibly can and sends 'rent a sucker' instead."

Degsy took another bite of his spicy chicken wrap, chewed thoughtfully then said: "Can't be that bad, surely?"

"Easy for you to say, Derek. You don't have to go to them," Thurstan replied lifting the top layer of bread from his egg mayonnaise sandwich and powdering the contents with black pepper before flattening the bread back in place and taking a mouthful.

Degsy swallowed hard and took a swig from his glass of milk.

"Technically, Boss, neither do you. Should be the Super, shouldn't it?"

Thurstan wiped some stray egg mayonnaise from his chin with his serviette. "Full marks for spotting that. You're quite correct, but he's an awfully busy man, apparently."

Degsy looked back at him incredulously, "Really? What with?"

The DCI took another mouthful of sandwich and washed it down with a sip of coffee. He thought for a moment then said, "Golf, I think."

Degsy smiled. "Anyway, it's a 'one on one' isn't it, Boss? More civilised," he concluded.

"You'd like to think so," laughed Thurstan, "but there's nowhere to hide. No one else there to deflect his attention."

They both looked up, suddenly aware Chalkie was joining them.

"What've you got today?" Thurstan enquired.

He sat down. "Beef stroganoff and rice. Thought I'd give it a go. Looked nice. How come you've not gone for it?"

Thurstan peppered his second sandwich. "They were changing the trays over and I couldn't be bothered to wait. I've been summoned to see the Chief at three."

Chalkie casually checked his watch and slid the tray to the far end of the table, rearranging his plate and mineral water before taking a mouthful of food. He chewed in silence for several moments.

"Mmmm. You missed out. It's really good."

Thurstan chewed his sandwich thoughtfully. "Is Lizzie on duty yet? I thought she might have come down here with you?"

Chalkie scooped up some beef with his fork and waved it towards Thurstan. "You *really* should have had this. Yeah, she is, but I had to send her out on an enquiry." He opened the mineral water which fizzed and spluttered into his lap. "What's the Chief want, do you know? McMahon job?" he said as he wiped the residue off his trousers with his hand then took a swig.

Thurstan shot Degsy a glance. "I expect so," he said.

As Chalkie slowly replaced the bottle top, Thurstan's and Degsy's eyes met and the DS gave an almost imperceptible shrug. "Look, can we move to that table over there in the corner? I need to tell you something, Chalkie. Well, *we* need to tell you something," Thurstan said apologetically.

A smile flickered across Chalkie's lips. "Yeah, no problem."

Safely ensconced in the quiet far reaches of the HQ canteen, Thurstan and Degsy told him everything.

"I knew there was something going on," he chuckled, waving his forefinger when they'd finished. "And I've got to say, I understand totally why you wanted to keep it under wraps for so long. I'd have done exactly the same thing. Honestly, I've got no problems with it at all." He glanced at his watch. "If you have to see the Chief at three, you'd better get a move on."

Thurstan looked at his wrist. "I've got another five minutes yet," he said.

Chalkie grinned, offering the bottle of mineral water "You'll need five minutes to get that egg stain off your lapel. Here, use this, works for me."

CHAPTER 68
Friday 16th May 2014

"Good morning, Derek!" Thurstan hailed his DS who was waiting for him in the office.

"That for me? Thanks very much," he said as he relieved him of the mug of coffee he was holding. "Not having one yourself?" He placed it by his computer and hung his jacket on the coat stand before sitting down behind his desk.

Degsy could only mutter, "Er, actually..." before he was interrupted.

"Well, the meeting with the Chief went well yesterday. In the wake of our 'alley' victim turning out to be the serial killer, he appears to have totally forgotten we haven't solved the McMahon job. Of course the major plaudits went to the St Helens Enquiry Team, and rightly so. They put in a lot of hard work. Not their fault the killer lived outside the area and wasn't known to the system. Anyway, it seems we've managed to fly in under the radar *and* we are, currently, in the Chief's good books because, Derek, he views us as 'sharing the responsibility for having solved the crime.' His very words." He smiled broadly.

Degsy hadn't seen him quite this ebullient and garrulous before, at least not this early. "Not what I expected when I reached his landing yesterday, I have to say, and I have to admit I was quite relieved when I saw Bill Cheesewright was there as well." He took a sip of coffee, emitted a satisfied sigh and then beckoned the DS to him. "What's that under your arm, Derek?"

"It's today's newspaper, Boss. I know you don't usually bother with this sort of thing, but I thought you might want to read it. Are you really sure you don't want to savour the moment a bit longer, or at least finish the coffee first?"

Thurstan shook his head. "No, no. Let's have a look," he replied enthusiastically.

Degsy handed him the office copy of the local newspaper. Unfolding it, the DCI took another sip from his mug then looked down at the headline which proclaimed: *'The Shadow!'*

The local crime reporter was theorising that a vigilante was responsible for the recent unsolved murders which had left the Police completely baffled. Leaving no forensic evidence behind, able to avoid camera surveillance and virtually disappearing into thin air, the mysterious figure began to take on an almost 'super hero' status by the finale.

A serious look replaced the previous jovial countenance; the DCI rubbed his chin several times. "Bugger!" he said quietly. "You know, Derek, I *did know* it wouldn't last for long but I was hoping for longer than that."

Degsy felt he should say something, but wasn't sure what.

The phone rang. Thurstan picked it up, signalling him with a raised palm to hold his thoughts a bit longer. "DCI Baddeley," he said. "Yes, Sir ... No, Sir ... I'm on my way, Sir." He put the phone down, slowly stood up and casually walked to the coat stand in the corner. "Derek, is there any chance we still have such a thing as the Yellow Pages in the office?"

Degsy looked confused. "Yeah, I think so, Boss. Why?"

"Why?" Thurstan threw him a weak smile. "Because, Derek, I might need to stuff it down the back of my pants," he replied slowly, putting on his jacket with a heavy sigh. He patted his colleague on the shoulder. "Should you need me, I'll be with the Chief. I may be gone for quite a while."

Standing by the lift, Thurstan knew he had to tell the Chief everything. He'd known it yesterday; it was why he'd decided to tell Chalkie. He felt bad he hadn't told his DI before but rationalised he'd enough on his plate investigating Monica Jean's murder. Still, he felt guilty he hadn't done it sooner.

Stepping out on the first floor, he saw his reflection in the hard plastic cover of a notice board. Adjusting his tie and quickly brushing his lapels, he took a deep breath and swiped his warrant card through the security device. In the outer office, he introduced himself to the Chief Constable's Personal Assistant. Pretty in an unconventional way and in her early forties, her short cut hair was almost white and she wore a dark grey, below the knee, pencil skirt with a crisp white blouse.

"I've been expecting you," she said pleasantly, flashing him a dazzling smile as she stood up and walked towards the large door behind her. "Follow me, please," she told him cheerily.

She knocked and entered without waiting for an invite.

"DCI Baddeley is here to see you, Sir."

She waved him in, then turned and gave him the same dazzling smile before leaving and closing the door behind him.

The Chief was seated in a large swivel chair behind an even larger oak desk. He was a lean man, in his mid fifties, with sandy coloured hair now greying rapidly. "Take a seat," he said gruffly. He waited until Thurstan was safely seated then lifted a copy of the local newspaper from his desk. He held it as if it were contaminated. "Tell me about this," he said, fixing the DCI with a stern stare.

And so Thurstan told him. When he'd finished the Chief leant back in his chair and said: "So you're convinced this information hasn't been leaked by one of your own team?"

Thurstan nodded. "Absolutely. There's too many inconsistencies, insufficient detail. I suspect it's come from one of the Departments we've been channelling requests through."

The Chief rubbed his chin. "I'll have someone carry out a 'routine audit' and see what it flushes out. If necessary, we'll deal with it by issuing a few postings to less interesting places. But just clarify something for me. You're *now* waiting for the result of a DNA analysis on a toothbrush you stole from your suspect's mother? Did I hear that right?"

Thurstan cleared his throat. "Borrowed, Sir. I borrowed it."

"Borrowed? Without permission? Is that not theft?" the Chief Constable enquired with the hint of a smile.

"Well, not exactly, Sir. There's no intention to permanently deprive. We intend to give it back."

He could feel the sweat trickling down his back as he sat forward to emphasise his point.

"Notwithstanding that technicality, you can't use the result in evidence should it indicate a positive match." The Chief held his hands out in an open gesture. "It serves only as an indication you're on the right road. You still need to get your suspect... what's his name? Nickson?" Thurstan nodded. "And match him against your sample found in the alleyway."

"That's right, Sir," the DCI replied tamely.

The Chief got up and walked over to the window. He stood for a moment in contemplation before returning to his desk to sit on its edge, one leg in contact with the carpeted floor.

"I'm concerned the wider implications of what you're telling me do *not* become public knowledge. To be honest, I don't even want the facts to be known outside the existing circles. It could cause all manner of unwanted reactions. Not least from Special Branch, who I'm not at all sure see me as their master. I think we both know who they do. I don't want them even *thinking* they could get involved in what we've discussed." He rubbed his chin again, pensively. "What we need is a bit of 'divide and conquer'."

He paused, deep in thought. Eventually, he slapped the desk with his palm and declared, "Right! What we're going to do is neither confirm nor deny the lone vigilante theory to the media. In essence, we'll ignore it. What *you*'ll do is issue a press release in relation to the MacMahon case to the effect, say, 'information of a positive but complex nature has been supplied by persons involved in organised crime which make protracted international enquiries necessary and we're hopeful of a satisfactory result'. Yes, that'll do. We'll leave it at that. That's enough to infer a distinct separation from the other cases.

"In the meantime, I'll have something 'confidentially leaked' to the local Press regarding the Councillor's murder. After all, SB say they carried out extensive and exhaustive enquiries and insist the Councillor's death resulted from an act of a lone previous victim who's since taken his own life. They don't fool me but I think the press will buy it. Yes, there's something to play with there. Nothing contentious, of course; something roughly along those lines will suffice. Seeing as the Security Service have thrown the label 'National Security' all over it, we can leave them to carry out any blocking manoeuvres required for the more persistent reporter. Personally, I think it's a can of worms that'll explode all over their faces, given what's appearing more regularly in the satirical newspapers. However, it would be nice, at the very least, to have unplugged the fan before that happens." A thoughtful look. "Yes. I think it's achievable."

He got up and wandered over to peer out of the window again.

"Now, with regard to our dead serial killer," he said quietly. "Well, perhaps it was just the result of a chance encounter. Maybe he tried to rob the wrong person. The city's not awash with guns, as some would claim, but we all know they're far too freely available." He stuffed his hands in his trouser pockets. "I need to speak to someone about that, but it sounds feasible."

He turned to face Thurstan. "And yes, I *realise*, should we get our man, it provides him with the basics of an almost instant way out, but

270

judging by what you're telling me, I'm sure it's not something he or *they* couldn't come up with themselves."

The DCI nodded sagely. He'd already considered the possibility of Nickson claiming he'd been stabbed in an attempted robbery not long before his assailant had been killed himself.

"That should do it, at least in the short to medium term. No more *serial* vigilante." The Chief looked pleased with himself as he returned to sit on the edge of the desk again. Leaning forward, he wagged his forefinger at Thurstan. "You *need* to get this man, Nickson, and get him soon, if at all possible." He paused, "If what you say *is* true, I doubt very much, once arrested, your man is going to contradict whatever we say in respect of his being a lone operator and I'm pretty certain some 'anonymous benefactor' will make sure he's provided with the very best of legal representation."

Another nodded agreement.

He extended his hand. "Thank you for being so candid, Detective Chief Inspector. It's refreshing. You should have spoken to me much earlier though."

Thurstan stood up and shook his hand. "I'm sorry about that, Sir. Thank you for being so understanding."

The Chief moved behind his desk and sat down. "I'll get someone I trust from the Press Office to write the Press release for you. Liaise with them when they've been in touch." The phone rang. He held his hand up to indicate Thurstan should wait. "Yes? Ok, Mrs Byrne. Thank you for that. Tell her to take a seat and I'll see her shortly." He replaced the phone and looked Thurstan in the eye. "Officially, I don't condone how you've handled this matter but, unofficially, I don't condemn it either. Keep me posted."

As he opened the door to leave, the DCI heard: "If need be, at the end of it all, we can always blame the Russian Mafia. They're hardly likely to complain and no one's going to ask them for an interview." He turned and the Chief threw him a mischievous grin.

CHAPTER 69
17th May 2014

He sat on the lounger, listening to the ring tone.

Eventually: "Hi son, how you doing?"

"Hi Dad, doing fine. Sunning by the pool. Just wanted to see how you both are," he replied.

"We're fine, but I can't talk now because we have to go and get your Mum another toothbrush. She seems to think I've used it to clean the sink or some such nonsense and she's waiting in the car. You know how impatient she gets."

"Ok, I'll call you back later then."

"Okey doke," Dad said then added as an afterthought: "Oh, and those two Detectives came back the other day, whilst I was out, and spoke to your Mum. Apparently they need to speak to you again to clear something up."

"Really? Did she let them in, Dad?"

"Yes, apparently the young lad's got a prostate problem and needed to use the loo. You should tell him to get it checked out. Would be silly to ignore it."

"Right. Yeah, well I'll tell him that when I speak to him. Take care and love to Mum."

He cancelled the call and sat quietly in thought.

Leaning over, he popped the cap off a beer, took a mouthful, swallowed slowly then muttered, "The sneaky bastards."

CHAPTER 70
19th May 2014

Quietly reading through a file, Thurstan looked up in response to the knock on his open door.

"Derek! What news can you bring me?" A slight smile played across his face. "I believe the results are out today, am I right?"

Degsy laughed. "You *are* right, Boss."

"And? Don't be shy now," he chided him.

"I passed." Degsy blushed as he shifted awkwardly from foot to foot. "I don't know how, but I passed."

The DCI rose from his chair and shook his Sergeant's hand firmly. "Congratulations, Derek. They obviously have more confidence in you than you have yourself. We all do."

He wasn't surprised by the news, he'd had a phone call earlier but protocol dictated it had to appear as if the successful applicant for promotion had received it first.

"Right, take a seat, I've had a rethink," he continued. "Nickson. We need to check all Ports and Airports from the seventh of May up to today. I want to know if he's come back. No stone unturned. I know he doesn't appear to have come back under his own details but we need to close down the possible Irish re-entry route so we're going to have to officially circulate him. No arrest, information only.

"He could be using false documentation. Speak to the Border Force and see if they can give us the data and *we'll* sift through it.

Names that reoccur and coincide with the periods we know he was here but for which, officially, he wasn't. Patterns, that sort of thing."

Seeing the look on Degsy's face, he waved his hand dismissively. "I know. It'll go down with that lot out there like a lead balloon but it can't be helped." He easily managed to simulate a look of genuine apology. He'd been a Police Officer a long time and was a great believer in the saying: 'If you can't feign sincerity, you shouldn't be doing the job'.

"If it has to be done, it has to be done, Boss."

The DS shrugged and managed to raise a smile. His DCI looked pensive.

"Thing is, Derek, I doubt he'll use the same false documentation twice. Judging by the array of stuff he's been producing at hotels along the way, he's got access to new stuff all the time. If I were in his shoes, I wouldn't use it more than once – increases the chance of being traced.

"If he *has* come back in under his own details, he'll have done us a favour. At least we'll know he's here *but* I doubt he'll be leaving us any messages anymore. He'll have guessed we found the knife and he knows its potential. Yes, it's 'needle in a haystack' stuff, I know, but I'd hate to ignore the possibility he's been more obvious and we missed it because we weren't looking for it. Bottom line? Those enquiries will probably amount to nothing, but if we don't do them, we'll never know." A genuine apologetic look this time. "Can you sort that, Derek?"

"No problem, Boss. They might moan a bit at first, but they'll get stuck in nevertheless. I'll get Gandalph and Taffy to head it up. They've been working well together doing the Welsh enquiries and at least we know Llangrannog seems clean in terms of potential 'victims'. I suppose even 'avengers' need to take a little break now and then."

Thurstan got up and closed the door. "I get your point, Derek," he said quietly, "and I'm glad you raised the matter. Don't think I haven't given this a lot of thought. I'm sure you have. I think we need to have a candid conversation and I need to know exactly what you really think."

"No probs, Boss."

Thurstan smiled his appreciation. "Look, as far as I'm concerned this is how it goes. Our job is, basically, to impartially report the facts, as we find them, and the CPS make the decision as to whether or not there is enough real evidence in those 'facts' to obtain a conviction. That's the actual bottom line. It seems that doesn't always work for some, but that's how it works for me and always has.

"Sometimes, if the first test isn't fully met, the CPS will decide it's in the Public Interest to proceed, which tips the scales. I think Nickson is going to be one of those cases. At this moment in time this is definitely a 'no cough, no job' situation. Unless we find him with the smoking gun, the best we can hope for is his DNA."

He waved the file he'd been reading then removed a report sheet. "It says, Derek 'there is a very, very strong probability the DNA from the toothbrush and the knife will match any sample obtained from your suspect, as named." He put the sheet back into the file and closed it. "We get him, we get DNA. That'll be enough to get him charged, well, that and the 'Public Interest' considerations. Is it enough for a conviction? Clever Barrister, I don't think so." Degsy nodded agreement.

"We both know sometimes a defeat at Court is hard to take, Derek." He paused and leant forward. "But, in this case, I *really* don't think it would bother me. Would it bother you?"

Degsy chuckled. "I know exactly where you're coming from, Boss. Of course *I want* to 'nick' him – personal and professional pride but I have to confess I've got a sneaking admiration for him *and,* whoever they are, what they're doing. I know it's probably not what I should be saying but the fact is it wouldn't bother me either if he got off with it." It was his turn to pause as he rubbed his chin. "In fact, I almost wish we didn't *have* to catch him. Is that wrong or weird, Boss?"

"No Derek, neither. I know exactly what you mean." He leant back and waved his forefinger. "But we *are* going to get him."

"Absolutely, Boss. Absolutely," Degsy said seriously.

There was a moment's silence then Thurstan added, "Oh, before I forget. Any movement on his accounts at all?"

Degsy shook his head. "I've been keeping an eye on that since he left. Nothing. Squat. He's obviously dealing in cash or ..." he shrugged, "maybe he's using someone else's money."

Thurstan placed the palms of both hands on his desk and declared, "Ok. It's good to know. Let's get to it then." He gave him a warm smile.

As Degsy opened the door to leave he turned back towards his DCI. "Incidentally, I hope you don't mind me mentioning it, Boss, but I assume you've told Lizzie everything as well now."

"Yes, I have. I thought it was about time and, in fact, I really shouldn't have left it so long."

Degsy nodded, sagely, then added: "Oh, I forgot to ask! How did your Sunday lunch go, by the way?"

"Sunday lunch?" Thurstan looked puzzled. "Oh, *that* Sunday lunch! Yes, it was lovely actually, Derek. Great bunch of people, very nice meal." He felt awkward and hoped it didn't show.

"Good. I'm glad." Degsy said, thoughtfully, noting the awkwardness. Turning to leave, he smiled to himself then casually said: "Maybe it's a love interest."

Thurstan looked at him quizzically.

"I mean Nickson. Maybe he's getting his money from a partner we don't know about." He smiled. "Door open or shut, Boss?"

278

CHAPTER 71
21st May 2014

"Ok, we're on."

Opening the door, Nicks turned to Simon.

"Goes to plan? Dowesfield, corner with Yewtree. If not, play it by ear."

Snuggled in the shadows at the far end, the only other vehicle in the car park rocked gently from side to side. Walking briskly to the entrance, he paused, shielded by the trees, plastic carrier bag in hand. Simon drove past him, turned right onto Yewtree and began his circuit.

Touching his lapel, Nicks replied to the message, stepped out from the trees and crossed the road. Silhouetted by a distant street lamp, a figure walked casually towards him.

CHAPTER 72

"Quite nice." Degsy sipped his coffee and looked up at the stars.

Thurstan smiled. "Yeah, not bad. That little touch of caramel syrup makes all the difference. There's more if you want. Flask's in my bag on the back seat."

They were leaning against Thurstan's car, blue lights from the road closures strobing the trees and bushes. In the darkest section of the street, portable lighting bathed the body sprawled on the pavement opposite; white suits calmly went about their business.

"Well, what do you think, Boss?"

The DCI drained his cup, shook it out and threw it on the back seat.

"I think we both know, Derek. Especially with that new unopened toothbrush lying on the floor next to him. It's a long way to the nearest shops. Why wander about with it in his hand? No. He knows. He's letting us know he knows and yes... he's taking the piss."

Degsy placed his empty cup through the open window, dropping it onto the seat alongside Thurstan's.

"So, what do you reckon? He followed him to the darkest part of the street and shot him from behind?"

Thurstan shook his head. "No. It *is* a perfect ambush point but I think he probably came out of the car park further down. There's no CCTV there." He turned to face his DS. "Approaches him from the front. Less suspicious. Nobody likes hearing someone behind them on a dark street. *I think*, he'd probably have engaged him in a short conversation. Asking the time, that sort of thing, to allay any suspicions. It's what I would do. Then, as they part company, a few steps, turn and 'pop'. Then he goes to the body, head shot to finish him off and leaves our little gift." He sighed deeply. "Do you know? If I didn't know better I might think he actually knew what rota we were on."

Degsy chuckled. "It *has* passed through my head before, Boss".

"What time did the FME reckon?"

Degsy flicked through the pages of his notebook.

"She said roughly about an hour before he was found, give or take, so that would put it around one thirty."

Thurstan poured himself another coffee.

"Help yourself, if you want one, Derek. I'm going to have a word with the Crime Scene Manager. In the meantime, start calling them in. I want them briefed, ready to go and feet on the ground by seven o'clock."

CHAPTER 73

Thurstan read the victim's profile while the rest of the management team sat in silence. Chalkie methodically dipped a custard cream. Eventually the DCI leant back:

"It beggars belief. How could this man be a candidate for early release? A mother and three kids? What he did was horrendous."

Chalkie spoke first.

"I've made some enquiries there and it seems it's all part of a new experimental release programme. He was judged not to be a threat to the Public, the one stipulation being he had to be as far away from the victim's family as possible and Liverpool fitted the bill."

"He might not have been a threat to the public, but he was certainly a threat to the next mother and kids he latched onto." Picking up the small bottle of mineral water from his desk, Thurstan struggled to release its top. Lizzie leant across, took it from him, twisted the cap and placed it back on the desk. "Thanks, Liz," he said absently before continuing. "Surely the PPU should have known about him?"

"They did. They were told yesterday." Chalkie replied.

The DCI pointed to the file in front of him. "But this says he's been here a week!"

"It seems someone was a bit lax in notifying them. They're looking into it. Apparently it's never happened before." Chalkie dropped his papers onto the coffee table. "They're definitely not happy at all. I know the DI there and she's not one to be messed with. It *will* be followed up."

Degsy chipped in. "Is that the little one with the eclectic clothing?"

Chalkie nodded. Degsy chuckled. "Yeah, I've seen her about. Attractive but I wouldn't want to fight her."

Thurstan pushed the victim file to one side. "What's the score with the 'hostel' he was staying in, Derek? How come he's wandering around at that time of night?"

"Apparently, again, experimental, Boss. Worked on trust. They have their own keys and self contained flats. There's four of them at this place on Allerton Road. Well, three of them now. Very low key. The neighbours seem to think it's to do with drugs rehabilitation. They're not entirely happy but I think if they knew what it was really about they'd see their arses. His room's still being turned over but early indications are he's already been researching local dating sites. Lonely mums, that sort of thing."

"Anything from the teams yet?" He looked at Chalkie who shook his head and shrugged his shoulders.

"Yeah, I'll be surprised if we get anything but it's got to be done. I even asked for forensic to check the toothbrush for DNA just in case. I'd hate to think what we didn't do was more significant than what we did." Thurstan ran his hand through his hair. "Look, if anyone disagrees with me about Nickson, please say so now?" They looked at each other and shook their heads. "I'm absolutely certain it's him. If nothing else, the toothbrush confirms it. He's back. I don't know how he's doing it, but he's back. I want a full intel check, anybody with sound contacts in SB then use them, any contacts *anywhere* let's use them. We won't expand the house-to-house, in fact once we've completed the immediate area let's close it down because I've decided to come at this from a different angle.

"I'm sick of chasing him around. I want to identify any potential targets and see if we can't get one step ahead and be there when he does the next one. It's going to mean a lot of work. A lot of hours. The only thing I've got for you and your families is just sit back and think of the money at Christmas." He stood up, putting on his jacket. "Right, I have to go. The Chief Constable wants to see me." He patted Chalkie on the shoulder as he walked past. "Make it so, number one."

"Chief Con not happy?" Chalkie enquired.

Thurstan turned in the doorway. "Do know what? I think he's actually enjoying it."

CHAPTER 74
28th May 2014

Gandalph stood at the door. A full week since the DCI had decided the unit would go on the attack and they still had nothing. Thurstan looked up wearily.

"Stephen, come in. What's the matter? You look troubled."

Gandalph, smiled sheepishly and shuffled into the office.

"Can I have a private word with you, Boss?"

"Go ahead," Thurstan said, slightly anxious; personal matters were not one of his strong points.

"Not here, Boss. I can't be certain. That SB bloke and the suits were in here, if you get my drift."

Minutes later they were strolling through the Albert Dock.

"So, why are you so worried Stephen?"

"I've got some information, Boss, but everything about it is very, very sensitive, including how I came by it."

"From an informant?"

Gandalph shook his head.

"Not exactly."

Thurstan looked at him searchingly.

"Is this something to do with your aptitude with computers?"

The slight smile told him everything.

"Have you hacked into something, Stephen? Something big?"

Gandalph nodded. "Something massive."

Without really being conscious he was doing it Thurstan had started to surreptitiously glance around. "Have you hacked into SB's systems?"

Gandalph sat down on an isolated bench. Thurstan next to him.

"That's only the start of it, Boss. Maybe I got carried away but it's all untraceable. Believe me. I'm good at this stuff."

"Please tell me you haven't hacked MI5?"

"Ok, should we go back now then?" Gandalph looked him firmly in the eyes.

They sat in silence.

"Ok, tell me," Thurstan eventually said, with a hint of exasperation.

"You said to pull in any contacts we had. So I did. An old mate from my SB days."

"You were in SB? I wasn't aware," the DCI interrupted.

"Yeah, I was only there eighteen months. I got caught shagging the missus of one of the DIs. In my defence I didn't know who she was originally and when I found out I was as gobsmacked as anyone else."

"I assume when you found out that was the end of the matter?" Thurstan looked at him hopefully.

A wicked little smile played across his face. "Not exactly. She was a good looker and horny as hell. The DI found out and it all went tits up. To keep things quiet, I got to pick where they were posting me, so I was happy. SB wasn't my thing, Boss." He paused. "Anyway, I spoke to my mate. He played the game. Didn't know anything, but I know him too well and he knows it. He gave me some very subtle clues, probably would have been missed by anyone else. I knew he

286

was pointing me in the direction of the Councillor file. Just before he left we ended up discussing that programme from years ago, "Call my Bluff". Remember it?" Thurstan nodded. "As he was going he said, 'There's a lot of strange words in the English language. Triskelion. That's odd.' Then he did one.

"I couldn't ignore it so I worked from the back of my camper van and parked up in a couple of quiet lay-bys I knew from my younger days and bam! I was in. Interesting stuff. But there was something missing. It wasn't quite interesting enough so I checked it all again and that's when I caught it. There was a mention of 'triskelion', sneakily hidden away. Although it didn't say so it was obvious, to me at least, it pointed to MI5." He leant back and glanced around as he did so. "Well, I'd started, hadn't I, so it had to be done. It was strangely easy, but then again I am fucking good at this. I've read everything. Basically there's two people who fit the profile we're looking at. Both are in Liverpool, although one of them is due to be moved shortly and the other spends a lot of time at his holiday plot in North Wales. There's too much for me to tell you here, Boss, so I posted it to you in a birthday card. When you get it just separate the back part of the card. Between the layers is a thin sheet with everything on it. It's sort of delicate so be careful."

"And you're absolutely sure you're not traceable?" Thurstan looked at him searchingly, looking for a glimmer of doubt.

Gandalph chuckled. "Absolutely. I bought myself a second hand laptop from a market up in Cumbria for cash and everything I used has been wiped, stripped down and disposed of. It's either in a canal somewhere now or part of a cube that used to be a car, on its way to Africa probably. Yeah, I'm fairly certain." He stood up. "Ok if I go back to the office now, Boss?"

The DCI looked up and replied absently, "Yes Stephen, go ahead."

He took a few steps then stopped and turned. "Oh, and you'll need a magnifying glass, Boss. For the card."

CHAPTER 75

Thurstan returned home to find a large, slightly bent and crumpled pink envelope waiting for him on the hallway floor. Without thinking he found himself peering, briefly, through the living room curtains before he returned to the hall and picked it up. Throwing it on the kitchen table, he removed his jacket and poured himself a large single malt. Later that evening, in a secluded part of his garden, he burnt the envelope, card and its contents in a metal bucket.

The following day, he took a blustery early morning walk along Thurstaston Beach where he periodically and surreptitiously scattered the ash contents of a plastic bag to the wind before going to work.

CHAPTER 76

In the Ship and Mitre, Don sipped his glass of Fruli. "It's really pleasant. I don't know why I haven't tried it before."

Nicks smiled, nodded his appreciation and took a mouthful of his own pint. Sitting in the shadows of the rear room, they were alone apart from a couple standing at the bar. Simon scuttled up the steps towards them.

"Apologies. Customer came in looking for a copy of Up and Running's Sorry. I knew we had it on cassette somewhere but it took ages to find the little bugger. You two ok?" He pointed at their drinks. They nodded.A few minutes later he placed his drink on the table, sat down, lay his coat on the empty seat next to him and said: "Ok, I'm ready."

CHAPTER 77
Friday 30th May 2014

Thurstan stepped from the lift to be met by Gandalph's: "Morning, Boss." They waited, briefly, whilst the doors closed. "Just came to tell you everything's fine," Gandalph said quietly. "I swept the place as you asked and I'm more than happy there's nothing there."

"You're absolutely sure?"

He smiled.

"Yep, absolutely."

"How much do I owe you?" Thurstan asked him.

"Five hours twenty and a scoff allowance will do me, Boss," he grinned.

The DCI patted him on the arm.

"Good lad. Go home and get your head down and we'll see you this afternoon."

Entering the office he bumped into Arthur.

"You're in early, Thurstan. Wet the bed?"

"Cheeky sod!" he retorted. "What about yourself?"

"At my age it's expected. You're only a youngster," he laughed. "Want a cuppa?"

Later that morning, like scouts round a camp fire, he, Chalkie, Lizzie and Degsy sat huddled around the coffee table in his office. The conversation was muted.

"So that's my thoughts on the matter. Even though one of the subjects, as far as we can tell, doesn't fully fit the profile, I think we should cover him as well."

Chalkie eyed the other two as he spoke. "I think it would be foolish not to." They nodded their agreement.

Degsy leant forward and took another chocolate digestive from the plate. "Given that we've only got two days until MI5 move their chap, how long are we going to be watching the other fella out in Wales, Boss?"

"Well, I've already spoken to the Chief who says we have the resources for three days max. He spoke to the Chief Con of North Wales whilst I was there. Apparently they're big buddies. Your man in North Wales agreed to pay a third of the costs on the basis it would probably cost him a lot more if he had the murder to deal with. If nothing happens within three days the guy gets locked up on child porn allegations. Any more questions?"

"You're obviously quite certain of the provenance of this information?"

"Absolutely, Chalkie. Couldn't be more certain. The uncertainty is whether Nickson will show up. It's the best shot we've got." He smiled apologetically.

"Seeing as we're 'encroaching' into MI5 territory, it sounds like this has come from a hacker or someone of the 'Deep Throat' mould?" Lizzie chipped in, looking at Thurstan expectantly.

Again an apologetic smile, with a hint of a sigh.

"I don't think I'm giving anything away if I say it's a bit of both but anything else I can't say, sorry. If this leaks there will be hell to pay so the only people who can know about MI5, as I said before, is us, in here." He pointed to the main office. "Them out there get told nothing but what they need to know to do their jobs. The same applies to the surveillance and firearms people with the exceptions of the Team Leaders who'll be on the job. They'll *have* to know about the MI5 close protection team, we don't want any accidents there." He bit into a chocolate biscuit then continued: "We'll be there to identify and arrest Nickson. We want to prevent what he intends to do or, if we don't manage that, we prevent his escape. That goes for both locations.

"With regards, specifically to the MI5 operation, anything that happens within the safe house compound is theirs to deal with. If it spills out onto the street in the immediate vicinity of the premises, say within 50 metres, they sort it out, we mop up if needs be. Anything further than that, we intervene. Hopefully we'll get him on the way in. I anticipate the safe house will be locked down at night so that's when we'll be getting some sleep. There'll be a skeleton staff at night just in case but I think Nickson will only turn up when they're ready to move their man, which will be sometime during the day on Sunday, between ten and four. Basically the first day of the deployment here will be a settling in period.

"Chalkie, you and Liz will be Bronze for the Welsh job. Alternate with the shifts. North Wales will provide Silver command.

"Derek, you'll be Bronze here in Liverpool, I'll be Silver. Gold command in both locations will be the Chief Constables."

He sat back in his chair. "Chalkie, you and Liz sort your own arrangements and plan, then get back to me."

When they'd left the room Thurstan beckoned Degsy closer. "We haven't got much room for error on this one, Derek. You and I will be communicating via our own personal channel. I may have to make decisions I don't want anyone else to hear. If something happens at that safe house which is not in the game plan I don't want people charging in. It needs to be controlled. We may even have to just quietly walk away."

CHAPTER 78

Thomas Weedsley was a worried man. The much respected former headmaster of a prestigious school in the Northwest had received a phone call. An anonymous 'benefactor' told him that Police Officers would come soon, to speak to him about 'certain' allegations.

Two things would be his downfall. His large collection of category 'A' child pornography and the remains of a 10 year old boy, a runaway, lying buried under the dirt floor in the cellar of his holiday home in North Wales.

His initial attempts to destroy the pornography had proven unsuccessful, so he'd transferred it all to his cottage, several miles outside the sullen little village of Llanfinog. Here he could do the job properly, away from prying eyes.

The impending threat brought him a strange new titillation, however. He knew the sensible thing was to destroy it now, straight away, but he wasn't ready to complete the final act. Drawing the curtains, he shovelled coal on the fire and began to indulge in a final feast of sexual gratification.

Outside, on the dark windswept hill, three CROPS men settled down in their positions. Between them they could see the whole building and its approaches. It didn't matter the house backed onto woodland. A twenty metre gap between the edge of the woods and the garden's stone wall, with its little wrought iron gate and French windows beyond, provided a safety margin.

Specialist Firearms Officers and a helicopter were on hand close by, ready to go at a moment's notice. Chalkie and a team from MIT sat in unmarked vehicles at various locations whilst Lizzie and the rest of the party took what relaxation they could in a hotel not too far away.

CHAPTER 79

Bramwell Peterson was pleased with himself. Not only had he survived but he'd managed to consolidate his position. It'd been a bold strategy, not without danger. Ideology wasn't the reason he'd passed classified information to the Russians and their allies. No, it had been necessity. They knew of his proclivity. They weren't the only ones.

Agreeing to be 'turned', by the Security Service, was a long awaited act of release. Ceding ownership of the diary in which he'd detailed his and the 'others' shared experiences was the stimulus for their offer.

They were *so* pleased with themselves no one had even broached the question of a copy. Well, copies to be exact; sealed in brown envelopes, addressed to two rival newspapers and safely tucked away in a bank safety deposit box. The new copy of his will and its instructions were quite clear, even the obscure solicitor the bank had recommended would be able to manage it should anything happen to him.

CHAPTER 80
Sunday 1st June 2014

Simon pulled up in front of the little shop.

"Here's a tenner. Get me a diet coke, a packet of cheese 'n' onion and a sandwich. See if they've got any vegetarian ones."

Nicks took the money and ambled in.

Si turned on the CD and drummed his fingers on the wheel, losing himself in the moment.

The door opened. Nicks plonked himself in his seat and turned the CD off. "Diet coke, packet of crisps and a spicy chicken wrap." He handed them, with the change, to Simon.

"Didn't they have a vegetarian option?"

"Yeah, they did."

"What was it?"

"Fuck off."

Si stared at his crisps. "These are beef. I wanted –"

"They didn't have any and I know you don't like salt and vinegar." Nicks gave him an exasperated look.

Simon ripped the packets open. "D'yer want some?"

Nicks hesitated then relented. "Yeah, go on."

They ate in silence.

Still brushing bits of crisps off his trousers, Simon stopped halfway down the lane. Nicks grabbed his little backpack and opened the door.

"No Si, sorry but you didn't. You still owe me a fiver," he said.

"I've told you. I paid that back," Simon protested.

"Not that fiver! Ages ago, the one for the sandwiches and the sports drink. I mean, a fucking sports drink. You're taking the piss," he laughed.

"It has a nice taste. Anyway, tight arse, don't fuck up."

"And you," he smiled, closing the door.

He took the public footpath and walked casually across the field, entering the tree line. At the opposite edge of the woods he knelt down; the wrought iron gate beyond. Threading the suppressor onto the weapon he left the bag in the undergrowth, next to a tree stump, and racked a round into the chamber.

Swiftly, he made it across the open ground, through the gate, to the French windows. Time was of the essence now. Quietly opening the door, he slipped into the room.

CHAPTER 81

In the library Bramwell Peterson calmly smoked his cigar. Taking a long draw he blew out the smoke slowly before picking up the brandy glass and gently swirling its contents. Inhaling the aroma, in two distinct mouthfuls he savoured its progress across his tongue and into his soul.

In the next room, through the French windows, a figure quietly entered and murmured into a concealed microphone. The glass panelled doors dividing the two rooms glided silently open and the figure slowly raised his arm.

Three vehicles waited on the drive. Two saloons, between them a 4x4. Although there'd been no intelligence of any specific threat, the doors were open, engines running, CP team standing; watchful, shades on, ready.

"Mr Peterson." The minder looked at his watch. "Time to go."

Opening the front door, two protection officers preceded Peterson down the steps, two behind. Bramwell smiled and his head popped open like a ripe melon hit by a sledgehammer, collapsing him straight down into a heap on the steps. Spattered in blood, bone and brain, the two rear officers sought immediate cover, weapons drawn, instinctively knowing their 'principal' was a lost cause. The other two, shielded by the 4x4, dragged him down the few remaining steps, leaving a pink trail of brain tissue behind him.

Degsy, watching from the observation van, simply said: "Oh!! ... Fuck!!"

900 metres away, atop one of the towers that made up the 'Dennings Towers Residential Complex' known locally as 'Dennings bollocks' two workmen folded the stock and tripod of an AWM sniper rifle, removed the suppressor, placed it all in a kitbag and calmly began descending the service stairs.

CHAPTER 82

"Thurstan!" It was Arthur. "Soapy's on the phone. Says he has to speak to you. It's urgent!"

The DCI huffed. "If it's about his sick note tell him I'm busy!"

Arthur shook his head. "He says you *have* to speak to him *now*!"

Thurstan picked up the phone. "David, this had better be good."

"It's Nickson, Boss. I've just seen him!" Soapy answered.

"Are you sure it's him?" Thurstan's heart rate immediately increased.

"I was just coming back from my sister's and I walked right past him. He was getting out of a motor driven by a little blonde guy. I'm absolutely sure, Boss. I've spent enough time looking at his photo."

"Where?" Thurstan was already scribbling on a notepad.

"Mossley Hill. He's just gone into a small wood that backs onto Granarth Close. I've googled it on my phone. He can't be going anywhere else."

"Where are you now?"

"I'm at the end of the road, sitting on a wall."

Granarth Close? Why did that ring a bell? "Ok, stay there. Don't approach him if you see him again!" He gave Soapy his mobile number and strode off to get his jacket. *Granarth Close.* He knew the address somehow. *Granarth Close. Granarth Close. Bingo!*

Reaching his desk, he ripped open the top drawer and grabbed the copy of the Echo. Rifling through it, he found the article. '*Holocaust survivor's final victory?'* There was a picture of an elderly man on the steps of a house. The door behind him had the number 15.

Driving out of HQ, in the unmarked MIT vehicle, Thurstan called into his radio.

"DS Drayton. DCI Baddeley."

"Drayton go 'head."

"Derek, any sign of Nickson?"

"No, Boss. We've got this place pretty much sewn up and there's been absolutely nothing." The surveillance guy next to him tapped his leg and whispered: "Movement."

"That's good. Soapy just called in, says he's seen Nickson in Mossley Hill. He thinks he's making towards Granarth Close. I want you, our team and the firearms to meet at 15 Granarth. Asap."

"Alright, Boss, hang on a mo' there's some movement here. They're bringing him out...Oh!! ... Fuck!!"

Thurstan pulled over to the side, hazard lights on. "What's happening?" *Nothing.* "Derek! Speak to me. What's happening?"

"His head just fucking exploded, Boss. Jesus Christ almighty!"

This was not what he wanted to hear. *Decision! Think! Think man!*

"Are they in the compound still?" No reply. "Derek! Are they still in the compound!"

A shaken Degsy replied: "Yes, Boss. They never got out of the place."

Thurstan could hear calm voices in the background.

"Callsigns with the eyeball, any clues where that came from?"

"One zero bravo. Maybe Dennings Bollocks. It's the best vantage point."

"Roger that."

Thurstan stuck his arm out of the window and placed the strobe light on the roof. He called Degsy again.

"Leave them to it! It's their problem now. Tell the surveillance guys to stay put, observe and report. The rest of you, 15 Granarth Close, now!"

He threw the radio on the passenger seat, bent forward over the 'blues and twos' control panel and muttered: "Now, how the fuck does this work?"

CHAPTER 83

"Berger! Berger! You fucking moron!!"

"Hauptscharführer!" the Unterscharführer called back.

"What is that fucking monkey still doing on that machine!" he screamed, spittle spraying from his mouth. "Where is that fucking idiot Zimmermann? I told him to tell you. Get rid of him now or I'll do it myself."

"But Hauptscharführer, it will take too long to train –"

"Don't give me that shit again Berger!" He pointed at Hersh.

"You! Get down off that machine!" He drew his CZ P27 pistol, cocked it and waved it wildly around. Hersh immediately leapt to the ground. He knew better than to argue with the Hauptscharführer.

"You!" He now pointed to one of the bone shovellers. "Get up there and make this fucking thing work or I'll shoot you where you stand!" He turned to the Unterscharführer. "Don't stand there with your mouth open! Take him away and get rid of him!"

The Unterscharführer grabbed Hersh by the scruff of the neck and dragged him towards the far exhumed pit. "I'm sorry Hersh, I'm sorry."

Behind them they heard a shot. The Hauptscharführer shouted: "Move, you piece of shit! You've been fucking promoted."

Berger glanced over his shoulder and saw a second bone shoveller climb onto the machine and scramble over the body of the first. Breaking into a run, he pulled the stumbling Hersh with him.

Forcing him to his knees on reaching the edge of the pit, Berger hissed: "Fall into the pit when I tell you. Don't fuck up and stay still, it'll be dark soon. It's your only chance." Hersh stared down at the top layer of soil splattered decaying bodies. He was oblivious to the nauseating smell; he'd been there too long.

Berger cocked his pistol, pushed Hersh's head forward, stepped back and called: "Now!"

Hearing the report of the gun, Hauptscharführer Sauer turned to see just another Jew tumbling into a pit. He smiled and turned his attention back to the Knochenmühle.

"If you want to live another fucking day keep that machine going!" he screamed at Hersh's replacement. The remaining shovellers feverishly fed the insatiable monster. "Work you scum! Clear those fucking bones!"

From the layered funeral pyres, black, fetid smoke billowed over the darkening field and through the adjacent woods. Jacob Hersh lay perfectly still. He'd no idea why Berger had done it.

This was Sonderkommando 1005, Chelmno, January 1945.

CHAPTER 84

'Jack' Hersh pottered around the kitchen. He still hadn't got used to where his friend Rose kept all the things, but he was 'getting there'. Dropping some tea bags into the pot he added the milk to his cup and switched on the kettle. *Rose.* He smiled at the memory of a friendship lasting the years.

Washed and dressed in her fresh nightgown by the nurses who'd moved on to their next call, she'd eaten the toast he'd gently fed her earlier and had taken some sweet tea from her 'baby' cup. She was asleep now. In Liverpool for a short series of talks about life and death in the Nazi extermination camps, he'd volunteered to help out, so Rose's son could take a short break.

At 88 years of age he was still a fit man. A long brisk walk every afternoon, snow and ice permitting, and daily use of some light weights kept him feeling sprightly. Both he and Rose were survivors of the camps.

After the war, he'd tried to put that existence behind him as best he could, then in 2002 he'd read an article about a wealthy German industrialist and had instantly recognised the photograph. Contacting renowned Nazi hunter Simon Wiesenthal's office he'd explained the man had formerly been known as Hauptscharführer Ernst Sauer, the man in charge of running the gas wagons at Chelmno, the man in charge of Chelmo's Leichenkommando Corpse Units during the

Aktion Reinhard clean-up operation; the man known and feared by the inmates for his enjoyment of the killing and barbarity.

It had taken a long time but shortly Jack Hersh would travel to Germany to give evidence in the 96 year old's trial; the last ditch attempt to bring him to justice. Witnesses had been few; Jack was now the last one still alive.

The doorbell rang. He dropped the teaspoon into the cup and strolled to the door. Opening it he saw a young woman in her early 40's.

"Alright luv, I'm Barbara's friend. You know? The cleaning lady? She was here yesterday, well she can't make it today so I've come to sort you out as a favour."

She grinned cheekily at him. He closed the door behind her and they walked into the living room. She seemed like a nice young woman but was about to lose points by insisting on speaking to him as if he was a 5 year old.

"You don't need to show me where all the things are, Barbara's told me. Is that a cup of tea you were making? Why don't you sit yourself down in front of the telly? I'm just gonna pop me handbag in the hall and I'll make you a nice cuppa before I get started." She smiled brightly. "Right, come on, you get sat down there. That's nice. There, the telly's on and here's the remote so you can choose whatever you like and I'll bring your tea shortly."

She left him, returning five minutes later with a tray upon which sat a cup of steaming tea, a sugar bowl, spoon and a plate of digestive biscuits. She placed it on the small table next to him. "I've just got to nip to the loo then I'll start with the hoovering."

She disappeared into the hall. He put two sugars into the cup, stirred, broke off half a biscuit and dipped it in his tea. In the hall she opened her handbag to remove the already loaded and cocked Smith and Wesson M and P 9mm pistol. Screwing a suppressor on it, she slowly returned to the door of the living room and quietly peered around the frame. She could see the back of his head as he sat in the armchair, sipping his tea and watching the news. Stealthily, she stepped into the room and began to level the weapon.

Either side of her ponytail, a slight, almost imperceptible, breeze caught her neck.

She was still trying to register its significance when the bullet hit her, crumpling her straight down onto the limp rags that were her own legs, her torso flopping on its side into the carpeted floor.

Nicks, who'd entered through the French windows and hidden momentarily behind the rich velvet curtain, strode over the body and recovered the Smith and Wesson. The pool of blood from her head was expanding.

Jack Hersh stood up and said: "I'll get some towels from the cupboard."

Returning a few moments later he and Nicks placed them around her head. Jack shook his hand. "Thank you young man. I could see her reflection on the silver vase. I have to admit I was worried. Look, I've spilt my tea." He wiped the front of his jumper.

Nicks clicked his radio. "Elvis, clean up."

"Yes, yes".

He went to the front door. Within a minute a black transit marked 'Private Ambulance' pulled up. Three men entered the building, one of them carrying a tool bag.

In the front room, two of them rolled the 'cleaning lady' and towels into a body bag and carried it out to the van. The third studied the blood stained carpet. Opening his tool kit he produced a Stanley knife, cut a square around the blood, removed the section and rolled it up into a plastic bag. He and Nicks moved the settee. The 'fitter' eyed the floor then quickly cut another square of carpet which he slotted into the space the bloodstained one had occupied. They replaced the seating. He examined his work.

Stuffing the knife and bloody carpet remnant in the tool bag, he shook Jack's hand as if he was just a run of the mill workman affecting a temporary repair and declared with a smile:

"Not a perfect match but it will do for now. Someone will pop round to replace the whole thing tomorrow."

Nicks handed him the unloaded Smith and Wesson with the fully charged magazine and saw him to the door.

In the distance, the emergency sirens closed in.

CHAPTER 85

Vehicles screeched to a halt, doors already open, uniformed firearms officers spilling out across the street, seeking the available cover.

At the rear, armed officers leapt from an unmarked van, quickly formed a crocodile and, with a shield man at the front, briskly walked along the alleyway until they reached the rear gate of number 15. An extendable ladder placed, one of them climbed up providing cover from the top of the wall. The rest, shield man in front, rapidly entered the garden, through its gate, fanning out as they did so.

Back at the front, the firearms Team Leader began to call out the occupants of number 15. Following the instructions being shouted at him, Jack reached the pavement to be whisked behind safe cover, searched and swiftly interrogated. A second crocodile formed up and strode to the entrance steps. A brief halt, then they entered and searched. After several minutes the TL appeared in the doorway. "Clear!"

Thurstan and Degsy stood in the living room.

"Are you sure you don't want a cup of tea or something?" Jack called from the kitchen.

They politely declined. Thurstan looked around the room. Nothing seemed unusual. Dated, but comfortable furniture and a busy carpet, not new but serviceable.

"Look, Mr. Hersh, I'm terribly sorry about all this but we had what we thought was very reliable information. I really can't apologise enough."

Jack strolled back in with his cuppa.

"Detective Chief Inspector, please don't worry. It's a long, long time since I've had such an exciting morning." He placed his cup on a coaster. "And believe me when I tell you, it's a great honour to have a man of your stature come to visit, although next time you could just ring the bell."

He laughed. They produced awkward smiles. Thurstan looked down at the floor slightly embarrassed.

"Well, we'll leave you to recover what you can of the day and sorry again for all the trouble."

Jack closed the door behind them. He'd checked on Rose already. She was still sleeping peacefully. When she woke, he would have a tale to tell her. That was for sure. Smiling he returned to his armchair, cup of tea and the remote control.

Sat in the car Thurstan rubbed his eyes, ran his hands up and down his face, hard, then brushed his fingers through his hair and kneaded the back of his neck.

"Where to now, Boss?" Degsy looked at him sympathetically.

He said nothing. Staring out of the windscreen he looked blank. Eventually, he let out a heavy sigh.

"We have to speak to the surveillance TL, Derek. Then we have to stand them down."

312

They travelled in silence. Apart from the 'cock-up' he'd organised, something else was troubling him but he didn't know exactly what it was.

After five minutes, he said abruptly:

"Turn around, Derek. Go back. Number 15. Something's not right."

The bell 'bing bonged'. After a few moments the door opened and Jack greeted them.

"Chief Inspector, you haven't just come back to practice have you? Come on in."

In the living room Thurstan explained. "I'm sorry for the intrusion but there's something I wanted to check, if I have your permission?"

Jack nodded.

"You have your job to do, Chief Inspector."

Thurstan moved the armchair and crouched down to the carpet. Degsy looked on intrigued. The DCI began to pull at the fibres, lifting a neatly cut square from the floor. He inverted it and placed it down. In the space created could be seen the underlay on which there was a slight, dark staining. Thurstan stood up and pulled the armchair over the gap.

He smiled politely at Jack then nodded Degsy in the direction of the settee. They pulled it to the side revealing a similar gap in the carpeting. Thurstan smiled at Jack again. He looked around the room intently. Suddenly he was down on his knees, peering under the sideboard in the back part of the room, closer to the French windows. He beckoned Degsy.

"Pencil or pen, Derek, please."

After several seconds, he produced a 9mm empty shell casing. Degsy already had a small evidence bag open.

Standing up, Thurstan brushed his trousers and smiled again at Jack.

"I think we *will* have that cup of tea now Mr. Hersh, if you don't mind."

CHAPTER 86

MIT was a hive of activity. Chalkie, Liz and the team were on their way back from North Wales. He'd pulled the plug, in light of the day's developments. The job's mobile began to ring and wobbled its way towards the edge of his desk. He watched it for several seconds then picked it up.

"Boss, it's Devon. Sorry we're not back yet but we got sidetracked. I'll explain fully later but we're in Sefton Park, the car park, Mossley Hill Drive and Greenbank. There's something you might want to take a look at."

"What is it Devon, it's been a long day?"

"Me and Ikky came across a couple of bobbies giving CPR to a woman they'd dragged out of a car that was parked up. We stopped to help them out. Paramedics have confirmed she's dead and I've asked them to stay 'til you get here. We went through her stuff, naturally. Nothing untoward until Ikky started reading her diary. Seems she's been having an affair with another woman. Today's entry is interesting though. It says 'Helen. Sefton Park. Can't wait.' Underneath she's written, '15 Granarth Close 11am'."

CHAPTER 87

"So, tell me, Boss?" Degsy asked, placing his pint back down. "What the hell was all that about?"

They were alone in the snug.

"It's a long and complicated story, Derek, but I'll do my best to give you the short version," Thurstan replied, wiping the beer froth from his mouth. "When they killed the Councillor they opened up Pandora's box. I think they were aware of that. "The Councillor had been privy to the dirty secrets of some very highly placed, influential people, including Peterson, who'd been spying for the Soviets for a long time, also for the East Germans.

"When the Warsaw Pact collapsed he continued with the Russians but, it seems, he was also spying for some other former Pact country, now an EU member. All highly embarrassing stuff.

"MI5 and MI6 knew about Peterson. SIS in particular used him to feed false information to his masters. The Security Service were aware of his 'predilections' and his connections with the Councillor and others.

"Subsequently, they felt they had to protect not only this knowledge but also the individuals themselves, believing having their co-operation and compliance in certain matters would conserve the status quo. What were a few kids from broken homes or care homes compared with the overall state and 'health' of the nation? Not my or your response but in the 'murky' world of politics and intelligence gathering such an outrageous thing obviously seemed viable."

"But where does Weedsley come in? Was he part of all this?"

"No, Derek, I don't think so. He *was* in the sense he was a paedophile, but it seems he'd no connection to the higher echelons. He was just the 'Patsy'. Found by MI5 and nurtured specifically so he could be fed 'to the wolves', should their operation be compromised by journalists or events. That's what 'Triskelion' was all about. The Councillor, Peterson and Weedsley. Of course, I'm not sure they knew about the body in his cellar. If they did, they may have been instrumental in steering him away from further activity of that kind. We'll probably never know.

He sipped his drink. "I think they knew about his fragile mental state though *and* I think they would have contributed towards it, probably with the idea that should they launch him into the media spotlight he'd kill himself rather than face the ignominy."

He took a mouthful of beer. "Want any peanuts?"

"Not for me, Boss."

Thurstan got up and walked to the bar, returning with a packet of dry roasted.

"Well, what about Hersh, then?"

Thurstan smiled. "I think Mr Hersh was targeted by the wealthy industrialist whose reputation he was about to 'sully'. Maybe it was a member of his family but it was probably more about money than reputation." He munched a few nuts. "You can't win them all, Derek. Peterson's out of our hands now, national security and all that. Hersh?

317

Well, we've got a suspect we can't find, a body we can't find and a witness who doesn't want to go on record. Looks like a non-event. Perhaps that's how it should stay.

"The cleaning lady in the park? If the opportunity arises, maybe we should overlook the little mark on her chest? I suspect, apart from that, we probably won't find significant traces of whatever her killer, our missing body, injected her with. I think the 'heart attack' in her car scenario would be the line the family would prefer, rather than the 'lesbian affair and murdered by her lover' we'd have to present. Who wins with that?"

He took a mouthful of beer and they sat silently eyeing their pints as Thurstan munched another handful of peanuts.

"So, where do you think he went?"

"Who, Derek?"

"Nickson. Soapy said he never came back out of the woods, so where did he go?"

"Fuck knows." He gave him a tired smile. "Wherever he is, I hope it's a long, long way from here." He drained his glass. "Another? I'm getting the train tonight."

Degsy finished his drink. "Yeah, go 'head, Boss. I think I'll do the same."

CHAPTER 88

Thurstan wondered why the large oak desk somehow looked even larger now than the last time he'd seen it.

Eventually the silence was broken by the Chief.

"Right. I think we're both certain there's absolutely nothing to be gained by alarming the Public with news or even hints of some sort of organised retribution organisation. It's going to cause all sorts of problems. You know what they're like. Any old excuse to plunder the nearest electrical store and set fire to all and sundry, not to mention nutter copycats crawling out of the woodwork." He rubbed his forehead then waved his open hand towards the DCI continuing with a hint of exasperation. "Similarly, no one will thank us if it's actually 'official'? Look what happened to the last chap who let the 'cat out of the bag', the Deputy Chief from Manchester." He let out a sigh. "No! Might as well go downstairs to the Firearms Range and shoot ourselves in the foot right now." He took a sip of iced water from the tumbler on his desk.

"I've asked the CPS and Courts to expedite the trials regarding the Masterson murder and Tommy Cole. Strike whilst the iron's hot, so to speak. Get it in and out of the papers quickly; leaves the MacMahon job to fade away gracefully. We've already blamed organised crime and hinted at international involvement so I think interest will wane given time. That only leaves MacMahon's wife to make a fuss but she's unlikely to pressurise us in respect of where our enquiries are going. From what I've been told, she firmly believes it was Tommy Cole that saw him off."

Thurstan interjected: "I think our saying it was organised crime with international connections, which ... sort of fits Tommy Cole to a tee, might have fuelled the fire a bit there, Sir."

The Chief stared at him questioningly.

"Oh, I see what you mean. Quite possibly. Never mind. I think it's highly unlikely he'll be serving his time here so if she pays some other inmate to see him off it won't be our problem. Maybe when she finds out Masterson was his mistress she'll lose interest all together," the Chief added thoughtfully then looked at Thurstan, who felt the time was right to give a little nod and a smile.

"The Councillor's murder? Well, totally out of our hands now *and* the 'one that never happened'."

He looked at Thurstan: "Coffee?" Thurstan nodded. He pressed the intercom. "Mrs Byrne, two coffees, please, and a small plate of biscuits."

He went 'walkabout'. "This chap, McGee, the St.Helens serial killer. To be honest, I've had some things altered. We've reversed the injuries so it sounds like he was shot from the front. Official line is 'commits an attempted rape and bravely fought off, then tries a knifepoint robbery. Picked the wrong person'. Of course, we'll tell the Press our enquiries indicate this just happened to be a member of Liverpool's 'gun toting' organised crime who's now left the country. Enquiries continue, no stone unturned. That sort of thing. They'll suck it up.

320

"And in case you're wondering, I've spoken personally with the Pathologist, old friend of mine, *and* the victim. It's sorted. Should they be asked any awkward questions they'll refer it all back to us. At the end of the day, if we get caught out by the Press, we explain it away by saying enquiries were of such a sensitive and protracted nature that a cover plan was needed so as to not alert the people we were seeking. Long term we'll have to play it by ear."

The Chief appeared to have a knack for this sort of thing, although Thurstan wasn't very keen on his using the word 'we'.

There was a subtle tapping low on the door. "Get that, will you, Thurstan? You're nearest." Mrs Byrne entered with a tray, and her dazzling smile.

"Thank you, Mrs Byrne," the Chief said, giving her a big smile. She dazzled them both again, closing the door behind her. Thurstan couldn't help noticing she had a curious but attractive sort of flick of her hips going on as she walked.

"Help yourself to milk and sugar," the Chief said, handing Thurstan his coffee, "and don't forget to have a biscuit."

The DCI poured some milk, slid a sugar cube beneath the darkly marbled surface and stirred. Leaning forward he helped himself to a custard cream. He decided not to 'dunk' as he didn't know exactly what the Chief's policy was with regard to dunking. His strategy today was 'play it safe'.

The Chief Constable sipped from his cup as he stared out of the window.

"Now, your man in Yewtree Road." He smiled benignly at Thurstan. "Information from the 'underworld', I think. Disgruntled, former prison inmate. Suspicions of some sort of fallout regarding drugs transactions, that sort of thing. Given time the Press will forget about it; what with summer fashions and then the football season almost upon us they'll have more than enough to fill their pages. It'll be dead in the water. Feel free to dunk, by the way."

Thurstan leant over and removed another custard cream from the plate. He had to admit the Chief was good, very good. He dunked, ate half and took a sip of coffee as the one sided conversation continued.

"Now regarding Nickson. I have to say he hasn't actually dispatched anyone either of us are likely to shed a tear over. I know you've circulated him 'All Ports and Airports' but he may be able, nevertheless, to slip back into the country. If that happens, then he's our number one priority. Use the Ways and Means Act if needs be. Personally, I don't care what you lock him up for. Walking on the cracks in the pavement, having a wonky smile or even drunk and disorderly would suit me fine, just make sure you get his DNA and, if necessary, we'll pay for someone to open their lab up in the middle of the night and give us the result in a matter of hours.

"Even if some well meaning Custody Officer refuses the charge, as long as we have his DNA sample we don't have to destroy it for six months. The point I'm making, Thurstan, is the DNA sample, when matched, is going to ensure he'll spend at least nine months remanded in custody, if not longer. Hopefully, the threat of that will keep him well away. In the meantime, do whatever you can to keep a track on him. Any problems you get regarding authorisations or Court Orders, come straight to me. Oh, and if you still haven't put him on the system, leave it that way."

"I will, Sir."

Thurstan stood up.

"Sit down, Thurstan, I haven't finished yet," the Chief told him returning to his desk. He dunked another custard cream. "I love these biscuits," he commented. Looking at the DCI, he nodded towards the last one on the plate. Thurstan shook his head.

"Right!" the Chief announced. "Different subject. I need to make some changes. Bill Cheesewright is being posted to the Matrix as Superintendent. I've decided to promote DI White to replace him as the other DCI at MIT. Taking note of your written request regarding young Drayton he'll be your new DI. Good news all round, I think?"

Thurstan was pleased. He'd known Chalkie had passed his promotion board, reluctantly resigning himself to the fact he'd probably lose them both within the next six months.

"Great news, Sir. When will they be notified?"

The Chief looked at some notes.

"Let's see. Yes, they'll be told on Monday, officially published Friday and effective as from the beginning of next month, so don't be letting the cat out of the bag." He smiled. "Okay, we're done, I think."

Thurstan stood up again. "Just one thing, Sir..." He was interrupted before he could finish.

"If you're concerned about the detection rate, Thurstan," the Chief said walking him to the door, his arm around his shoulder, "I wouldn't worry. Personally, I have full confidence in you. You need to take a pragmatic view of things. The figures will sort themselves out. Look on the bright side: Christmas is only around the corner. I'm sure there'll be one or two easily solved domestic murders over turkey dinners to even things out. Who knows? If you're really lucky there could be even more." He smiled affably and opened the door. "Oh, and your personal file?"

The DCI looked puzzled; he'd never mentioned the matter to anyone.

"I think you'll find you won't have any problems. He's always been a spiteful little shit. Between you and me, he won't be here much longer. I had to recommend him for a job with the Met just to get rid of him. Part of my 'reclaim the SB' strategy."

As he watched Thurstan disappear into the corridor to the lifts, Mrs Byrne sidled up to him, smiled and said: "Did you mention it to him?" He looked down at her, smiling back: "No. I didn't have the heart. It'll dawn on him soon enough, I'm sure." He moved further into her office and clapped his hands together enthusiastically. "Right, Mrs Byrne, you get the tray and things from my desk and I, in the meantime, will make you a well earned cup of Earl Grey with one sugar." He checked the kettle, switched it on and began to arrange the tea things.

"Thirstin' badly and dehydratin'," he said to himself, shaking his head and chuckling.

CHAPTER 89

Don leant one arm on the table and spoke in a low voice.

"Well, I have to admit, this Baddeley chap is being a bit of a nuisance, and it *is* going to be quite difficult to continue to use you in the UK for the foreseeable future, especially now they've circulated you. It could be done, but…" He caught Nick's gaze and smiled. "Why don't you take a break, make it a long one, and we'll wait for it all to blow over."

"It's not going to 'blow over', Don," Nicks replied with a hint of exasperation, sliding the 'job's mobile' across the table to him. "This isn't the sort of guy to let it happen."

Don smiled condescendingly. "There *are* ways we can alleviate the problem. Things are always going missing and people are always getting posted to all sorts of other departments, don't you know? It's just a matter of time."

"You can't do that with this fella." Nicks shook his head. "No, if you make what he's got disappear or fuck him about, it'll just make him more determined. I know his sort." He let a little laugh escape. "It's what I would do. It'll become a crusade for him. I'm sorry, not only is it no longer tenable but, as I said before, I just don't want to do this anymore. I've had a glimpse of my own mortality. I think I've done enough."

Don reclined in his seat agitatedly.

"For goodness sake, Nicks! It was a mere scratch."

Nicks smiled at him.

"It was more than a *mere scratch.* And anyway, I only said I had a glimpse. Nevertheless, it was enough." He held his hands palm up in an open gesture. "Why the hell am I doing this shit at my time of life?"

Don leant forward, jabbing his finger towards him.

"Because someone *has* to, Nicks! And, besides, you're good at it."

"Yeah? Well, I think I'm losing my touch. I should have taken a bit more time to find that damned knife. He'll have my DNA profile from it by now. Once he's matched it to DNA off my Mum's toothbrush, the one *I know* he's nicked, I won't just be an interest to him. I'll become an obsession." He sipped his coffee thoughtfully.

"Look," Don said soothingly, "you know as well as I do he can't use that in a court of law. At the moment he's got DNA for someone who was in or near the alleyway around the relevant time. We've discussed this before, Nicks. It's nothing a damn good lawyer can't adequately explain away to a jury." He delicately sipped his coffee, replaced the cup on the saucer and said quietly: "Of course, we wouldn't be in this position if you hadn't stuck your nose into something that was none of your business."

Nicks looked at him hard. "I couldn't just ignore it."

"No, no, of course." A hint of sarcasm then more deliberately, "But it seems you couldn't *just* phone the Police either."

"By the time they'd have arrived it could have been too late," Nicks countered, defensively.

Don glanced up as two young men walked past, hand in hand. He watched them as they climbed the stairs to the exit. "That may well be," he murmured. Looking back at Nicks, he picked up his drink. "And besides, you just couldn't resist it, could you!"

Once again, Nicks felt like an errant schoolboy experiencing the crushing disappointment of his Form Master.

"Nicks, listen to me!" Don was insistent. "We can sort this out. As I've told you. Things go missing. Departmental personnel change all the time. It'll take a while, but it can be done." He pushed the 'job's' phone across the table with his forefinger. Nicks slid it straight back.

Don looked down at it. "It's not *just* about this Baddeley chap, is it?"

Nicks looked him square in the eyes.

"I'm done," he said.

Leaning back in his chair, Don sighed, then pocketed the phone and said quietly:

"I've always liked you, Nicks, so I won't try to talk you out of it." He smiled and Nicks thought it was the only genuine smile he'd seen Don produce.

"I respect *your* decision. Everything has a shelf life, as they say." He paused. "I *do* have to remind you, though I know I needn't, none of this can ever be spoken about *or* conveyed in any manner *whatsoever*." He smiled his usual smile before adding: "The consequences would be quite dire." He wasn't smiling anymore.

Nicks toyed with his coffee and replied quietly:

"I can imagine."

"No. I don't think you could."

Don lifted his cup, draining the remnants. He placed it back down, stood up, picked a minute piece of fluff from his jacket and deposited it carefully into the cup.

Extending his hand, he smiled again; two genuine smiles in five years and both on the same day. Nicks began to feel flattered. They shook hands firmly then Don was gone. Nicks leant back in his chair with a sigh of relief then toyed aimlessly with a napkin. Slowly, he drank the remnants of his caramel Latte.

Suddenly, Don was back.

"I forgot to mention," he said pleasantly. "She's done a wonderful job with the flowers."

Nicks looked back at him vacantly.

"Who? What flowers?"

"Why, Anca of course. The window boxes? They look absolutely delightful. Geraniums have always been my favourite." He placed the phone back on the table. "On second thoughts, you *will* need this. It's not over yet, Christopher. Take care."

Nicks watched him walk away. "How long have you known?" he called.

Don swung around to face him. For a while he just stood there. Then he returned and said, quietly:

"Your cosy arrangement? Having your little German friend mind your phone then forward our messages on to you? I've known all along." He paused. "I know you want your own little bit of paradise on earth, Christopher, but the road to Eden's not easy." A wistful look. "It's... somewhat overgrown."

He climbed the steps to the exit, glanced back, a last smile; the door slowly, silently, closing behind him as he faded away into the crowds bustling along the Kurfürstendamm.

As Dan Wheatcroft

The Leveller Trilogy

The Road to Eden is Overgrown

Ask the River

No Room for the Innocent

John Gallager series

The Summer of 66

The Summer of 75

As Paul Addy

Pad's Army

And for children 6 - 9

The House in the Wood

Printed in Great Britain
by Amazon

63595974R00199